Beside Still Waters

THE WYLDHAVEN SERIES

by Lynnette Bonner

Not a Sparrow Falls – BOOK ONE
On Eagles' Wings – BOOK TWO
Beauty from Ashes – BOOK THREE
Consider the Lilies – BOOK FOUR
A Wyldhaven Christmas – BOOK FIVE
Songs in the Night – BOOK SIX
Honey from the Rock – BOOK SEVEN
Beside Still Waters – BOOK EIGHT

OTHER HISTORICAL BOOKS

by Lynnette Bonner

THE SHEPHERD'S HEART SERIES

Rocky Mountain Oasis – BOOK ONE
High Desert Haven – BOOK TWO
Fair Valley Refuge – BOOK THREE
Spring Meadow Sanctuary – BOOK FOUR

SONNETS OF THE SPICE ISLE SERIES

On the Wings of a Whisper – BOOK ONE

Find all other books by Lynnette Bonner at:
www.lynnettebonner.com

Lynnette BONNER

USA Today Bestselling Author

Beside Still Waters
WYLDHAVEN, Book 8

Published by Pacific Lights Publishing

Cover design by Lynnette Bonner of Indie Cover Design, images ©
Depositphotos_21219423_DS – Texture
AdobeStock_606424995 – Décor and Dividers
Depositphotos_9724376 – Flare
Depositphotos_543190338 - Smoke

Other images generated by Lynnette Bonner using Midjourney and Adobe Photoshop.
Book interior design by Jon Stewart of Stewart Design
Editing by Lesley Ann McDaniel of Lesley Ann McDaniel Editing
Proofreading by Sheri Mast of Faithful Editing

ISBN: 978-1-942982-30-2

To "The Old Gang."

We've come a long way from the years when we were just getting to know each other on Christian Writers! You all have been such a support and encouragement to me. I dearly miss those who are waiting for us in eternity, but the rest of us who remain must work while the fields are still white. I count each of you among my closest friends (even though I haven't met most of you.) Your friendship has been such a blessing to me. Love you all!

Psalm 23:1–3

The LORD is my shepherd;
I shall not want.
He makes me to lie down in green pastures;
He leads me beside the still waters.
He restores my soul;
He leads me in the paths of righteousness
For His name's sake.

Chapter One

Just looking at Washington Nolan standing there next to Kin at the front of the church made Zoe Kastain mad. Madder than mad. Every part of her shook with a fury that she realized had likely been building for months.

Today was supposed to be a day of happiness and joy. The whole community was overjoyed to celebrate Kin and Cora's marriage. Cora was radiant in her gown of champagne silk and Kin looked dashing in his suit with a bowtie at his throat. The day should fill her with peace and serenity. Joy. A gentle thrill at the wonders of love.

Instead, she wanted to leap up and scream for the happy couple to be wary because love was a fickle fiend. Wouldn't *that* set the town's tongues to wagging?

Zoe wriggled, irritated with the hardness of the bench beneath her. She tried to keep her face impassive and summon an attitude of celebration for her friends, but red had started to creep into the edges of her vision.

Washington Nolan had made her promises. Dazzled her with what she thought had been sincere kisses. And, on that fateful day when he'd ridden the train out of town to join the cavalry, had even asked her to wait for him.

And then he'd come home—or rather, Kin had dragged him home by the scruff of his sorry, self-pitying neck.

Injured and broken, Wash had told her he wanted nothing to do with her. He'd shut his door in her face, leaving her to gather the scattered pieces of her broken heart. And all for what? Because he'd suffered an injury to his leg that had taken some of his mobility?

Did he really think she would love him less because of it? How little he apparently knew her!

She rolled her lips in and pressed them together so tightly that pain penetrated the fog of her frustration. She pulled in a long slow inhale. Tried to relax.

So he now used a walking stick to get around—what did that change? If he'd truly loved her, something so insignificant shouldn't—*wouldn't*—have dampened his ardor. If he'd known her at all, he would have known that her love for him wouldn't change just because he was maimed. Certainly she understood that an injury such as his would take time to move past. But it wasn't as life-altering as he was making it out to be. Not like it might have been if he hadn't come home to her at all.

Her eyes scrunched against a roil of nausea. She shifted again, and again found no comfort.

If he would let her, she would help him determine what came next. But he'd been stubbornly maintaining his distance. In fact, this was the first time she'd seen him in town since his return home.

Since his focus lay on the ceremony, she let herself study him. He looked fine. Better than fine if she were honest, in the tailored suit that Mrs. Holloway had sewn for him. Standing as he was, with his walking stick leaning against the far wall, no one would even know that he'd been shot. His hair was a little on the long side—something to be expected, she supposed, since he'd been so reclusive. But his broad shoulders stretched the gray wool of his suit near to bursting, and tapered down to narrow hips that gave no indication of a man who'd faced trauma. He looked sturdy. Robust. Handsome.

Realizing she'd been staring for too long, she forced herself to examine the others in the wedding party instead. He was no longer her concern. The realization was a bitter concoction to swallow after a lifetime of loving him.

Beside him, Sheriff Callahan wore a matching suit, and across from the men, Mrs. Griffin and Belle wore gorgeous identical green gowns. They each held a nosegay of white lilac blooms interspersed with ferns and soft pink tulips. They were fitting bouquets for Cora's gentle personality. Beautiful, just like she was.

For some reason, the sight of those bouquets knotted Zoe's stomach as tight as a tangle of worms in a bait bucket.

She, too, should be getting married this spring. Well, if Wash hadn't gotten hurt, she supposed he would still be in the cavalry, but since he was home, if he were still a man of his word, they should be celebrating their own marriage. Yet he hadn't spoken to her—other than to tell her he wanted nothing more to do with her.

A sudden thought made her eyes flash wide. What if he'd been testing her? Testing her love for him? Testing to see if she'd be willing to remain committed to him though he was injured?

And she'd been so hurt that she'd simply walked away! And now, for all these months—*oh, merciful heavens*—he'd been thinking that she never really loved him!

She had to prove him wrong. But how? What was the biggest gesture that proclaimed one person's love for another?

Marriage!

The idea was so preposterous that she gasped.

Ma glanced over at her. Even Papa Harrow leaned forward to peer at her from Ma's other side.

Zoe snapped her mouth shut and gave them a subtle shake of her head. "I'm fine."

But she wasn't fine, because this seed of an idea had set her mind to whirling and her heart to racing.

No. She couldn't . . . Could she? It would be madness! And yet . . .

She pressed one hand to her churning middle.

The idea swirled, threatening to rise up and take all her rationality captive.

She thought back to that fateful day last autumn when she'd worked up her courage to go see Wash at the cabin his father had built for him—his hideaway from the real world. It was a memory better left six-feet-under. The good Lord knew she'd tried to bury it many times with tears of repentance for her anger and bitterness, but it kept rising from the grave like a ghoul in a tale from Edgar Allan Poe.

She gritted her teeth and studied the gloves she strangled in her lap.

No. If she followed through on this idea, the rejection would feel so much worse. So much more final.

Beside her, Ma leaned close to whisper, "If you are imagining those gloves are Wash Nolan's neck, it doesn't seem to be bothering him any."

Zoe's shoulders sagged. She understood Ma's message plain and clear. Her anger and despair hurt no one but herself. She raised her chin. Loosened her grip on the gloves. Ma was right. She had to find a way to let this go.

And marching to Washington Nolan's house and demanding marriage is certainly not letting it go, Zoe Kastain!

Her cheeks burned at the mere thought, and she glanced around to make sure no one was looking.

Her gaze crashed into Wash's. Of course he'd looked at her at that precise moment. It was deserved punishment for her insensible thoughts. Fair-skinned as she was, and with her red hair a constant torment, she'd never been able to hide a flush of embarrassment. In fact, she could feel the burn of her humiliation, even now.

One of Wash's brows winged upward in question.

Zoe snapped her attention to where Kin was just slipping a ring on Cora's finger. Let Wash wonder. She wouldn't pay him or her crazy idea another thought.

But she could feel him studying her. Could see from the edge of her vision that he hadn't turned away. Despite the promise she'd made to herself in the mirror this morning that she would not make a fool of herself, her scrutiny drifted back to him. Something indefinable tugged at his features—something that held her fast. His gray-green eyes softened as they swept over her face, warming her clean through.

And for one moment, Zoe's heart soared with the hope of what might be.

His throat worked, and he shifted.

"You may kiss the bride!" Parson Clay's exultant proclamation sent a jolt down Zoe's spine that yanked her attention to where it should have remained.

A loud cheer rose through the congregation as Kin leaned close to lay a lingering kiss on Cora's lips. After a moment, with a side-eyed glance at the congregation, Cora pulled back, but he leaned after her, and she indulged him in another series of kisses and retreats until she was nearly bent over backward. This caused endless ripples of laughter. Cora finally halted him with an embarrassed flush. Kin gave her an unrepentant grin, and then straightened slowly, pulling her with him. Cora responded by darting up onto her toes to give him one more peck, much to the amusement of those gathered.

Zoe couldn't resist a smile. She could only hope that their love would prove to last.

Parson Clay's laughter melded with the congregation's, and then he presented the couple with a broad, proud gesture. "May I present to you, Mr. and Mrs. Kin Davis."

Kin and Cora faced the congregation and Kin thrust their joined hands toward the ceiling in a gesture of triumph. "She said yes!"

Even Wash's somber lips tilted at that.

Cora's giggle was like a creek during spring melt—joyous and bubbly.

From the back of the church, Ewan McGinty shouted, "Three cheers for the happy couple!"

"Huzzah!" The joyous shouts nearly lifted the roof. "Huzzah! Huzzah!"

Still laughing, Kin and Cora hurried down the aisle, followed by the four who had stood up with them.

Zoe noted that Kane Carver, across the way, couldn't seem to take his eyes off of Belle as she passed. But Wash didn't look Zoe's way again. He must have gathered his walking stick sometime while her attention had been on Kin and Cora, for now he kept his attention steadfastly pinned to the portion of the aisle directly in front of him as the tap of his stick accompanied his hasty escape.

Zoe's gloves were once again choking for air.

Wash stumbled on nothing as he escaped the confines of the church into the warm spring air.

"Careful there." Thank heavens, Sheriff Callahan did not reach to steady him. "You okay?"

Wash concentrated on balancing on his good leg as he tugged at the tie that suddenly felt much too tight at his throat. "Fine." Striding to the rail, he leaned is cane against it, and planted the heels of both palms on it. He clenched his teeth at the pain that throbbed in his leg as though the bullet had only mutilated him moments ago.

He scrunched his eyes closed against the images that tormented him.

Zoe looking mighty fine in that soft-blue dress that could make a man forget his limitations.

Zoe trying not to let him see how hurt she was, and yet failing miserably at the task.

Zoe blushing over some part of the ceremony and making his insides twist with regret and a feeling of loss at the way life had forced him to relinquish her.

It should have been them at the altar. Not that he begrudged Kin and Cora their day. But, if not today, one day soon it should have been him and Zoe teasing each other with kisses in front of a church full of people. If only he'd come home whole and without the worry of how he would now make a living and provide for a family.

The crowd emptied from the church and spilled off the porch and onto the lawn. Kin and Cora had paused in the shade beneath the large oak and most everyone fell into a line that filed past the couple so they could offer congratulations.

And there at the end stood Zoe's parents and twin sisters. Aiden and the boys had no doubt run off to play baseball as soon as they were released from the church—he knew that was what he and Kin would have done when they were lads. And Belle was there at the foot of the stairs helping to unload cauldron after cauldron of food from the wagon that Dr. Griffin had just arrived in.

He shouldn't search for Zoe, but he did nonetheless. She was . . . there, helping Charlotte Callahan spread cloths on the tables that several men were hurrying to set up. Ewan had apparently donated his tables from the alehouse for the occasion.

Her red hair glinted like fire in the spring sunlight. The hem of her dress skimmed the grass, and the sleeves were wide and puffy at the shoulders, drawing his attention to a waist so slender that he could span it with the breadth of his hands. He knew because . . . well, some memories were better left in the past.

The very distant past.

He scrubbed one hand over his face. Why had he let Kin talk him into being here today? He should have maintained his reclusiveness and insisted that Kin have Joe or Jackson stand up with him, but his friend had been persistent. And he hadn't had the heart to say no.

But now . . . his leg, more specifically his knee joint, was going to burst into flames if he had to stand much longer. He should go down and make himself useful somehow, but just the thought of facing those stairs made sweat break out on his forehead. Not only would the pain of navigating them be severe, but everyone would be watching him.

Behind him, something scraped across the porch decking.

He spun to find Sheriff Callahan placing two chairs and a big cedar bin filled with ears of corn. "Don't suppose I can get you to help me shuck some corn? Charlotte and I planned to do this last night, but I got called out to Camp Sixty-Five because of a burglary, and Isaiah has been sick. Last night Charlotte was stuck to his side keeping cool cloths on his forehead."

Relieved, Wash sank into the nearest chair. He stretched out his injured leg and tried not to release too big of a breath of relief as the flames abated to mere coals. He picked up an ear of corn. "Is he okay?"

"He'll be fine." Reagan set to work on the corn. "Doc thought it was just something he ate. We let him and Lincoln and Grant sleep out by the creek a couple nights ago. They caught a fish and claimed they cooked it well, but all three of them got sick the next day, as you might know."

Wash didn't know, but he didn't want to let on. Truth was, he didn't often leave his little cabin other than to wander down to the bigger house to restock his food supplies.

Thankfully, Reagan didn't push him. "Doc figured they just needed a couple of days to get whatever it was out of their system and sure enough, Isaiah's fever broke in the early hours this morning. It was a short night, but we are both relieved that he seems to be on the mend. We left him home, sound asleep." The sheriff shucked an ear and scrubbed off the silks before asking, "How are Lincoln and Grant?"

Wash placed his shucked cob to one side of the cedar bin. Maybe he hadn't escaped so easily after all. He lifted one shoulder. "I didn't even realize they were sick."

"I see. Scarce can blame you. I know you've got plenty on your own mind lately."

That was true, he supposed. But not so much that he shouldn't have known his little brothers were sick. With Pa off to the woods each day to fell trees for Heath Logging, who had been watching the boys? Had anyone been there laying a cloth on his brothers' heads? Jackson also worked all day away from the house. Linc was old enough that he could probably manage to care for himself, but he would have been more likely to torment Grant than help him. Maude then. Yes. Likely it had been Jackson's wife who had helped his brothers. But that didn't lessen his feeling of guilt. She'd taken on a big job when she'd married Jackson, Christmas past. They'd moved into his brother's room in the main house until Jackson could get their own place built. Cooking and cleaning for Pa and the boys couldn't be easy on a newly married woman, but she'd risen to the task, and from what he'd seen, with a great amount of joy.

He dropped another ear of corn onto the stack and took up another to shuck. Maybe he needed to start doing more around the place. After all, he couldn't just sleep the rest of his life away. He had to find a way to wrangle through the pain he suffered. If only he didn't feel so constantly tired. The agony was a ceaseless energy drain.

Mrs. Callahan bustled up the church steps, a large empty pot cradled in her arms. "Reagan, the fire is good and hot and the water is boiling, are the cobs ready?"

"We've done about half. Here, let me get them for you. Wash is helping us." Reagan took the pot from Charlotte and set to filling it with the ready cobs.

"Bless you, Wash." Charlotte squeezed his shoulder.

Wash offered what he hoped passed for a smile and not a grimace. "Happy to help." Lies. What he really wanted to do was go home and sleep. So much for his realization that he ought to be doing more.

"I felt so bad that we didn't get it done earlier," Charlotte said. "But the bride and groom haven't even escaped their guests yet, so I don't suppose I needed to worry." She hurried after her husband, calling over her shoulder, "Reagan will be right back."

Charlotte and Reagan hadn't been gone for more than a minute when someone stopped only a few feet away.

It was the short blond doctor who had come to see him on occasion with Dr. Griffin. He sported a drooping walrus mustache that reminded Wash of his commanding officer at Fort Vancouver.

"Howdy," the man said.

Wash gave him a nod but feared that a frown may have settled on his brow. He didn't want to spend energy creating conversation with a stranger.

"You may remember me. I'm Doctor Polson. Alexander Polson." The man shifted a bit nervously and twisted a bowler hat through his fingers.

Wash managed, "I know who you are."

The man thrust out a hand. "Good. Then you'll know that I work closely with Doctor Griffin. He instructed me to wait until you were ready, and I figured seeing you here today was a good sign. May I have a few minutes of your time?"

Ready for what? Wash didn't want to know. But . . .

"Can you shuck corn?" Wash nudged the empty chair with the boot of his good leg. The man could sit if he would work. Because the sooner this job was done, the sooner he could hightail it on home before this agony made him bite somebody's head off.

"Uh, yes. Thank you. Happy to help."

The man sat, but he didn't get to work.

Wash lifted him an irritated glance. "How can I help you, Doctor?"

"Mr. Nolan, I think I'm the one who can help you. With your leg I mean. It would require an exploratory surgery, but I am trained and have performed many such surgeries when I worked in California. I suppose you've heard that we are building a surgery right here in Wyldhaven?"

"I have not, no. And if you'll pardon me for being blunt, I've had enough of doctors butchering my leg. Thank you, though." Just the thought of going back under the knife made a shudder work through him. He'd been through two such surgeries back-to-back after the accident and neither had given him his leg back nor taken away the pain.

"I understand that, but if you'll just let me explain—"

"The answer is no, Doctor." A movement drew his scowl toward the porch steps.

Zoe stood there, unmoving, like a doe, curious, but ready to flee at the first whisper of a sound she didn't recognize. Perfect. Just what he needed. Her getting one of her ideas. She was unrelenting and tenacious when she felt she had a good plan.

Wash tossed down a cob and stood with the aid of his stick. He touched his brow and gave the doctor a nod. "You'll forgive me, but I have to go."

His cane tapped out a steady betrayal of his infirmity as he approached Zoe by the steps. He kept his focus on the boards. The last thing he needed was to look into the depths of those blue eyes of hers. When she didn't move out of his way, he fiddled with his cane a little. "Zoe—" He'd meant to ask her to please allow him to pass, but her name emerged broken and barely audible. He cleared his throat.

"Sorry." Her reply was nearly as breathy as his had been. She stepped to one side, giving him free access to the stairs.

He turned sideways, gripped the rail, and descended the stairs one halting step at a time. He didn't dare raise his gaze to those gathered, or he'd never have the courage to leave his cabin again. The last thing he wanted to see was the pity many of them were certainly directing toward him at this very moment.

When he reached the foot of the stairs, he carefully adjusted his balance and settled his cane against the grass.

"You ready to go home, son?"

A small bit of tension eased in Wash's gut. "Yes." He counted it a blessing that Pa was a thoughtful man with a kind heart.

Mrs. Griffin hurried up with a basket that she thrust toward Pa. "Here, Butch. For you and the boys this evening."

"Thank you kindly, Mrs. Griffin." Pa hooked the basket over one arm.

She turned and gave Wash a gentle hug. "It was so good to see you here today, Wash. Try not to be a stranger, hmmm?"

He nodded, but only because he knew that would make her leave him alone.

"Lincoln! Grant!" Pa's beller practically made Wash leap out of his skin. "Let's go, boys!"

Wash felt a measure of relief to realize that his brothers were both here today. That must mean that they hadn't gotten as sick as Isaiah. Or maybe they just had iron stomachs from all of Pa's cooking through the years.

Wash bit off a smirk.

His younger brothers would come running from behind the church at any moment and likely beat him to the wagon. And with the obstacle he faced to hoist himself up to the bench, he'd better get moving or the whole family would be waiting on him.

Keeping his focus on the path before him, he moved forward, thankful to see that no one had hemmed their buckboard in. They would have free access to the road.

Just another hour and then he could lose this anguish in blessed sleep.

From her place on the church porch, Zoe watched Wash retreat. She pressed her hands together.

She would not march to the man's house and demand that he marry her. She simply wouldn't.

It would be unseemly . . . yet it was all that she'd ever wanted.

It would cost her the Wyldhaven teaching position . . . maybe.

It would give Ma no end of angst over her actions . . . but she'd recover.

It would put Wash in an awkward position . . . but it would also prove her love for the man once and for all.

And then maybe Zoe could talk Wash into the surgery she'd overheard Dr. Polson speak about. Surely Wash owed it to himself to try?

And surely she owed it to him to prove that she still loved him no matter the condition in which he'd returned home?

Her stomach churned like a white-water cataract.

Parson Clay trotted up the church steps, obviously intent on heading into the sanctuary for something, but Zoe stepped toward him. "Parson?"

He paused. "Yes, Zoe?" His eyes were kind, the corners crinkled in greeting.

Her fingers fidgeted worse than Jinx when he was about to get fed. She laced them together. "I wondered if you'd be able to meet me at Washington Nolan's cabin tomorrow morning? Say nine o'clock?"

The minister frowned. "I . . . can."

The hesitation with which he said the words made her realize he wanted to know why she was asking, but all she offered was "Thank you very much," before she hurried down the stairs.

Lord have mercy. What was she doing?

She was going to throw her whole life and reputation away!

And all for a man who swore he no longer loved her!

Chapter Two

Harlan White rode from the forest with his men beside him. They all reined up on the hillside and paused to survey the land below. Harlan leaned to one side and spat, without removing his scrutiny from the small ranch that lay in the valley before them. Smoke spiraled from the chimney of the main house, and from the smaller cabin down the road. Farther to the north, a new cabin had just been started.

"Why haven't they moved on, boss?" Ted Beck was loyal, if not very bright.

Harlan liked the man, even if he was the newest of his crew. Harlan had rescued him from a barfight in Cle Elum a few weeks back and the man had stuck fast by Harlan's side ever since.

Harlan spat again. A long white strand of his hair escaped and blew across his eyes. He gathered it back and resecured it with the leather strap at the base of his neck. "Because we apparently haven't made it difficult enough for them, Beck. We simply haven't offered them enough incentive to give up."

"You've cut fences, driven off their cattle, butchered the pigs. What more is there to do? Maybe we ought to just pick another spread to buy?"

"Shut up, Ted. You just follow instructions, and everything will be fine."

Ted slunk back. “Yes, boss.”

Harlan sucked on his lower lip thoughtfully. Setting aside the fact that it would give him great pleasure to run Butch Nolan off this spread, he wanted the buildings intact if at all possible. The smaller cabins would make good bunkhouses. And the main house could use some maintenance, but it would get him through a winter or two until he could make a few sales. He was honestly surprised that the family was still on the land. He’d been trying to keep his head low and create the problems without bringing too much attention to it. He’d thought that Nolan would cave easier. The man he’d been years ago would have done so by now. After all, he didn’t make his living off the land. It would be easier for him to move into town with his family. But so far, he had simply been repairing the fences they’d cut and absorbing the loss of the livestock. The few times he’d visited the alehouse in town, he hadn’t even heard any tales about the issues, which must mean that Nolan had been keeping his troubles close to his vest. Why would that be the case?

The wretch was making it difficult for him to carry out his plans!

It wasn’t like he wanted to steal the place. He only wanted Nolan to put it up for sale so he could swoop in with a cash offer. A low cash offer, but a cash offer none the less.

Harlan yanked his horse around to retreat. He heard Beck’s horse fall into step beside his. The rest of the men fell in behind.

“Seems we’ll have to tackle this problem from another angle. But don’t worry, we will get them to sell. And for a rock-bottom price to boot.”

It would serve the man right. He mostly wanted it because it would hurt Butch. But even if it wasn’t Butch who owned the land, Harlan had to admit that it was a prime lot. Grass so thick that if a man lay down, another could walk right past him and never know he was there. And plenty of water with Wyldhaven Creek running right through the center. Such land would keep cattle fat and happy. And fat and happy cattle would feed plenty of hungry loggers, the growing town of Wyldhaven, and plenty of homesteads beyond. There were other places around that he could choose, but this one suited his needs, so he'd decided to look no further. It was just his starting place. It was the closest ranch in the valley to the source of Wyldhaven Creek up in the mountains. And once he had control of the headwaters, he'd be able to leverage the rest of the valley into giving up their spreads as well. There was nothing a man could not accomplish with the right pressure. Trouble was, the process was taking longer than he'd expected it to.

And he hated waiting. It was time to up the ante.

Time to take his revenge.

Belle stood to one side of the bustle in the churchyard and took in the scene. She wanted to commit every detail to memory so she could lay it to canvas for Cora and Kin to keep as a treasure of this day. It would be her gift to them.

They were seated at the head table now, whispering sweet nothings to each other as though no one else were present. Parson Clay stood to one side with his arm around Aurora's shoulders as he watched Kin with fatherly pride. Aurora's hand lay curved gently over the roundness of her let-out skirt and she smiled lovingly up at her husband.

Rays of light filtered through the leaves of the large oak to gild patches of the grass with lemon yellow in an uneven pattern. Closer to the church, Charlotte, Dixie, and Jacinda hurried to lay out a buffet, and Dr. Griffin and the sheriff each grabbed a cookie when they thought their wives weren't looking. But Mrs. Callahan caught them and gave her husband's hand a playful slap.

A colorful quilt in the shade beneath a nearby wagon had been spread for Dr. and Mrs. Griffin's girls. Ellery Rose, who lay on her stomach with her little legs bent into the air behind her, chattered away to her baby sister, who watched the chaos with curious wonder as drool dripped from her chin.

"Memorizing the scene?"

Kane's voice spun her to face him. Her heart cavorted at the closeness of his proximity. "You know me too well. I'm hoping to paint—"

Something in his expression silenced her. His brown eyes were ever so soft and full of light, and he studied her the way she'd seen Papa Harrow study Ma on occasion. Forget cavorting. Her heart was engaged in an outright frolic now—like a child just set free from school for the Christmas holiday.

"I have something for you."

Only at that moment did she realize he'd been standing with his hands behind his back. He was hiding something.

Involuntarily, the fingers of her right hand touched the empty ring finger of her left. Was the man finally going to make all her dreams come true? "You do?" Joy bubbled through her.

He whipped his hand from behind his back and held up—her shoulders sagged—a rolled-up tube of paper? She hoped he couldn't read the disappointment radiating through her. Slowly, she reached for the document. "What is it?"

"Just look. I've been saving up."

Territorial University of Washington arced across the top of the first page. Beneath that lay a jumble of words—too many to read at this moment. A second smaller paper was a train ticket to Seattle.

She frowned. Looked up at him. "I don't understand."

His brows slumped and he worked at one side of his lower lip with his teeth. "I enrolled you into the art school. I figured you'd be happy."

So he hadn't missed her disappointment. She looked at the pages again. At one time, her only dream had been to go to art school, and yet in recent months her dreams had grown to involve so much more than that. "It's lovely, it's just—you want me to go away?"

He took a step back. "I thought it was what you wanted?"

"It is. I have wanted it for a very long time."

His features eased. "Well, good then. I wanted you to be happy. You deserve to focus on your art, Belle. The world needs your gift."

"And what about you?" She gasped and pivoted away, slapping her fingers over her mouth. She hadn't meant to blurt anything so forward. But to go to school would be to leave him. Was that what he wanted? For her to go away?

The warmth of his hand clasped hers. He pulled her around to the relatively private side of the oak's trunk, pressed her back to the tree, and leaned one hand by her head.

His intense gaze drilled into hers. "I need you, Belle, like the clouds need the sky. Like a soaring eagle needs wind beneath its wings."

A tremor worked through her, and she eased out a breath of relief.

He continued. "But it would be utterly selfish of me to ask you to give up your gift to be the wife of a horse trainer."

A boldness stole over her. She straightened and settled a hand against his cheek. "And what if I want to be the wife of a horse trainer?" She studied him, looking for any indication of resistance to the idea. They had danced around this for months now, but never spoken of it so openly. Perhaps it was the wedding atmosphere that had made them both intrepid.

Kane loosed a low growl before turning his head to press a firm kiss into her palm. “Don’t tempt me, Belle. First, I want you to pursue your art. Being a wife—my wife—would split your focus.”

“I wouldn’t mind.”

“You have such a beautiful gift. I don’t want you to throw it away on account of me.”

“Love and learning can exist together.”

“Yes.” His voice was gruff. “But the one would distract you from the other.”

Her disappointment surged again. “And what if the lack of one distracts me from the other?”

Kane’s focus sharpened on her. He stepped close and took her face in both his hands. “There is no lack. Only delay. You will go to school and become the best artist you can be. I will write to you every day so you don’t forget my love for you. And then you will come home, and we’ll talk of marriage again.”

Her pulse stuttered. He’d actually said it. But it hadn’t been a question. She tilted him a smile. “Oh, will we?”

His face twisted into the dearest scrunch of frustration. “I mean, you know, if you will have me?”

Such a joy bubbled up that Belle felt she might explode with it. She tipped her head back on a laugh and wrapped her arms behind his neck. Then leveled him with a look. “I wouldn’t have it any other way, Mr. Carver. Unless you want to let me become your wife first?”

Kane pressed his forehead to hers and closed his eyes. “You are temptation itself, lady.”

She grinned. “Am I? Is it working?”

He shook his head, stepped back, held out a finger to stop her from leaning after him. "No. No, it's not working. Schooling first. Then we'll see if you still want to be the wife of—" He threw up one hand. "Well, me."

Belle snatched his hand, dropped a kiss to his knuckles and pressed the back of it to her cheek. "I will always want to be your wife, dear Kane. So much so, that I dread being apart."

"I know. Me too. But the time will pass. And I would never forgive myself for selfishly standing in the way of your gift."

Belle frowned. "Am I so awful that I need so much schooling?"

He shook his head. Swept a strand of hair behind her ear. "So good that you owe it to the Lord to develop it to its peak."

Her chest tightened. "That's a lot of pressure, Kane."

His thumb caressed the curve of her cheek. "The Lord always gives us the strength to do what He's called us to do."

She exhaled, long and slow. There was no winning this battle. "I will miss you."

"As will I you."

Someone made a noise of disgruntlement to her left and Belle looked over.

Papa Harrow, hands plunked on his hips, glowered at them.

Belle stepped back and clapped her hands silently. "Papa, Kane just asked me to marry him!"

The man turned the force of his ire on Kane, who shuffled uncomfortably.

Oops. She probably should have let Kane ask her stepfather for her hand. "Well, sort of. Not really, actually." She pressed her palm to her forehead. "I mean, at least not yet."

Kane shook his head and ran a thumb across his lips. He still hadn't met Papa's probing glower. Maybe she was digging his hole deeper. She pinched her lips tight before she could blurt any more.

"Well did he or didn't he?"

Belle thrust out the notice from the school. "He's paid for me to go to art school in Seattle."

Her father's brows nudged up. "I see. That's wonderful."

She lifted a hand. "It is, but I was trying to talk him into marrying me first."

"And he said?" Papa narrowed a glance on Kane.

Belle felt her shoulders sink. "He said schooling first." She rolled the two papers together once more.

Papa gave one short nod. "Smart man. Now, if you'll both join us on the busy side of the tree, I think that might be best."

Belle clamped her teeth against a giggle. "Yes, Papa."

"Yes, sir." Kane poked his toe at a clump of grass.

Papa retreated, and Kane angled his eyes toward her, a sparkle of humor in their depths. "He's sure to deny me, when the time comes."

Belle tapped Kane's chest with the tube. "I will convince him otherwise." She started to follow her father, but Kane pulled her back, gave a surreptitious glance to make sure they were still alone, and then dropped a quick kiss against her lips. He gave her a smile and a wink and motioned that she should lead the way.

She did. Feeling much lighter than she had only moments earlier.

Zoe woke on Saturday morning feeling like she might be sick. She rolled onto her side, curled into a ball, and clutched her stomach.

Was she really going to follow through on this?

Lord? Is this the right thing to do?

She held her breath. Listened to the silence.

Well, that wasn't a "no."

And if she didn't do this, she would end up as an old maid schoolmarm for the rest of her life. Was that what she wanted? No. She wanted to be Washington Nolan's wife. Had wanted that for nearly as long as she could remember.

Taulby Ecklund's face suddenly flashed into her thoughts.

She sat up, heart wrenching at the thought of what she must do. And if she were to do that, she needed to hurry or she might miss Parson Clay.

After leaping out of bed, she flew through straightening and tucking the blankets and then into her best dress. It wasn't white, nor did it have any lace, but the brushed blue wool brought out the color of her eyes and she needed to feel pretty, today of all days. She braided her wild red curls and pinned them into a semblance of order at the back of her head.

She snatched the small traveling case from the bottom drawer of her wardrobe and stuffed it full of as many items as she could fit. Two complete sets of clothes, her extra boots, an extra petticoat, hairbrush, extra hair pins. And after she used her toothbrush and powder at the washstand, those too.

Satchel in hand, she hesitated. Should she ask Ma and Papa to meet her at Wash's? Ma especially would be hurt if she didn't. But on the other hand, if she was to once more be humiliated, she didn't want them to be witnesses.

Better to act and ask for their forgiveness later.

She strode across to open the window, dropped the bag outside, then pressed the sash firmly closed once more.

That done, she took a fortifying gulp of air, shot up another prayer for strength and guidance, and then stepped out of her room.

As she'd known they would be on a Saturday morning, Ma and Papa were already at the table. Papa reading the paper and Ma darning a pair of Aidan's socks.

Ma popped from her seat. "Morning, dear. You're up early for a Saturday." She strode to the kitchen, which was just across the counter from the table. "I made cinnamon buns."

"Thank you." Zoe swallowed. Had they heard the tremor in her words? "I just have a few errands to run today." Humiliation flamed at the lie. She had never been one to fabricate the truth. "Okay, that's not quite true. I have one main thing to accomplish today, and I'm rather nervous about it."

Papa tipped down the corner of his newspaper. "And what one thing is that?"

Drat. She couldn't tell them for they would surely tell her she was crazy and forbid it. She tipped up her chin. "I'd rather not say at the moment. But I would ask for your prayers that all would go well."

Ma and Papa exchanged a glance as Ma set a sugary cinnamon bun and a cup of coffee before Zoe's normal seat. "Sit, Zoe. Eat. Relax. I know that seeing Wash yesterday couldn't have been easy."

The very mention of his name sapped the strength from her legs and she plopped into her chair. The gulp of coffee she took nearly scalded the roof of her mouth.

"I, for one, was glad to see that he's able to stand and walk. As much as he's been keeping to himself, I wasn't certain." Ma returned the coffee pot to the stove.

Zoe did not want to talk about Wash. Neither did she want to eat that cinnamon bun for fear that it would come right back up, but if she didn't eat, her parents would know something was wrong. She forked off a bite, trying to ignore Papa Harrow's searching scrutiny.

He straightened, folded the paper closed, and set it beside his empty plate. "Are you going far? Need me to saddle a mount for you?"

Her bite of roll halted partway to her mouth. If she took a mount, she would need to bring it back, and she didn't want to have to face her parents again for a few days—unless of course, things didn't go as she planned. "I don't need a mount. I have to go speak to Taulby Ecklund on a matter." That was true and he lived close enough that her parents wouldn't insist on the horse. She stuffed the bite in so she might be prevented from having to say more. If she left out what she planned to do after, that wasn't exactly a lie, was it? Just a bit of omission.

Again, Ma and Papa exchanged a glance. Ma lifted one shoulder and Papa eased back in his seat. Ma took up her darning again. "You've always been a good girl, Zoe. And a sensible woman. I, of course, pray for you every day, but I'll be praying for you especially today."

The bite of sweet bread felt like a hot ball of shot going down. And it dropped into her stomach with as much force. She pushed her plate back. "Thank you, Ma. I'm not much hungry this morning, but your rolls are as good as ever." She stood. "If you'll excuse me, I'd better be on my way. I don't want to miss Taulby before he leaves for the mill."

The twins burst from their room at that moment, arguing about something that Zoe couldn't quite decipher, but she'd never been more thankful for one of their scraps.

It distracted Ma and Papa, and Zoe made her escape before they could pester her with more questions that she wouldn't be able to answer.

Guilt rushed over her as she hurried around to the side of the house and hefted her valise, but she threw back her shoulders and set out resolutely for Taulby's house.

Jinx padded along beside her, but that was okay. She would send him home later this evening. It gave her some ease to reach down and feel the warmth of her beloved companion's furry head.

Taulby Ecklund was in the middle of his morning ablutions, when he noticed movement on the path to his cabin. With a towel over one shoulder, he turned toward the window for a better look and his heart leapt into his throat.

Zoe Kastain and her faithful dog—heading his way!

He snatched up his comb and hurriedly thrust it through his tousled hair, smoothing it back against his head. He hadn't even shaved yet, but there was no time.

Grabbing up his wash basin, he tossed the week's worth of dishes on the table into the tub. The towel, damp from his washing, did an ample job of swiping crumbs onto the floor. He dropped the basin full of dishes into the kitchen sink, and then sprinted for the seating area across the room. He gathered boots, discarded shirts, pants, and socks and tossed them into his bedroom just as a soft knock came at the front door. He yanked the bedroom door, but a pair of pants prevented it from shutting. He gave the pants a swift kick, and thankfully, the door did close that time.

Taking a bolstering breath, he scanned the length of himself. A bit damp. A little rumpled. But he would have to do.

He hauled open the door.

Zoe's fist hung in midair as though she'd just been about to knock again. She leapt back with a start and a squeak. "Oh! Goodness. You gave me a start. I thought maybe you'd already gone to the mill."

"Ach. I did not mean a start to give you. Forgive me." Curiosity burned through him. What had brought her to his door this early in the morning? And with luggage at that.

Zoe made a little sound in the back of her throat.

He realized he'd kept her standing on the porch while he scrutinized her bag. "Forgive me. Some coffee you would like?" He stepped back and held the door wider.

Zoe lowered her focus, and he couldn't miss the pink that filled her cheeks. "Uh, on the porch, perhaps?"

"Right!" *Dumme ku!* "Please . . ." He motioned that she should take one of the wooden chairs on the porch. "Coffee I will bring, ja?"

"Thank you, Taulby. That would be lovely."

In the kitchen, his hands trembled as he hurriedly placed two mugs and the coffee pot on a tray. He rushed into the pantry. Did he even have any sugar? Did she want it in her coffee? More polite to offer it, even if she refused. But where had he put it? He started the hunt through the assortment of cans and canisters.

What had brought her here? Yesterday, he'd arrived at the wedding a little late and slunk into the back row. But he'd been able to see Zoe from his seat and it hadn't escaped him how she'd fidgeted and squirmed, nor how she'd studied Washington Nolan as he retreated down the aisle at the end.

That carpetbag . . .

He gave up finding sugar on the current shelf and turned to the one on the other side.

He'd been plain about his feelings for Zoe ever since she'd captured his heart when he'd rescued her after she twisted her ankle in a gopher hole. But she'd been careful to put him off any time he even broached the subject of the future.

Where was she heading, packed as she was?

Ach! There was no sugar to be found in his pantry. He couldn't leave her waiting any longer and would simply have to make his apologies.

His hands shook so badly that the cups rattled when he hefted the tray. He took a calming breath and tossed up a prayer to the good Lord that he would not make a fool of himself in front of the woman he wanted to spend the rest of his life with. Then he pushed through the front door and onto the porch.

He hurried to place the tray on the table between the two chairs, seeing that she had set her bag near the cabin wall. Her dog slept peacefully in a patch of sunlight that warmed the grass at the foot of the stairs.

"It is an apology I must make, for no sugar I have found."

"Please don't worry. Black is fine."

The coffee pot chattered against the rim of the mug he filled for her. Drat his big clumsy hands!

"Thank you." She accepted the cup. It dwarfed her slender fingers.

He filled one for himself, but was too on edge to sit, so he leaned his hip against the porch rail, instead. She looked a little pale this morning. Like she might not have slept well last night. He wanted nothing more than to pelt her with questions about what she was doing on his porch at this hour of the morning. Instead, he forced himself to calmly sip his coffee and wait.

Zoe seemed to be searching for words as she lifted her coffee to her lips. Her brows shot up and her eyes widened and fluttered a few times. "Wow, Taulby," she chuckled. "I'll be awake for a week after just that one sip."

Amusement danced through him. He lifted his cup. "This is coffee as God intended."

She smiled, and oh the ways that smile tangled his insides.

"Taulby . . ." She shifted in the chair, set her cup back on the tray, and then stood to look up at him from beneath the shade of one hand. "I'm about to do something, and I felt that I owed you an explanation before I did it."

He felt his brow slump. "On you go." Whatever she was about to say, he hoped his heart would keep on beating.

"At the wedding yesterday, you may have noticed Washington Nolan? He stood up with Kin."

"He and the sheriff, ja." He took a large gulp of coffee and let it burn the whole way down.

"Yes. Well, as you know from past conversations, a few years ago, before you came to town and before Wash left for the cavalry, he and I . . . we had . . . an understanding, you see. But then he came back injured and, well, things changed. However . . ."

She shifted and there was a subtle change in her expression that left him suddenly very clear on where he stood and why she was here. He jolted upright. "Stop, Zoe. Before more you speak, I must have a say, please." He carefully balanced his coffee cup on the rail.

She hesitated, waiting for him to continue.

He stepped toward her, taking both her hands in his. He turned her so she wouldn't have to peer into the sun. Then, looking down at her, he willed her to read all the love he felt for her in the gentleness of his gaze. "Marry me, Zoe Kastain. A good husband I will be to you. Love . . ." He shrugged. "I know you do not for me feel as I do for you. Not yet. But with all my heart I love you, and I will every day work to be a man worth your love, ja?" He clamped his teeth to keep himself from blathering more.

She looked up at him. Opened her mouth, then snapped it shut again. With her hands still settled firmly in his big, calloused ones, she looked from his porch across the fields, her lower lip tucked between her teeth.

A breath eased from him. He could hardly believe his good fortune that she hadn't immediately told him no.

Chapter Three

Zoe felt the surprise of Taulby's proposal sweep through her. She supposed it was her fault for allowing him to escort her places on a number of occasions. But she'd felt that she'd always made it plain that she saw him only as a friend.

Taulby was a wonderful gentle giant of a man, and it wasn't that she worried he wouldn't be good to her. It was simply that her heart had already been taken captive by another. Yes, Wash had taken her captive and then thrown open the doors of her jail cell and told her to vamoose, yet she couldn't bring herself to do so, no matter how sensible that would be.

So, now she must let Taulby down. But softly, for she wouldn't hurt the man for anything.

She looked back up at him. "Taulby, you deserve someone who will love you with the same sweet love that you show to others."

He squeezed her hands. "This love you will learn, Zoe."

She shook her head, feeling the sting of tears in her eyes. "I wish that were true. But I will only ever love you as a friend, Taulby, because my heart already belonged to another before you even arrived in town."

A muscle hardened in his jaw. "A man who has offered only disdain and disregard."

Zoe swallowed. That was true enough. Recently. "He loved me once. And I believe he will do so again."

Taulby grunted and released her hands. He paced to the end of the porch, gripped his neck, and then turned to face her with pain filling his eyes. "What is this you are about to do?"

Zoe folded her arms over the terror that kicked to life in her chest. She angled to study the fields once more. "I'm going to marry Wash Nolan."

She heard him plunk into one of the chairs. "So why is it you tell me this?"

Zoe's shoulders sagged. "I guess I simply didn't want you to hear it from someone else."

"And yer mama and papa? They know of this that you have planned?"

Zoe clamped her teeth, uncertain how to answer, for the truth would surely condemn her in his eyes. Her hesitation must have been the only communication he needed on the matter, however.

He stood and lightly touched her shoulder. "A mama, she should be at the wedding of the daughter, Zoe. It would be a terrible mean thing to deny her. In the house I am going now." He started down the porch toward his door, but then stopped and looked at her over his shoulder. "But one more thing I will say. If this Nolan is again a dummkopf, a place you will always have with me." He strode inside and quietly shut the door, leaving her in the silence.

Zoe hefted her valise and swiped her eyes as she stepped off Taulby's porch. Jinx scrambled to his feet, and she bent to pat his head before heading once more toward the path. But at the fork in the road that would either take her back home, or toward the Nolan place, she hesitated.

It *was* a terrible mean thing to deny Ma a place at her wedding, and Belle too, for that matter. But if she went back home they would only talk her out of her plan. No. The only way she was going to get Wash to keep his promise to her was to force him to do so. He needed her. That had been as clear as the waters of Wyldhaven Creek yesterday. She must convince him that his life was not over. That he deserved to be happy. And that her love for him had never faded.

And if she couldn't? If he rejected her offer once again?

She would choose the life of an old maid, rather than unfairly marry Taulby, who would never have her whole heart.

Dear Lord, please don't let it be.

She would never find out if she didn't get moving.

Throwing back her shoulders with determination, she turned onto the forested path that led to the Nolan spread. Her heart hammered in anticipation, causing sweat to break out on her forehead. *Calm down.* She forced a long, slow inhale and turned her attention to the area around her rather than on what she might do if Wash refused her yet again.

The day was beautiful. Sun streamed through the evergreen branches to gild the forest floor. In this area of the wood, the trees had grown tall and broad, and most of the branches didn't start for many feet above her head. She could have paused to study the beauty of the vast array of tree trunks on either side of the pathway, but she didn't want Parson Clay to beat her to Wash's cabin, so instead she marveled over them as she hurried along.

There were the wide, deeply etched orange and gray barks of the ponderosas—some as orange as her hair, while others wore their color with more subtlety. Here and there she glimpsed the stringy gray trunks of the cedars whose bark could be peeled away in long strips. She and her sisters had woven many a fairy crown from those when they were little. A few of the trunks wore the softer, daintier, dove-colored bark of the white pines. These were interspersed with the stark white of a few birch trees that were just now coming into full leaf here in the foothills of the mountains.

Such a variety of textures and colors! What creativity the Lord had used in His creation!

Zoe sniffed the air, loving the loamy fragrance of the evergreen forest warming to the sun.

A chipmunk with a pinecone darted along the length of a fallen log before he perched on the far end and chattered at her as though scolding her for disturbing his breakfast.

And then she was through the wood and standing on the hill looking down on the Nolan spread. Just like that, her heart took to misbehaving again and if she didn't get hold of herself, she was going to arrive at Wash's door looking as if she'd just been chased by a mother grizzly.

She set her bag on a patch of moss along the top of the embankment and took a moment to straighten her hair and take several deep breaths.

This was it. Her last chance to convince the man she loved that she was the right woman for him.

Her pulse surged and tumbled over itself like a jubilant cluster of kittens with a ball of yarn.

Mornings were always better. A good night of sleep seemed to abate the agony of Wash's bum leg. But he knew that if he stayed on his feet too long, he would be right back into the weeds again.

Impatiently, he stirred the pot of boiling oatmeal and gathered milk, butter, and brown sugar near his bowl. His coffee already waited at the table. It was only a moment before the oats were cooked to his liking and he scraped the contents into his bowl and took the pan to the kitchen sink. Pa had piped running water right into the house from a high storage tank, so he didn't even have to work a pump handle to fill the pot.

A knock came on his door just as he returned to the sideboard by the stove.

He frowned.

Was it one of the boys? Coming down to see how he was faring after his long day yesterday? He wouldn't put it past Pa to send one of them to make sure he was all right.

He was fine. All he had planned for today was sitting on his bed with his legs propped up so he could finish *The Red Badge of Courage*. It had been out for a few years now, but this was the first chance he'd had to read it.

Leaning heavily on his cane to keep from putting any more weight than necessary on his leg, he strode to the door and settled his hand on the knob. He yanked it open. "Tell Pa that I'm—Zoe!" He fumbled to lean his cane against the wall and straighten.

She stood on his porch with Jinx sitting beside her, a small brown satchel clutched in both hands.

Truly, the last person he'd expected was Zoe. He tried not to notice how pretty she looked, but failed miserably. She'd attempted to corral her red curls, but as always, some strands had escaped to caress her cheeks. He released the door, widened his stance, and clasped his hands behind himself so that he wouldn't give in to the temptation to reach out and finger those curls.

"Good morning. I wasn't expecting you." Understatement. "How can I help you?" He didn't want to help her with anything, truth be told. Just standing here for these few seconds was already reminding him that he'd overdone things yesterday.

The familiar flame flared to life in his calf and every muscle tensed as though preparing to fight the blaze.

Zoe opened her mouth, but no words came out. She angled her head. Tried again. Still no words emerged from her open lips.

Wash frowned. This wasn't like her. All his life Zoe had been the one who knew what to say in whatever circumstances they found themselves in. "Is everything okay?"

"Yes. Sorry. I'm struggling to find the right words. Obviously." The last word seemed to be a barely audible afterthought to herself. She snapped her mouth shut and turned to study the railing at the other end of the porch.

Wash shifted a little, unsure what he ought to say.

Jinx took advantage of his movement and slunk past his legs into the house.

"Oh! Jinx, no!" Zoe called.

But the dog ignored her, strolled over by the fireplace, and curled up on the rug.

Wash smiled. "Guess he knows the meaning of making himself at home. I'd invite you in, but . . ."

"Yes. Please don't worry. I understand." Embarrassment blushed her cheeks and her hand trembled as she reached up to swipe one of those tempting strands behind her ear. She couldn't seem to meet his gaze and a little jitter of concern flared.

They'd always had an easy camaraderie. Of course that was before he'd gone back on his word and sent her in tears from this very porch. He clamped his teeth, willing away the painful memories of that day, but he couldn't banish the memory of what he'd done after closing the door in her face. He'd sunk onto a chair, pressed his forehead to his knees, and bawled his sorrow into the silence around him.

He had wanted to yank open the door and tell her he was sorry. Call her back. Hold her forever. But love demanded that he let her go. She deserved a man who could do right by her. Protect her. Provide for her.

What could Wash give her? Nothing. Nothing but the few dollars he got each month of a cavalryman's discharge pension. At first, the family of the man who had accidentally shot him had sent money to cover his expenses, but it had been months now since he'd received anything from them.

"What can I do for you, Zoe?" The words burst out much more harshly than he'd intended.

Her pert little jaw jutted to one side as a sheen of hurt filled her eyes. Her chin lifted. "Taulby Ecklund has asked me to marry him!" She dropped her valise and plunked her hands on her hips.

Weakness threatened to steal the strength from his knees. He gripped the posts of the doorway, searching her face, but one thought flared to life.

Her satchel. He suddenly couldn't think of anything but that blazing satchel.

Was she going to marry the man today? Had she packed her things and come to say her farewells before she married the miller?

It was a good thing he hadn't had a chance to eat yet. He might be sick.

His focus drifted to the bag on the porch at their feet. "So you've come to say goodbye." He'd meant it as a question, but it had emerged a statement. A statement he desperately wanted to snatch back.

The realization ought to have filled him with relief. Ecklund was a good man, from all he'd heard from Pa. And he was certainly of means. Zoe would be taken care of in the way she deserved.

Yet his traitorous heart thundered with a yearning to haul her into his arms and beg her to believe that he hadn't meant his rejection. To promise that he would never let her go.

She was quiet for so long that he finally dragged his scrutiny back to her.

Zoe's stance had softened. Her hands were clasped before her now—though her knuckles were white as though she might be struggling with the temptation to reach out to him. However, she didn't move. She merely looked at him with her blue eyes soft and filled with . . . something he couldn't quite pin down. The injured part of him wanted to label it pity, but that didn't quite ring true. If not pity, what then? Sorrow? Yearning?

"I thought we already said our goodbyes, Wash? At least that was the impression you gave me the last time I was standing in this exact spot."

He coughed a little and forced a nod. So he was right. This was goodbye.

God, give me strength.

He focused on a little bit of nothing past her shoulder. It hurt too much to look at her. "Yes. You're right of course. I truly do wish you all the best, Zoe. I know he will love you and care for you as you deserve." He ground his teeth to keep from imploring her not to accept the man's proposal.

"Wash Nolan, you are a stupid fool!" Her hands were once more firmly lodged on her hips.

"What?" His gaze zipped to hers.

He blinked. Once. Twice. Three times.

He'd known Zoe to have opinions, but she'd never spoken so harshly to him.

She leaned closer, eyes no longer soft, but hard and glittering. "And yes, I know the Bible says to call no man a fool, but Lord forgive me, what else am I supposed to call you?"

"I—I . . . don't understand."

She thrust her hands wide. "Of course you don't. So why am I so determined to make this work?" She shoved her bag with one foot, nudging it more firmly against the cabin wall.

Before he even realized what he was doing, his hand shot out to clasp her arm. "Make what work?"

His heart hammered so hard that he could feel the slam of it against his ribs.

A rider emerged onto the path to the cabin. It was Parson Clay riding their way.

His focus snapped back to Zoe.

Why would the parson be out this way so early in the morning, unless . . .

Wash searched Zoe's face. Surely she hadn't meant . . . Realization dawned so suddenly that he let go of her arm and scooped both hands into his hair. He clasped his fingers behind his head and simply looked at her, holding his breath and waiting for her reply.

God, please don't tempt me with this again. I don't think I have the strength to reject her a second time.

She fidgeted worse than Grant did when he was trying to work up the courage to confess something. After a long moment, she angled a quick look toward the parson, who had dismounted from his horse and was tying it to the hitching post, then returned her focus to him. "I'm not marrying Taulby, Wash. But I *am* going to marry you."

His eyes fell closed, and he literally clamped his teeth against his tongue to keep from blurting, "Yes! Yes! Yes!"

Reason warred with desire.

She worried her lower lip. Chin dipped down, she studied him through her lashes as she waited for him to speak.

His love for her ought to slam the door on this errant hope, but it was too late. Hope had already slipped inside and curled temptation around his heart.

She shifted. Swept her tongue over her soft red lips.

Hang it, looking at her lips wasn't helping him win this battle. His heart begged him to give in to her outrageous request. His love might be enough to sustain them through the lean times, right? But what would happen down the road? She would have to be the breadwinner. He could barely stand on his leg for a few minutes! He couldn't work the ranch or even take a job with Heath Logging.

No.

He snatched his cane and paced across the kitchen, keeping his back to the whole package of temptation standing on his porch.

God, why are You tempting me with this?

The heavens remained silent.

Wash gripped the back of his neck and squeezed at the tension.

A picture flashed through his mind. Zoe traipsing through town with her arms linked with his. His leg gave him no pain and he walked easily. Zoe smiled up at him with love in her eyes. Wash bent to drop a lingering kiss against her lips. A little boy trotted beside them with Zoe's red hair and his broad build.

The pain of it was so strong that it made him shudder. His fisted hand pressed hard against the tabletop. He pulled in a draught of reality, pushed out the dream on a long slow exhale.

Lies. It was all lies.

If she married him, she would be worked to the bone, making up for his limitations. He couldn't do that to her. He must not give in to the weakness of this desire.

He just had to get the words out. Again.

God, please. I need words.

His tongue felt thick. His mind waded through sludge trying to string together the thoughts that had helped him let her go those months ago.

Behind Wash, the porch boards creaked, and Parson Clay asked, "Zoe? Is everything all right?"

"Why, yes, Parson." Zoe's voice rang clear and serene, no trace of her nervousness from moments earlier. "Wash Nolan is just coming to grips with the fact that you are about to marry us."

Wash spun so quickly to face her that he almost lost his balance. He stabbed the floor with the tip of his cane to regain his footing. Good. Let his disability tether him to reality.

Hands clasped before her now, Zoe smiled sweetly at him, but he could see the stubborn set of her jaw.

"I'm what?!" The parson's mouth gaped as he glanced between them.

Wash held out a finger. He meant to say an emphatic no. Instead, what emerged was "What if I say yes?"

Chapter Four

Zoe backed up until she felt the solidity of the porch rail behind her.

He was going to say yes?

Merciful heavens! He was going to say yes!

Joy swelled through her like she hadn't felt for years. So much wonder and excitement that she felt jittery and lightheaded.

Wash's finger was still held out as though to keep her silent, so she waited for him to continue, clamping her teeth over her lower lip so she wouldn't blurt joyous nonsense.

Beside her, Parson Clay shuffled his feet. "Wash? Are you saying yes?"

Zoe felt warmth in her cheeks. It was, after all, a little humiliating that she'd had to be the one to force the issue. But she couldn't bring herself to care about that at the moment. Elation had her feeling as though she were lounging in the clouds!

"No! I'm not saying yes."

Zoe blinked. Clutched for the rail. "What?" The word was breathy. Barely a sound in the sudden silence.

So much for lounging in the clouds. She'd just crashed right back down onto Wash's porch.

"What I'm trying to say, Zoe, is that you need to think through what you are asking."

Irritation surged into the places left empty by her dissipating joy. "Do you think that I'm standing here on your porch, Washington Nolan, risking your rejection once again, without having thought through the consequences?"

"Yes, Zoe, I do think that!"

"Well then, you are indeed a—" She angled a frown toward the minister standing quietly beside her. No matter that it had been only a few minutes since she'd called him a fool, she couldn't bring herself to repeat the travesty with the minister standing so near. She nudged her chin up a notch. "What I mean to say is that I stand by my earlier proclamation, then. Because you are wrong. I *have* thought through the consequences."

"No! You haven't!" He tossed a gesture toward his crippled leg. "I would be naught but a burden, Zoe! I can't work! I can barely find the fortitude to stand for a few minutes. And Lord forgive me, I'm no good company when the pain gets so overbearing."

She stepped forward. "I will work, Wash. I'll gladly work. I'll teach if the school will still have me. We've made it to 1899! In just a few months, it will be a new century! Surely it's time for schools to realize that a married woman still has something to contribute to the students. And if not, I'll tutor and work hard to do the chores around the place. Dixie is always looking for some help, so I could do that part time." She reached through the doorway to touch his hand where it gripped the cane he leaned on. "Please, Wash. We'll figure it out. Together. I walked away once out of shock and hurt. But I need you to know that I love you enough to stay. To stand by you through this. Don't ask me to leave again." She pulled in a tremulous breath, willing herself to remain calm. "Please, don't ask me to leave again."

His voice was low and dejected when he spoke. "And what of chil—" His gaze cut sharply to Parson Clay.

The man shifted his feet and gestured with his hat toward his horse. "I'll just be over there." He took two steps and then, with a glance over his shoulder divided between them, tacked on, "Praying."

Zoe couldn't help a small smile at that proclamation. The poor parson likely thought she'd lost her mind and would be praying for her to find it again. But one look at Wash's serious contemplative expression straightened her countenance.

"What if children come, Zoe? If you are working and trying to do all the chores, who will take care of them?"

A boldness stole over her that she didn't know she possessed. She sidled a step closer to him, took his hands, cane and all, and slid them around her. His warmth enveloped her. He didn't pull back. But he did close his eyes and swallow hard.

She reached up to touch his chin. "Wash Nolan, I've loved you I think from that moment when you burst into the classroom all those years ago and found me tied to my chair with a broken arm. Do you remember?"

She watched him carefully, willing him to look down at her. The stubble of his cheek prickled as the gentle pulsing of his jaw rose and fell beneath her fingers.

Finally, he looked down. A swirl of emotions winged through his eyes. "Oh, I remember, Zoe." His voice was gravel and rocks.

Satisfaction swelled inside her. "And you've loved me almost as long, right?"

"Longer."

The proclamation filled her with peace. She nestled her cheek against his chest and inhaled, long and slow, as she simply relished the scent of him. It was a smoky aura touched with a hint of pine and the lemon soap that Jerry sold down at the mercantile. This was where she was meant to be—safe in the circle of Wash Nolan's arms.

She knew she had won him over. And now she must proceed with caution.

"Then let us love each other, please, Wash. I want to have the freedom to hold you just so for the rest of our lives. And I want the joy of knowing you'll hold me in return. I want to spend the rest of every moment with you and only you."

"Zoe." The word was almost a groan in her ear. His cheek came to rest against hers. His arms tightened around her.

She straightened. Turned her head toward him just a little, in invitation. And then his lips covered hers. Warm and soft and gentle. Searchingly at first, his lips caressed hers slowly, but then his arms tugged her closer and his mouth moved against hers with more urgency. His breaths came hard and fast and a low groan slipped free. She kissed him with abandon, rising on her tiptoes to give as good as she got. His curls slipped through her fingers, filling her with a possessiveness that surprised her. Salty tears mixed with the taste of his kiss, and she realized then that she was crying.

With a little laugh, she eased back from him.

He reached up with one hand to swipe her tears away. "Zoe." His voice broke on her name. "I'm the most selfish of men."

She shook her head. Covered his hand with her own. "No. You aren't. Marry me, Wash. Let's love each other so that burdens and hard times are halved and the joys are doubled."

His shoulders drooped, but he said, "Okay, Zoe."

The thrill of it had her bouncing on her toes. "I have one more request."

"Oh?" He studied her with caution in his eyes.

"Can we do it at the church? On Saturday? I planned to ask Parson Clay to do it today, but, well, my family ought to have the privilege of being there. And yours should too."

His tension seemed to ease as he leaned forward to press his forehead to hers. "Okay, Zo. Saturday sounds good."

"Thank you, Wash," she whispered. "You won't regret it. I promise I'll never let you regret it." Stepping back, she hefted her valise. "Jinx, come."

Fortunately, the dog decided to be obedient today. He slipped past Wash and trotted off the porch.

She had to find the strength to leave this man for just one more week. "I'll tell Parson Clay. Shall we say three in the afternoon?"

He dipped his chin. "Three's fine."

She felt the corners of her mouth nudge upward, as she retreated a step, unable to tear her gaze from his.

He didn't return her smile. He merely shifted his feet and gave her another small nod.

Her heart stuttered. Was that doubt in his eyes? No. She wouldn't acknowledge that. Not when he'd just said yes and promised her the future she wanted. Not when happiness was so close to her grasp.

He lifted a hand of farewell.

She did the same, taking another step.

His eyes shot wide. "Mind the step!"

She clutched at the support post just in time to keep herself from tumbling backward down the two steps. Flames licked at her cheeks. "Until Saturday then."

With that, she forced herself to turn and walk with calm serenity toward the parson, who was pacing on the other side of his mount. She heard the door of the cabin click shut behind her.

"Parson?"

The man jolted to a stop and searched her face, brows raised. "Yes?"

Zoe swallowed. "I'm sorry to have troubled you to ride all the way out here, but we've settled on Saturday at three o'clock."

"Oh, thank God." His whole stance seemed to sag with relief.

Zoe giggled. "You were over here praying that we wouldn't ask you to help us jump the broom today, weren't you?"

A gentle smile lifted one corner of his mouth. "I confess that my prayers were along those lines, yes."

Zoe could have felt miffed, but she was too happy to feel anything but joy at the present. "Will you be able to do a ceremony for us on Saturday at three?"

"Yes. Yes. That will be fine." He tilted his head. "What will you do about the school?"

"I'm going to drop my bag at home and then go straight to talk to Mr. Heath. It would be terribly sad to leave the school just when we finally have our own building which is so wonderful. But . . ." She lifted one shoulder. "I wouldn't have peace doing anything but marrying Wash."

"Of course the school board will be the ones to have the final say . . ." His words trailed away on a note of warning.

Zoe swallowed. "Yes. Of course that's true."

The face of each member of the board flashed through her mind. Charlotte and Reagan Callahan wouldn't be a problem. In fact, maybe Charlotte could come back to the school as a teacher part time herself. With the logging camps growing, Zoe was in sore need of some help to split off the younger grades from the older ones. No, it wasn't the Callahans that she'd have to worry about. Mr. and Mrs. Olann, however, were another matter altogether. As well as Mrs. Hines. However they'd recently had their decision to oust poor Isaiah Coleman from the school overturned when Mr. Heath surprised them by having the town vote on whether to uphold their decision or not. So maybe this time they would vote with a little more caution. At any rate, it didn't matter.

All that mattered was that Wash had said yes.

She would soon be Zoe Nolan!

Harlan White thanked the postmaster for the letter and stepped from the building onto the porch. He hoped the missive would contain the leverage he was looking for. He likely could have received the information much quicker over the telegraph, but that would have involved the telegraph operator, and it was always better to keep ones information to oneself.

His fingers slid along the edges of the envelope as he paused at the lip of the porch and looked out over the town. His men were in the alehouse across the street. The barman, Ewan McGinty, was amiable, but not to be trusted. Even though he was likely the best information source in town, he seemed much too friendly with the locals.

But that didn't matter now.

He smiled, flicked the corner of the envelope, and trotted down the stairs. Near the Wyldhaven bridge, he sank onto a sunny patch of grass along the riverbank. It was a perfect spring day with birds chittering in the trees, not a cloud in the vibrant blue of the sky, and the soft music of the water underscoring it all. Maisie would be very happy in this little town—once he secured them a place to live.

Carefully, he tore open the corner of the envelope and then slipped a finger inside to rip along the seam.

Only one page? Disappointing.

With a frustrated grumble, he glanced behind himself to make sure no one was in sight, and then tugged his spectacles from his vest pocket where he kept them carefully concealed. No need for his men to know he had any such weakness. They were wolves that would pounce at the first scent of blood.

He spread the letter open against one knee.

Dear Cousin,

Wonderful to hear from you and it was my pleasure to look into the backgrounds of the names you sent. Unfortunately, I found no criminal history on any of the families, save one.

Save one!

Harlan tugged the page a little closer.

The family of Olann that you mentioned . . . Perhaps it is a different family. However, I found mention of one Merle Olann, whose wife is Elizabeth, or Betsy as she was more familiarly called.

The banker and his wife! That was indeed their names! Perfect!

This Merle Olann served time in the New York Penitentiary for the crime of embezzlement and tax evasion.

Harlan smiled.

It is also said that the family's daughter was born while the man was away to prison and at such a time as she cannot possibly be of his seed.

But as stated, of the rest of the names you sent, I was unable to find anything of interest.

Yours sincerely . . .

Harlan didn't bother with reading his cousin's signature. Thankfully, his work with the Pinkertons seemed to have come in handy. Even if acquiring the information from him had necessitated a lie to convince his cousin to send the information.

Tucking his spectacles away, Harlan twisted on the grass to angle a look down the street to the far end near the livery. The bank stood on the west side of the street, looking stately and professional.

Harlan leered.

It was time he opened a bank account, looked like.

Maisie, darlin', we'll soon have a sweet little spread to call our own!

Better yet, Butch Nolan would pay for his past indifference.

Zoe woke the next morning with nerves cavorting in her stomach. She pressed one hand over the ache.

Yesterday, she'd gone to speak to Mr. Heath, and he'd promised to call a meeting of the school board as soon as possible.

She'd planned to share her news with her family at dinner. But Belle had beat her, sharing her own news about leaving for art school in just a few short weeks. And then Ma had rushed Aidan off to his chores and the twins off to their studies and Belle and Papa Harrow had been engaged in a deep conversation about various artists whose work Belle admired, and Zoe simply hadn't found a moment to get a word in edgewise.

She would need to be bolder at breakfast. *Just be courageous and blurt it out.*

It was Sunday morning, which would present an additional challenge as everyone rushed to get out the door for services. Though come to think of it, maybe Sundays were slightly calmer than weekdays when she and the children all hurried for the schoolhouse.

So this morning was her only chance to share her news with the whole family at once—which would prevent anyone from being hurt that she hadn't told them first.

She rolled from bed, ignoring her queasiness, and slipped behind the dressing screen to don her Sunday dress. Shoes in hand, she padded through to the dining table and dropped into one of the chairs.

Ma already bustled around, frying eggs and pancakes. She thrust her chin at a ham on the counter. "When you get your shoes on, wash up and then slice that, please? The pan is ready for frying." Another jut of Ma's chin indicated the empty pan waiting for the slices of meat.

Zoe went to work quietly. She would wait until everyone was around the table.

Aidan and Papa tromped in from the barn with the milk pail and while Papa went to the sink to wash, Zoe forced herself to remain calm as she helped Aidan skim the cream from yesterday's bucket and then transfer the milk to the pitcher for this morning's breakfast table. The cream, she covered and hoped Aidan wouldn't notice the trembling of her hands as she leaned down to place it into the icebox.

"Goodness," Ma said.

Zoe jolted, drawing a curious glance from Ma, who hovered just above her shoulder.

"Sorry to startle you. I was only thinking that we've got quite a collection of cream at the moment. Perhaps we should make iced cream this afternoon?"

Both the twins, who had arrived a few moments ago and were now setting the table, flew into a frenzy of excited chatter.

Aidan's eyes sparkled, but in typical teenage boy fashion, he only offered, "A passable way to spend the afternoon," and then headed over to wash in the sink next to Papa.

Papa grinned over his shoulder. Ma and Zoe exchanged a smile with him.

Belle arrived with an apology for oversleeping and helped take platters to the table.

Far too soon, everyone was seated, and grace had been said.

Now or never.

Zoe shored up her nerves. Opened her mouth.

"I hear that Aurora will be singing a solo this morning," Ma said. "I'm so looking forward to it."

"Oh yes!" Belle added as she carefully sliced her eggs and ham. "I just love her voice."

Zoe dipped her chin in agreement. "I—"

"I saw a baby bunny in the meadow by the barn yesterday!" Sharon spread jelly on a biscuit. She took a huge bite and spoke around it. "It was the cutest thing you ever did see!" Eyes widening, she covered her mouth with one hand. "Sorry."

"You didn't touch it, did you?" Papa asked, ignoring her ill manners. "The mother might not care for it, if you touched it."

Sharon chased her bite with a swallow of milk. "I didn't touch it, no. But it was the darlingest thing. Barely the size of a teacup with grass towering over its little head. Its ears were only about the length of my littlest finger." She held up her pinky for them all to see. "It was all gray with one white patch around an eye and the tiniest pink nose with black whiskers!" She chuckled. "It had nibbled off a blade of grass that was probably as long as my arm, and it was practically inhaling it with such fast little chomps that it looked like the planer down at the mill!"

Even Zoe had to laugh at that.

Belle's fork hovered partway between her plate and her mouth. "Sharon, you are a wonder with words. I can see it so clearly that I could paint it!"

Papa Harrow reached over to squeeze Sharon's arm. "She really is great with words, isn't she? Perhaps being a writer is in your future, Sharon?" Papa and Ma exchanged a gentle look.

Sharon blushed and poked at her last bite of ham.

Shiloh flounced in her chair. "Why did Sharon get all the talent? It's just not fair!"

"Now, Shi," Papa said. "You do yourself a disservice. Why, I haven't seen anyone better than you with the animals, and I'm not just saying that. The way you fixed up that chicken mash? The chickens have been laying a third again as many eggs as before."

Zoe lamented the rapidly ticking clock as Shiloh looked to Ma for confirmation.

Ma sipped her coffee. "It's true. We made an extra two dollars last week from the eggs we sold at the mercantile."

Shiloh beamed.

Papa Harrow pulled out his pocket watch. "Oh my, we'd better get—"

"I have news!"

Everyone jolted to silence and blinked at her outburst.

Zoe covered her mouth to hide her grin. Perhaps ill manners ran in the family. "Sorry. But I do have news."

Papa Harrow lifted his pocket watch. "We really should—"

Zoe held up a hand, intent on being heard. "I'll be quick, I promise. I want you all to hear this at once."

But then her mind went blank.

Was Ma going to be so very disappointed that she had a daughter who'd practically had to force a man to marry her? Or that they'd be losing her income? At least she could be grateful that the family was doing so much better now that Papa Harrow's clock shop was well established in town.

"Zoe?" Ma prompted.

There was nothing for it. She blurted, "I'm marrying Washington Nolan on Saturday at three o'clock."

Ma dropped her fork. It pinged off her plate and jounced like a jackrabbit. Ma scrambled to slap it against the table before it clattered off the edge.

The twins and Aidan simply gaped at her.

But Belle whooped and leapt from her chair. She rushed over to throw her arms around Zoe. "That's wonderful news! I'm so glad he's finally come to his senses! When did he ask you? I didn't think you'd had much time for conversation recently?"

Zoe returned Belle's hug, avoiding her questions with, "Thank you. I'm so very happy. Goodness, we'd better hurry or we'll all be late for church."

She needed to move or she was going to tremble right off her seat. She rose and gathered her silverware into one hand.

Unfortunately, Ma was not to be deterred. "Zoe? When did he ask you?"

"I'll wager that was yesterday when you left here with a valise in hand?" Papa asked.

Zoe froze. Looked at him. "You saw?"

He nodded. "Your ma and I wondered if you'd come back last night."

Zoe stacked Aidan's plate on her own and then reached for Shiloh's. "Well, I did." She smiled. "And the wedding is this Saturday, like I said." And now she'd better distract them again before they realized she hadn't exactly said that Wash asked her. She turned her focus on Ma. "Are you mad at me, Ma?"

"Mad? Child, I could never be mad about Wash finally coming to his senses and asking you to marry him."

Zoe swallowed.

"It's such happy news!" Ma continued. "I'm just . . . surprised, that's all. I didn't think Wash Nolan was ready to get on with his life?" There was a hesitation in her words and a cautiously shared glance with Papa that made Zoe rush toward the sink with the stack of plates.

"Well, I'm going to help him with that."

"What about the school?" Papa's gaze still drilled into her steadily from where he remained seated at the table.

"There will be a meeting of the board later this week." Zoe washed her hands and dried them on the towel. "Hadn't we better get off to church?"

"Yes. I suppose we had." Papa offered her a quick wink.

Relief surged and Zoe gave him a smile of thanks for letting her off the hook so easily. There were too many questions that she didn't know the answers to yet. But she was thankful to have the news out in the open.

As they headed out the door, Ma looped her arm with Zoe's. "I'm so excited I can hardly stay inside my own skin. We'll need to make a trip to the mercantile for some things that every bride should have and I'd like to ask Dixie to make a special cake if that's all right with you?"

Before Zoe could even respond, Ma was off on another stream of excited chatter. Something about flowers.

And Zoe was content to simply let her blather.

It was wonderful to have the support of a family who loved her so much!

Chapter Five

First thing Monday morning, Harlan stepped into the bank and sauntered toward Olann, who stood behind a thick wooden wall protected by bars and a locked door. The fancy metal bars that separated him from the main part of the bank had just enough room beneath them for a few bills to be exchanged.

Harlan leaned his elbows on his side of the counter and smiled at the man through the grate. "Howdy." Using his crossed arms and leather duster to conceal the movement, he reached beneath his jacket and quietly withdrew his pistol from the holster he kept strapped under his arm.

Olann eyed him suspiciously. "Morning. How might I help you?"

Thankfully, they were currently the only two in the bank. Casually, Harlan lifted his hand and jabbed the barrel of the gun through the bars, again using his body to keep the gun from being seen by anyone who might step in behind him. "Well now, friend. I think you've asked the right question."

The banker gaped like a fish on a hook and he thrust his palms to shoulder height. "Don't shoot. I'll do whatever you want."

"Shhhh." Harlan motioned for him to lower his hands. "Just put your hands down. I don't intend to harm you. Not as long as you listen real careful and do just exactly what I say."

Olann swallowed convulsively. "All right." His hands fidgeted near his waist.

Harlan was satisfied to have the man's attention. "First, Mr. Olann . . . Merle Olann, am I right?"

The man offered a slow nod, cautious eyes never leaving Harlan's.

"Merle, I need you to know that I know about your past. I know about the time you spent in the hoosegow. I know about the fact that the little wife stepped out on you, and that your firstborn isn't even yours."

A hard glint crept into Olann's eyes. Tight grooves rimmed the edges of his lips. And his brows slumped low.

Harlan was thankful to be the one holding the gun. This man suddenly didn't seem to be someone to be trifled with. He needed to proceed with caution. However, he'd also just had a rather unsettling thought. It was a shot in the dark, but if he was right it would give him the additional leverage that he needed. "I also know," he continued, forcing his voice to remain calm, "that the man who was the father of that child disappeared and hasn't been heard from in several years."

Olann had stopped fidgeting now and a cold anger stiffened his posture. "If so, there's nothing tying it to me."

Harlan's brows lifted. Interesting. Maybe the man *had* offed his wife's dalliance? It had only been a guess, but it was what he would have done in the man's situation.

"Never mind that. What I want you to mind, is how we can help each other."

Merle tilted his head. "Go on."

Harlan eased upright and jostled the barrel of his gun for Merle's attention. "I need you to remember that I could have hurt you if I had wanted to."

"Oh, you can be sure that I'll not forget it. Get on with what you want."

He swallowed, not liking the man. Not even a little. He sucked his teeth. Maybe he should have thought this plan through a little more carefully. But there was nothing for it now but to charge ahead. "I keep what I know to myself, friend, and you help me get a little piece of land I've been wanting just outside of town."

"And how am I to help you with that? If it's a loan you want—"

Harlan shook his head. "I certainly don't need your money. But I need you to deny a loan."

"Deny a loan? To whom?"

Harlan smiled and holstered his gun. "Let's just say there's a small spread outside of town that's going to have a little trouble with a fire. They're going to need to rebuild. And when they come to you, you're going to find a reason to deny them a loan, understand?"

Olann shrugged one shoulder. "That sounds easy enough."

Harlan allowed his smile to grow. "Good. Yes, it is easy. Now." He dropped a stack of bills onto the counter. "I'd like to open a bank account, please. I think I'm going to be in town for a while." He shoved them beneath the bars.

Oh, Olann didn't like it. He didn't like it one bit.

Harlan's grin broadened.

Zoe tried not to fret as she stood at the blackboard in the less-than-a-year-old schoolhouse and wrote today's math problems in columns for each age group. But stopping herself from fretting was tantamount to stopping the sun from rising.

Wash had not shown up for church yesterday. She wasn't sure why she'd thought he would when he hadn't been attending ever since his return from the cavalry. But she truly had expected him to come. His acceptance of her proposal was a good sign, right? So she'd hoped it would spur him on to doing right in other areas too.

She'd felt downright discouraged as Ma and Papa divided worried glances between each other, the Nolans' pew, and her.

Now she had to wonder if he would even show up for the wedding on Saturday at all. Would he embarrass her like that?

Today she was anxious that he might. And all she could think about was the brief moment of doubt that she'd glimpsed in his eyes as she'd been leaving.

On top of that worry, Mr. Heath had tottered in just before she'd rung the morning's bell to let her know that the school board meeting was set for a week from today. It was the soonest they could arrange it because Mrs. Hines was out of town on a buying trip with her husband, Jerry, for the mercantile and wouldn't return until late Saturday.

At least if Wash left her waist deep in a rain barrel, the school board would know come the time of their meeting next Monday.

One week. Land almighty. She pressed a hand to the terror in her heart.

"Mith Kathtain?"

Zoe came to with a jolt, realizing that little Carmen Olann was standing by her side, looking up as she held out the slate in her hands. Though neither Mr. nor Mrs. Olann had red hair, Carmen's curly locks were the color of a maple leaf in autumn. The child's hair coloring had always been a curiosity for Zoe. Of course it had also given her a special affinity for the child.

Zoe bent until she was on the girl's eye level. It was time she set aside her own concerns for the day and focused on the children. "How can I help you, Carmen?"

The little girl thrust out her slate. "Thith math ith too hawd!"

"Is it now?" Zoe tilted the slate toward herself so she could see the problem Carmen struggled with. It was a simple addition problem but did involve double digits.

From the section of middle grade boys, someone giggled. "Her father is the banker!"

"He obviously didn't pass down his skills with numbers," another voice replied.

Zoe snapped upright and leveled the section with narrowed eyes. "I'll thank you to remember that kindness and compassion are the qualities required of any gentleman, gentlemen."

A few of the boys squirmed in their seats. None of them seemed able to meet her gaze.

"Back to work, if you please."

"Yes, ma'am," they chorused.

"Now then . . ." Zoe squatted by Carmen's side. "Let's see if I can explain how to do this a different way to help you understand . . ."

That was how the week passed. Each day that took her closer to Saturday filled her with more angst and trepidation. Wash didn't come into town. Didn't stop by to discuss any wedding plans.

She'd thought about going out to see him, but was too afraid to give him the opportunity to back out of his agreement.

Between her long hours at the school, Ma dragged her to Mrs. Holloway's house for dress fittings. Zoe had insisted that she could simply wear one of her Sunday dresses, but Ma had rejoined that every bride ought to have a special dress for her wedding day. And oh my, how Zoe loved the dress that Mrs. Holloway was crafting. It made her feel like bright white sunbeams, the palest of rose buds, and tiny fluffy baby swans had all gathered to create a blessing just for her.

If she and Ma weren't going to Mrs. Holloway's for a fitting, they were at the mercantile, buying things Ma felt Zoe would need to set up house. Ma had purchased a set of cast-iron pans, a large wash tub, tableware, and mixing bowls in several sizes. There were canning jars, and a large canner to seal them, several crocks for storage, and just about every utensil that Mr. Hines had in stock. That didn't even count all the food that Ma had insisted on packing in crates from their cellar at home.

"Just a few staples to get you started," she had said.

Zoe had no idea if Wash's tiny kitchen would even hold it all, but she hadn't been able to talk Ma out of any of it.

And now here it was, late Friday afternoon. She'd just wrung the bell and the last of her students had tromped from the room, leaving her in the silence of the lingering chaos.

She went first to the boys' section, as she always did, to straighten desks and hang up the coat that one of them had left on the floor. Then she moved to the chalkboards and carefully erased all the lessons that they'd already tackled. If she wasn't the one to return, she wanted the next teacher to know where she'd left off, so she carefully penned out instructions for the accomplishments of each grade. She'd given the students the entirety of next week off. If she wasn't to be the returning teacher, that would at least give a few days for the board to find her replacement. And she wanted a few days to get settled into Wash's cabin, even if she would be the one returning to the classroom.

Oh, how she hoped she would be returning!

After sweeping the last of the dust out the door, and giving the entryway rug a good shake, she returned the rug to its spot and then surveyed the room with a critical eye. The pine boards that lined the walls gleamed gold in the slant of the afternoon sun. A splash of pink drew her attention to the desk that Taulby Ecklund had purchased as a donation when the school was built last year. An apple sat on the desk, polished to a sheen. Zoe smiled, blinking back tears. Which of her dear students had left that there?

She returned the broom to the little pantry and then took the aisle to gather her things. Her stomach rumbled. With her stack of books in one arm, she lifted the apple and took a hearty bite.

"Mmm!" Tart, sweet juices danced on her tongue. She'd given her lunch to young Tom Channing at noon because he'd forgotten his and it had been a long time since this morning's pancakes.

"Zoe?" Ma called from the back door.

"Coming!" Zoe hurried to meet her. Today was the last trip to the dressmaker. She would see the completed gown and then tomorrow, she would walk down the aisle to Washington Nolan and become his wife.

Please, God. Please, God. Please, God.

Wash paced through his cabin, annoyed with the tap-tapping of his cane. He'd been pacing for too long because his leg already felt like it was clamped in a bear trap, but he'd put this off long enough.

Last Saturday, still a little elated from the thrill of having Zoe in his arms for those few moments, he'd gone up to the house and told his family about the wedding. He'd even let Maude coax him into staying for dinner and it had seemed like they were a family once again. It had felt nice to be normal for a while. He'd even managed to ignore his pain for a few strung-together hours.

The first two days he'd set his mind to trying to come up with legitimate work that he could do with his bum leg. He could carve a fair bit, and that was something he could do while seated. He could make toys, or carved decorations for furniture. But no one in these parts would have need of something so fanciful. It would be a sparse living. Deputy, lumberman, hostler, and farmer were all immediately crossed off his mental list. He'd thought about starting a store of some kind, but even that would require the stamina to load and unload supplies, stock shelves, and stand behind a counter all day. He'd racked his brain, but every potential job he'd thought of, like the carving of toys and decorations and such, would require a move to a city. He didn't think Zoe would want to leave her parents and siblings behind.

There was nothing for it but to march into town, steel his resolve, and tell Zoe that it wouldn't work.

Taulby would likely still want to make her his wife.

Wash's gut turned sour at the thought, but he'd determined to do the right thing.

He'd walked down to the house and left Pa a note that he needed a ride into town, but for the next three days, Pa had gotten home late from his work in the logging camps—too late to take Wash into town. Last night, Pa had sent Grant over to tell him that Jackson would pick him up around noon to take him into town today.

Friday.

The day before the wedding.

Noon would have been perfect—or at least as perfect as it could be in such a situation—because he could have found Zoe on her lunch hour at the schoolhouse. There would have been a deadline when she needed to get the students back into the classroom, offering an easy excuse for ending the conversation. And it would also have kept Zoe busy for a few hours after he broke her heart again. Maybe that would have helped her ease into the reality somehow.

But now it was already four o'clock. If Jackson didn't get here soon, it would be too late to call on Zoe's family.

Heartache rippled through his chest.

He couldn't simply not show up to the ceremony tomorrow. He wouldn't be so cruel as to leave her waiting for him with the whole town looking on. No, he had to find her and talk to her tonight.

Finally, he heard the creak of the wagon as Jackson pulled up out front.

Wash jerked open the door. His pulse pounded in his ears and his temper was about as fine as a pig in a parlor.

Jackson blinked at him. "Sorry to be a little later than we said. I got hung up at the mill." He came around to Wash's side of the wagon and actually reached out a hand like he wanted to help him climb aboard!

Ignoring his hand, Wash tromped past him, allowing his cane to plant for a brief moment on Jackson's arch.

"Ow!" His brother leapt back.

Wash hauled himself up onto the bench, grinding his teeth to keep from yelling out at the knife of pain that had just thrust itself through his calf. He dropped onto the bench with a huff of frustration at his ill temper. "Sorry about that."

Jackson gimped around to the other side of the wagon and eyed him warily as he took up the reins. "Where to?"

"Kastains, well, the Harrows." He waved a hand. "You know." Wash had the presence of mind to feel remorse over his childish actions. What had come over him lately? "I really am sorry about your foot."

"It's fine." Jackson made no other comment other than to chirp to the team, and the ride into town was tight with a silent tension.

When they pulled into Wyldhaven, Mr. Harrow, Zoe's mother's husband, was just locking up his clock repair shop.

Jackson pulled the team to a stop and called a hearty greeting. "Hello, Mr. Harrow!"

Wash wished he'd been quick enough to shush him. It was too late now.

The man looked up and smiled as he walked their way. "Evening. Lovely day today."

Wash hadn't noticed.

Jackson tipped a nod toward the Wyldhaven Creek bridge. "We were just headed out to your place. Want a ride?"

Mr. Harrow narrowed a look on Wash. "Looking for Zoe?"

A roil of queasiness made Wash squirm. He nodded. He never had properly asked the man for his daughter's hand, he realized. Too late for that now, he supposed, since it was the night before the wedding—or in this case *not* the night before the wedding.

"You won't find her at the house. She's over at the Holloways' trying on her dress for one last time before the wedding tomorrow."

There was a hint of warning in the words that let Wash know the man was daring him to hurt his daughter this close to the ceremony.

Wash shut his eyes. Blazes, he was a fool, just as Zoe had said. He should have found a way to get into town much earlier in the week.

Beside him, Jackson shifted. "Right. Well, we'll just . . ."

His brother waited, but Wash didn't have any words of instruction to fill the silence. He felt adrift. At sea. Uncertain what to do.

". . . head on over to the Holloways' then."

The wagon rumbled over the strips of newly corduroyed street, jouncing red-hot coals through Wash's leg with each bump. It was as if the Almighty Himself was reminding Wash how low He had rendered him and urging him not to drag Zoe into the depths as well.

Finally, Jackson pulled the wagon to a blessed standstill before the Holloways' door.

At least Jackson seemed to have learned his lesson, for even though he tied off the reins and climbed down, he didn't come around and offer to help Wash down.

Wash landed on the ground on his good leg, but had to hop several times and almost took a header onto the Holloways' porch before he managed to catch his balance.

"Ready?" Jackson eyed him. "You don't have to do this, you know."

His brother had not asked what he was doing here looking for Zoe the night before his wedding, but Wash could tell from the look on his brother's face that he was none too happy with him and likely knew why they were here.

"Let's just get it over with."

Jackson grunted. "You're an idiot." He strode onto the porch and rapped soundly.

Wash blew out a breath. At least he hadn't been called a fool this time. He used the stair rail to haul himself up the steps onto the porch, threw back his shoulders, and lifted his chin. Both his hands rested on his cane.

Mrs. Holloway opened the door with pins between her lips. Upon seeing them, she snatched the pins from her mouth. "Oh, it's you!" She grinned conspiratorially at Wash. "Looking for the bride-to-be, I suppose?"

He swallowed. "Yes, ma'am."

"Well come on in." She waved them into the entry.

It felt crowded with Jackson standing shoulder to shoulder with him in the narrow entry. To their left was the parlor and to the right was the dining room that opened onto the kitchen and a hallway beyond that led to the house's bedrooms. "I'll just go let—"

"Jacinda, I think we need one more feather right—" Zoe rushed into the dining room and stopped so suddenly that she might as well have run into an invisible wall.

Wash felt his jaw go slack. Zoe stood before them, encased in a white gown that hugged her in a tight sheath from shoulders to hips where it flared into yards of white frills. He perused the length of her, his mouth dry. No curve remained hidden. Had he ever noticed how utterly perfect she was?

Zoe's hand fluttered nervously over a swath of scrunched up bits of material that were interspersed with a sweep of feathers over one of her hips. He figured the ladies thought the material looked like flowers. But all he could think about was the perfect, beautiful bride wearing the dress.

"Oh, goodness, I didn't want you to see me in this until tomorrow." Zoe's cheeks turned a pink that was a perfect pairing with her red curls all piled on top of her head.

If he'd felt adrift and uncertain before, the feeling multiplied and then multiplied again. Struck dumb, he knew his mouth was hanging open, but he was powerless to close it.

Jackson reached over and did it for him with an understanding grin.

"Well, you've seen me now, so never mind. There's no point in crying over spilled milk. What is it you need, Wash? I assume you're here looking for me?"

Wash's gaze remained dumbly glued to that curve-hugging dress. After a long moment, he realized that all four of the room's occupants—for Mrs. Harrow had stepped in behind Zoe at some point without him noticing—were staring at him with humor lighting their eyes.

"Uh. We. Well, we—"

Jackson stepped forward, partially blocking Wash's view of Zoe. "What my brother is trying to say is that we're here to see if Zoe has any belongings that she would like transported to Wash's cabin tonight? That might make tomorrow after the ceremony a sight easier."

"Oh, what a relief," Zoe chirped. "I halfway wondered if you were here to tell me you'd changed your mind." She leaned to peer around Jackson's shoulder. There was hesitant uncertainty in her eyes.

Wash shook his head. "Not that." The deception tasted bitter. Why had God cursed him so? First with a love for this woman, then with a debilitating injury, and then with the weakness of character not to be able to let her go?

Somewhere deep inside, he knew the accusations that he leveled at the Almighty were unfair and irreverent. But pain and bitterness were his constant companions these days.

"Well, since you asked." Zoe tossed an amused glance at her mother over her shoulder. "Ma has assembled quite a compilation of things that she wanted to bless us with. But it's all out at the house."

"We'll go get it." Wash turned for the door before he could make more of a fool of himself by staring again. "See you tomorrow." He froze and spun back to get one more glance. "Zoe, you look . . ." He gulped. "I can't come up with . . . Sakes alive . . . Grand doesn't come close to covering it."

The last thing he saw before he fumbled his way out the door was her pleased, shy smile.

He stopped on the porch and hauled in a long slow draught of the cool evening air.

He really was going to get married.

Zoe was right. He was a fool.

Jackson was right. He was an idiot.

He gave his cane a quick twirl.

Chapter Six

Harlan was happy to have a plan. Now he just needed to figure out how to execute it.

A fire was one thing. But killing someone, well, that wasn't something he wanted on his conscience. So the fire had to be set in such a way as to ensure no one's life was endangered.

So far, when either he or his men had been watching the Nolan place, there hadn't been even a moment where all the people were gone from the place.

It came close to being empty on Sundays. But the one who lived in the cabin up the road from the main house very rarely left the property. And most of the time the main house was also occupied by the woman who lived there.

She reminded him of Maisie. Pretty. Auburn haired and petite. But married. At least he thought she must be. Likely to the oldest brother who lived in the main house.

And he oughtn't be pondering on some other woman when he was doing all this work to get that spread for Maisie anyhow.

He hadn't quite figured out the whole Nolan family dynamic yet. He'd been too leery to ask many questions around town. The last thing he needed when tragedy struck their place was for people to remember that he'd been asking questions about them. But now he might have to risk it. He had everything in place, and it was time to pull the trigger on this plan.

Tragedy would strike and he would simply swoop in as the rescuing angel who offered to buy their spread when they were forced out by the bank.

With someone on the property at all times, he could have simply started a fire at the barn, but he feared that whoever noticed it and ran to put it out could be injured. And also, if only the barn burned, the family might simply rebuild without the need of a loan from the bank.

He hated to lose the buildings. But he and his men had roughed it before, and they could do so again until he could rebuild. He would rebuild the house first, of course. For Maisie.

He just had to figure out a good time to set his plan into motion.

He wandered into McGinty's Alehouse with his men. They needed a meal, but more than that, he hoped to draw out some news. If he was careful, he might be able to direct the conversation toward the Nolans without raising any suspicions or causing anyone to remember it.

He and his men settled around one of the round tables in the far corner.

"What can I get you gentlemen?" the barman called from his place behind the counter.

Harlan swung a finger in a circle. "Beer all around. And whatever meal you're serving."

"I got chili or chili."

"That'll do."

A moment later, the barkeeper stopped by their table with a tray. He set beer and chili in front of all four of them. "Seen you gentlemen around a fair bit the last few days. You moving to town?"

Careful.

Tension tightened Harlan's gut. But a search of the man's face proved the question had merely been conversational.

Harlan eased against the slats of his chair. "Thinking about it." He rushed ahead before he could talk himself out of it. "Saw a pretty little spread up at the headwaters of Wyldhaven Creek. Think those folks will ever sell?"

Beck shifted in his seat, a spoonful of chili halfway to his mouth, and looked up at him.

Harlan ignored him.

The barkeeper tucked the tray beneath his arm and plunked his hands on his hips. "That would be the Nolan spread and I'd say you'd have about as much luck talking him into selling as you would talking a bear from its winter den."

Not what Harlan wanted to hear. Of course he'd known the man was planted deeply because as many things as they'd done to the place would have driven a less invested man to sell long before now.

Harlan casually raised a shoulder. "Figured as much. Sure is a pretty little spread though."

McGinty nodded. "It is that. But the man has too many sons to be talked into selling. He wants to leave them something when his time comes. In fact, his family is about to grow again. His oldest is getting married tomorrow." The barman looked like he really was happy about that. "Well, I'll let you all enjoy your meal. Just holler if you want another round." The man returned behind the bar.

Harlan resisted a whoop of excitement. It was exactly what he'd been hoping for!

He took a bite of chili, grunted, and about spit it right back into the bowl. Blazes that stuff was hot enough to peel whitewash from a fence. He breathed past the bite and forced himself to swallow, chasing it with a gulp of beer.

The barman grinned at him across the room. "Good, right?"

"Sure," he lied with a cough. He glanced at his men. None of them seemed bothered by the heat of the chili. Hang it! He was going to have to eat it and pretend he liked it.

But it didn't matter. The good news was worth the torture. He scooped up another bite, beer at the ready.

When Zoe woke on Saturday morning, she started to rise, but then realized what day it was and collapsed back against her pillow for a moment, hand over her heart.

It was the day of her *wedding*! To the man of her dreams.

Last night when she'd first seen him standing in Jacinda's entry all stern and scowling, she'd had such a foreboding sensation. But then his expression changed the moment he caught sight of her in her dress. The way his jaw had hung!

A smile stretched her lips. He'd liked what he'd seen, which made her feel all soft and warm inside.

She may have had to force him to marry her, but he was still attracted to her.

It was a start. But would it sustain them?

The foreboding threatened to return in full force.

Best she get on with her day before she worked herself into a tizzy of unease over whether he was going to leave her standing at the altar.

She leapt from her bed and dashed to the wash tub with a twirl and a sway. Papa Harrow had brought it into her room last night. It was already half full of water. She drew her hand through it and was pleased that it had warmed to room temperature. She just needed to pour two large pots of boiling water in to warm it.

In the kitchen, she found that Ma already had their two largest canners full of water and heating on the stove.

"Thank you, Ma!"

Ma smiled. "Can't have our girl doing manual labor on her wedding day."

Zoe chuckled. "I'm sure there will be plenty of that in my future."

Ma's brow tugged, and even though she whirled away to quickly tuck a towel around the pies she was bringing for the wedding reception, Zoe hadn't missed the look of concern.

"Best you eat while the water finishes heating." Ma swung a hand toward the table. "Oatmeal and hard-boiled eggs are on the table already."

The way her stomach was suddenly cramping, Zoe didn't think she could manage to swallow a bite, but it would only add to Ma's worry if she didn't try. She put one egg and a dollop of warm oats on her plate. Oats were not her favorite. But butter and brown sugar always made them more palatable.

Ma usually kept the white sugar only for guests, but today she set the sugar bowl by Zoe's plate. "Put a little in your coffee this morning."

Zoe complied, adding a healthy dose of cream from the pitcher. She savored a slow sip. Mmmm. Sweet coffee was her favorite.

Her younger siblings and Papa arrived in spurts, each sleepily serving their plate and sinking into their chairs around the table. Belle hadn't arrived yet, but that wasn't unusual. She often was the last to wake.

Sharon asked if she was nervous.

Zoe lied when she said, "No."

"I sure hope he actually shows up to the church," Shiloh said around a bite of oats. "It would be so embarrassing for us if he—"

"Shiloh Louise Kastain!" Ma snapped from her end of the table.

"Sorry," Shi mumbled.

Zoe suddenly felt more than a bit sick. She set her half-eaten egg on her plate next to the untouched oats. Pushed the plate back.

Papa gave her a sympathetic look of understanding.

Zoe tried to smile. "I think I'll just take my bath now. I'm afraid what might happen if I eat any more. Aidan, would you mind helping Papa with the hot water?"

Aidan and Papa hefted the first of the large pots of hot water from the stove and carried it to her room.

Unwilling to give up her sweet treat, Zoe took her mug of coffee when she followed them.

When they'd dumped in the second pot, Zoe closed the door behind them, and set her coffee on the little stool she'd placed by the tub. After undressing, she sank into the hot water clean over her head. She remained under until her lungs threatened to burst and then surged up to gasp a lungful of air.

Swiping hair and water from her eyes, she leaned back against the side of the tub and grabbed her coffee. "Lord, if You could, please remind Wash Nolan how much he loves me. And help him realize that with our love buoying us up, everything will be just fine!"

And please don't let him leave me stranded at the church.

She couldn't quite bring herself to voice that last part of the prayer.

After a fortifying sip of coffee, she returned the mug to the stool and went back under the water.

Belle woke on the morning of her sister's wedding with a massive yawn. She'd stayed up much too late the night before trying to finish a painting that she wanted to give to Wash and Zoe today as a wedding present.

She cast a critical eye across the room to where the painting still sat drying on the easel. The scene had mostly been finished, but she'd wanted to add some final strokes of lighting the evening before. She hoped that the light touch she'd used would allow the oils to dry by this afternoon. But if not, she'd just have to present it to them in a day or two.

The night before, when she'd finally laid down her brush, she hadn't been sure if she was happy with it, but here in the light of morning, she decided it was done.

She'd chosen a scene that she remembered from their school days. Miss Brindle had taken them on a field trip to study nature, and Belle remembered clear as day that Wash had plucked an apple from the wild apple tree they'd all sat under during lunch that day and had handed it to Zoe. It had been the first time Belle had realized he was soft on her sister.

With the Rodantes' barn in the distance, and the sunlight filtering through the leaves of the apple tree, and Zoe smiling softly up at Wash as she accepted the fruit, the painting had turned out just right. Of course, they were older now. But Belle hoped they would like this bit of nostalgia and that it might take them back to the happiest days of their childhoods if they ever needed that.

She blew out a breath. Who was she kidding? She had a feeling they were going to be in dire need of a reminder of happier moments multiple times over.

Worry over whether Zoe was making the right decision filled Belle. What if Wash was too broken to ever return to being the man they'd once known? Would Zoe have the strength to make it through that heartache?

If she didn't know that Zoe would see it as a betrayal, Belle might try to talk her into waiting a while longer before making such a momentous decision. She was marrying a man who had climbed into a shell and didn't seem intent on coming out of it anytime soon. But Zoe would be hurt if she brought it up, and Belle didn't want that.

She dressed and made it to the breakfast table just as Papa and Aidan returned with an empty canner. "Water for a bath for Zoe?"

Papa nodded.

"Good. I hope she can relax and enjoy today."

"Me too." Papa squeezed her shoulder as he passed by. "Did you get the painting done?"

Belle put oats and an egg on her plate. "I did. I was worried I wouldn't like it, but looking at it just now, I think it will do." She smiled.

"That'a girl!" Papa's eyes sparkled with pride.

He was continually reminding her to see the good in her work and not only the critical things that needed to be changed. Love for the man filled her.

They sure had been blessed when the Lord orchestrated for Ma to meet Papa.

"I can't wait to see what you've done!" Ma's eyes sparkled.

Belle blinked at her. For many years, Ma had been nothing but critical of her desire to paint for a living. So to have her showing such enthusiasm warmed her heart. "You may go look if you like, but the paint is still a touch damp. It's on the easel in the corner of my room."

Ma leapt up from her chair, wiping her hands on her apron. "I won't touch it, I promise. Elijah?"

Papa surged to his feet. "You don't have to ask me twice!"

Belle smiled as they dashed down the hall like a couple of giggling teenagers.

Shiloh sniffed. "I don't see what the big deal is! It's only some blobs of color on a canvas."

Belle narrowed her eyes at her sister. "You know, Shi, one of these days your bad attitude is going to turn around and bite you if you don't learn to curb it. Why can't you try to see the sweet side of things instead of always the sour? Don't you think life would be much happier for you if you chose to be positive?"

Shiloh tilted her head. "I don't know how to do that."

Belle hoped her sigh wasn't too audible. "When the negative thing pops into your head, you make a practice to rethink and see the positive. If you ask the Lord, He will help you."

"Like how?"

Belle poured herself a cup of coffee. "Well, for example, if you go out to collect the eggs and you only find eight, instead of complaining that there are only eight eggs, you could find a bright spot like the fact that you collected enough eggs to make a pound cake. And that was only today's eggs!"

"Only eight eggs! Why, that would be an abysmal amount of eggs. We might as well dispense with the chickens and fry them all up for dinner!"

Across the table, Aidan chuckled as Sharon huffed her irritation. "It's no use, Belle. She's got the sourest disposition of anyone I know!"

Belle reached to squeeze Shiloh's arm. "I won't belabor the point. All I'm asking is that you think on it. The Word tells us that we should rejoice in the Lord always. To constantly grumble is not a heart like the Lord would want us to have. Now." She rose as she stuffed the last bite of her oats into her mouth. "If you girls can get this table cleaned up for Ma, I'll go help Zoe with her hair. Aiden, a blanket on the wagon bench would help with Zoe's dress today, I believe."

Belle knocked on Zoe's bedroom door and then poked her head inside. She'd expected to find Zoe a bit nervous.

What she hadn't expected was to find her weeping in her bath water.

Zoe dashed water against what she could only assume was her splotchy face and motioned for Belle to enter. "Come in. I'm done. Was just about to get out."

Belle approached with a large towel held out to both offer Zoe privacy and the warmth of a wrap the minute she stepped from the water. When Zoe wrapped herself in the towel, Belle encircled her shoulders with one arm and gave her a gentle squeeze. "Are you okay?"

Zoe used a corner of the towel to dry her face. "I'm fine. Just as nervous as a calf at branding time."

Belle chuckled. She motioned to the screen in the corner of Zoe's room. "Into your underthings and then we can talk."

Zoe scooted behind the divider, hands trembling as she donned her undergarments and camisole. "I don't know what came over me, honestly. I was doing fine and then I got to thinking about what Shiloh said and I just fell apart."

From the other side of the partition, Belle snorted. "What did that little jackanapes say this time?"

Zoe couldn't help a huff of laughter. "She said she hoped Wash wouldn't embarrass our family by not showing up."

Belle sputtered a sound of dismissal. "He wouldn't do that to you, Zoe. He loves you too much to hurt you like that."

Just the encouragement of Belle's reassurance eased the tightness in Zoe's stomach. "I thought he was stopping by last night to tell me he wasn't going to go through with it."

"You saw him last night?"

"Yes. When I was at Jacinda's place trying on the dress." She slipped her long petticoat over her head. "I didn't know he was there and came out to talk to Jacinda and he was in the entry. He looked all stern and foreboding and then when he caught a glimpse of me he sort of froze and couldn't seem to find words."

Belle giggled. "That's because he loves you, like I said."

Zoe could only hope her sister was right. She stepped from behind the privacy screen, rubbing her long red curls with the towel. "Am I making the right decision, Belle?"

Belle patted the chair before her vanity. "Sit."

Zoe did as she was told, handing the towel off to Belle, who went to work drying the ends of Zoe's locks. She watched her sister in the mirror. "You don't think I'm making the right decision do you?"

Belle froze. Met her gaze in the reflection. "I know that you two have loved each other for a long time. But I worry that he's . . ." She waved a hand. "Not ready to get on with his life."

Zoe pushed a long slow exhale between her lips. She swiped at invisible dust on the vanity's top. "Me too. But . . . I'm going to help him with that."

Belle's expression softened. "If anyone can do it, you can, Zoe." She tossed the towel aside and squeezed Zoe's shoulders, giving her a hug from behind, her ear pressed to Zoe's. For a long minute, they just looked at one another and Zoe appreciated the strength she drew from her sister.

Finally, Belle released her. "Okay, what are we going to do about your hair."

Zoe felt the last vestiges of her nervousness flit away. "You're the artist. But I think I would like to put it up in pin curls for a few hours until it dries."

"That's what I was thinking too! We'll make you so beautiful that you'll knock Wash Nolan right onto the floor when you walk into that church today."

Zoe smiled. Then laughed. She reached to touch her sister's hand where she'd begun to form the first curl. "Thanks for being my sister, Belle. I know we've had our ups and downs through the years, but I wouldn't trade you for anyone in the whole wide world."

Belle's eyes misted. "Nor I you. Now . . ." She flapped a hand. "Let's get on with this or we'll both arrive at the wedding with red swollen eyes and blotchy cheeks." She grinned through her tears.

Zoe dashed at her own eyes and gave a nod. "Then instead of falling on the floor, Wash might turn and run right out the side door."

They shared another laugh in the mirror.

But just like that, Zoe's nerves returned in full force. She laid a hand over her stomach and closed her eyes. Why oh why had she eaten that half of an egg?

Wash tugged nervously at the cuffs of his dress jacket as he stood at the front of the church with Jackson and Kin Davis beside him. His attention was glued to the back of the sanctuary, where Zoe would step in at any moment.

Belle and Zoe's twin sisters were standing up with her, and Kin, Jackson, and Lincoln were standing up with him. His brother, Grant, and Zoe's brother, Aidan, hadn't seemed to mind in the least that they'd been tasked with escorting attendees to their seats. They'd done a fabulous job and were now seated next to their families on the front benches on either side of the aisle.

Wash had been on his leg much too long already today and it was shooting small flames that threatened to turn into the white-hot raging tongues of fire that never abated until he slept them away. But he was determined to remain in the present and enjoy this day without the aid of his cane. He could pretend he was a whole man for just one day, couldn't he?

After he'd seen Zoe at the dressmaker's yesterday and caved to his weakness for her, he'd decided to let go of his reservations and simply accept that there was no fighting his love for this woman.

He and Jackson had gathered the things Zoe had mentioned from her mother's place, and this morning when he left the house, there had been crates scattered all over the kitchen. He'd figured it would be best to let Zoe decide later what she wanted to do with them.

He still got a physical pain in his chest every time he tried to cypher out what he was going to do with his life from here forward. Not just his own life now, but Zoe's as well. He'd been good at book learning, but every job he'd ever done had been physical labor.

Throwing hay for old man Jonas before he passed.

Riding as a deputy for a short time when Sheriff Callahan had needed help.

And of course his work around the farm for Pa, and his short stint in the cavalry.

He swallowed down the bitterness that crept to the back of his throat every time he remembered that he would never be fit for that kind of work again.

Maybe he ought to revisit his idea about the carvings. He could create things and they could make some trips to the city to sell what he couldn't sell locally. The problem was, he wasn't really sure he was any good at that. He'd never carved anything more for his younger brothers than rough-looking shapes that could pass for a cow or horse.

He released a pent-up lungful of air and clasped one wrist with the opposite hand so he'd quit fidgeting. *Lord, I've not been much good at keeping in touch lately, have I? But here I am, about to give my heart completely to this woman and I don't know how I'm going to provide for her. So if You could just—*

Zoe stepped from behind the back wall that partitioned the sanctuary from the entryway and knocked his prayer galley-west-from-Sunday.

Wash tried to swallow, but all moisture seemed to have vacated his mouth.

Aurora started plunking a tune on the piano and the congregation rose, blocking his view. He leaned to see around Ewan, whose annoying shoulders were much too broad. Then she was there, at the end of the aisle, walking toward him with a shy smile. She carried a bouquet of purple lilacs and greenery tied with a big white ribbon. A matching bloom had been threaded into the curls near her ear.

If possible, she was even more beautiful today than she had been yesterday. A short swath of lace trailed in the aisle behind her.

Mrs. Holloway had sure gone all out on that dress.

He perused the length of her and tugged at the tightness of his collar, as the flames from his leg dissipated and instead worked their way into his heart. In just a few short minutes this beautiful woman would be his. What miracle of blessing was this for someone so undeserving?

Peace swept in to cover all the tension and anxiety of the past week.

They could do this.

Together.

He wasn't the complete man that he longed to be, but even the apostle Paul had suffered a thorn in his flesh, yet look at all that man had accomplished. Wash didn't deign to compare himself to such a giant of the faith, but if that man could do all he had done, surely Wash could figure out how to be a good husband and provider for this woman who filled him with such a protective spirit.

As Zoe and her father paused at the front of the aisle only paces away, movement at the back of the church drew Wash's attention. Taulby Ecklund slid into the back row, head hanging as he studied something before him.

Wash's heart went out to the man. The miller obviously had very strong feelings for Zoe. Yet . . . he swallowed. She had chosen *him* even after the man's proposal.

His gaze reconnected with hers.

He could get lost in the soft blue of her eyes for all eternity. He'd loved her for almost as long as he could remember. And *she'd chosen him.* Another wave of awe and unworthiness washed over him.

He was taking on a lot of responsibility simply by being here today. But it was for Zoe. Just as she'd chosen him, he was choosing her. And somehow that made the burden anything but a burden. It was a joy. A privilege. An act of self-sacrifice that would give him opportunity to prove his love for her all the days of their lives.

He suddenly forgot about his concerns over how he would provide for her. The worries over whether he was doing the right thing. The concern over how he was going to manage his constant pain. It would all work out because he loved her enough to fight through any obstacle.

He smiled at her.

"Oh, hi!" She returned his smile with a puff of relief that eased the tension in her shoulders and had the congregation chuckling.

Wash relaxed into his legs. He'd worried her by showing up at the Holloways' yesterday, hadn't he? Well, she could worry no longer because he was committed now. This was happening.

"Who gives this woman to be married to this man?" the parson asked.

Mr. Harrow laid his hand over Zoe's and looked down at her for a moment. "Her mother and I do." He leaned down and kissed Zoe's cheek, and then offered her toward Wash.

Wash was careful to maintain his balance as he stepped over to take her hand.

She eased to his side, smiling up at him. "I'm glad you're here," she whispered.

"I wouldn't want to be anywhere else." He squeezed her fingers reassuringly.

"You may be seated," Parson Clay said to those gathered. After the rustling of the crowd died down behind them, he continued. "We are gathered here today in the sight of God and this company to join together this man and this woman in holy matrimony . . ."

Wash lost focus on the words because Zoe's hand, soft and warm, had settled into the crook of his arm, and the scent of the lilacs tantalized him to lean down closer to her. He shuffled his feet instead, and laid one hand over hers. His palm curved over her knuckles. Her fingers tangled together with his. And in that moment, all was right with the world.

He heard her say something, and then his own voice confirmed his wish to marry her. The parson held out his Bible to reveal the rings as he spoke a few words about how gold was untarnished and a ring unbroken.

Wash was ever so thankful that Pa had pulled him aside this morning to offer him Ma's wedding band because it was a detail that he would have completely overlooked what with all the kerfuffle of emotions that had been tormenting him this week.

Now he looked down at the ring on the parson's Bible, teeth clenched. He'd only been nine or so when Ma passed after giving birth to Grant, but he could still remember her smile, the soft touch of her hand, the sound of her voice when she used to read them stories of an evening. She'd been fine one afternoon. And then she'd gone into labor and been with the Lord by the next.

Could something like that happen to Zoe?

The thought struck Wash so forcefully that he snapped his head up, gaze blurring on the cross that hung on the wall behind the parson.

"Wash?"

The parson's gentle question brought him back and he realized that Zoe had turned and extended her hand to him, and that the parson had stretched his Bible close so Wash could take the ring.

He shook away the concerning thought. They would deal with the discussion of children when the time came. For now, there wouldn't be any until he could get himself established in an income. If there were to be no children, they would need to refrain from—He felt heat wick past his collar.

He cleared his throat, snatched up the ring, and faced Zoe. Slipping the ring to the middle knuckle on her finger, he repeated after the parson. "With this ring, I thee wed. With my body, I thee protect and cherish. With all my worldly goods, I thee endow. In the name of the Father, the Son, and the Holy Ghost. Amen." He pushed the ring the rest of the way onto her finger but didn't release her hand, because he knew what came next and hang it if he wasn't about to kiss her before the parson gave the go-ahead. No one ever conceived a child with only a kiss. Those were an intimacy he could enjoy worry-free.

"I now pronounce you husband and wife!"

Wash tugged Zoe's hand to draw her closer and both the parson and the congregation chuckled. Zoe's blue eyes widened a little, but she did sidle closer and rest her hands on his shoulders. Something in her bouquet tickled the side of his ear and he reached up to slap it away. Zoe smiled and moved the bouquet farther behind him, which was okay with him, because it brought her nearer. Wash grinned down at her. Gave her a wink.

"You may kiss your bride, Wash Nolan."

Ah, those precious words. But, now that the moment was upon him, he wanted to savor it. To memorize the way her waist lay small against the splay of his hand, the way her gaze was soft and inviting, the fullness of her lips that she tilted up to him. The pink tip of her tongue that darted across those lips.

He placed one hand to the back of her head and slowly, carefully, drew her the rest of the way to him. Her lashes fluttered and dropped to rest against her cheeks.

He closed his own eyes then, too, and memorized the feel of her soft lips moving beneath his. One of her hands settled against his cheek, her fingers cool and gentle. Her thumb stroked the corner of his mouth. She tasted of mint and salt.

Salt?

He eased back.

Tears streaked down her face.

She chuckled nervously. "I truly am happy, I promise you."

He smiled and cupped her face with his hands, using his thumbs to stroke her tears from her cheeks. "I love you." The whispered words surprised him. He hadn't meant to say anything.

But it was worth it when she went up on her tiptoes and kissed him again. "I love you too." She returned to flat feet.

He leaned after her, but at the parson's sharp clearing of his throat and the warm laughter that filtered through the church, he stopped himself from kissing her again. He hugged her instead, pressing his cheek to hers so they could both look out over those gathered.

"May I present to you, Mr. and Mrs. Washington Nolan!" the parson proclaimed.

The congregation surged to their feet, cheering and clapping.

Zoe took his hand and started down the aisle.

He'd only taken one step when his leg collapsed from under him.

On instinct, he tightened his grip on Zoe's hand, but he was going down fast and hard. And Zoe's petite frame was no match for his weight, especially since she hadn't been expecting it.

He landed hard with Zoe right on top of him.

"Wash!" She scrambled to press her hands to his chest and search his face. "Are you okay?"

The heat of embarrassment flushed through him, but there was no sense in making matters worse by getting angry. He drew her to him with one arm, catching sight of the startled expression on Mrs. Griffin's face as she peered down at them from the bench beside which they'd fallen.

"Well, that was unexpected." He laughed.

"You're supposed to wait to do that sort of thing until you get out of the church, Nolan!" Ewan McGinty guffawed from his bench at the back of the room.

Zoe's face turned a color almost to match her hair, and anger hurtled in like a flash flood. He surged to his feet with a strength he didn't know he still possessed, drawing Zoe with him. He spun to find Ewan, and hoped his glare would convey his displeasure.

Ewan's cocky grin remained in place.

Wash took a step.

Dr. Griffin thrust out one hand and pushed past his wife into the aisle.

Wash could still see Ewan over Doc's shoulder.

His bawdy smile faded and he raised his palms. "Sorry. That was ill-thought of me. I didn't mean disrespect."

Wash let his anger seep away, shoulders easing. He gave the man a nod, then turned to look at Zoe. "I'm so sorry. Are you all right?"

He searched her over. She seemed all right, but he'd pulled her down to the floor with him! And all because his pride had wanted to make it through the day without his cane.

"I'm fine! Truly, I am." Zoe said. "I'm just glad you are too."

Jackson was there by his side then, holding out his cane. When they had fallen, Jackson must have retrieved it from the corner of the sanctuary where Wash had placed it before the service started. Wash accepted it.

"Thanks." He offered his brother a nod.

Chapter Eight

Zoe willed away the pain in her shin and did her best not to limp as she followed Wash down the aisle. When they'd fallen, her leg had shot out on instinct in an attempt to catch her balance and she'd whacked it on a pew. But Wash was embarrassed enough and the last thing she would do was add to that.

Something drooped against her arm and she looked down. One of the lilac stems had broken. She plucked it off and shoved it into the center of the bouquet so Wash wouldn't notice.

She lifted her focus just in time to meet Taulby's assessment as they approached the back of the sanctuary.

Concern filled his expression and when he dropped a look toward her leg, her pulse pattered in dread. He'd noticed her injury, which likely meant that others had too. The pain would abate, but she would certainly have a good-sized bruise showing later.

However, it was of no matter.

Bruises would fade, but she and Wash would remain together for the remainder of their days!

He'd shown up! Said his vows! Kissed her with a passion that had allayed all her fears over the question of his love.

He still loved her! And that was what would see them through. Their love for each other. Nothing else mattered.

She followed Wash onto the church porch and drew in a lengthy lingering breath. *Ignore the pain. Everything is fine.*

Wash had paused at the porch railing, palms pressed to it. He hunched into his shoulders as he scanned the churchyard.

Zoe stopped by his side.

A few tables were already scattered across the lawn, and as Belle, Aidan, the twins, and Wash's brothers all breezed past and descended the stairs, Belle was already bossing them. The guests would be coming out at any moment, and they would be expected to greet them, but . . . did Wash need to get off his feet?

She laid a hand on his shoulder. "We did it."

"Yes. We did." He didn't sound happy.

She swallowed. "Want me to get you a chair?"

He whirled on her so quickly that she took an involuntary step back. He hesitated and then his shoulders and face relaxed—even if only slightly. "Let's get something straight right from the start, Zo. You don't treat me like an invalid, and I'll do my best not to be one, all right?"

His words had the same effect as if he'd punched her. "I didn't mean to—"

"Well look at you two! Aren't you just the loveliest couple!" Mrs. Hines sailed toward them across the porch, arms outstretched. And a passel of people were spilling out of the church doors right behind her.

Wash fell into place by Zoe's side. He stood closest to the church doors, while Zoe stood nearest the porch steps. Wash shook Mrs. Hines's hand and then the woman pulled Zoe into a hug.

With her lips near Zoe's ear on the opposite side of Wash, the woman whispered, "I surely hope you know what you've gotten yourself into. Please let me know if I can ever be a help in any way!"

Zoe stiffened. She mumbled an automatic, "Thank you." But the last person in almost the entire world that she would ever go to for help would be Mrs. Hines.

Zoe looked up to find Taulby standing before her. Wash stood stiffly by her side, but he was already speaking to Ewan, who was next in line.

Taulby didn't reach out to shake her hand or even touch her. Instead, he briefly paused, touched his fingers to his forehead and mumbled, "All the best I truly wish you, Zoe. All the best." And then he trundled down the stairs and lumbered away from the gathering toward the mill.

Zoe felt a mixture of sadness and relief as her heart went out to the man. She truly hadn't meant to hurt him. And yet it was so wonderful to have Wash here by her side.

Hopefully, Taulby would find happiness again soon.

Taulby left the church with an ache in his gut and a cold sweat on his brow despite the heat of the day. He'd carefully kept his face neutral as he shook Nolan's hand. But when it came to Zoe, he didn't dare to touch her. He gave a stilted salute instead, mumbled some boring platitude, and then fled, relieved to have the task done.

The moment he was past them, he marched to his mount, yanked the reins from the hitching post, and swung into the saddle.

He should go to the mill. Work to do. But hang if he could sit still and work with all this *sjalusi* roiling in his belly.

He turned his horse for the open road and put his heels to its sides. The horse complied and gave him the speed he was looking for.

He must put Zoe Kastain—no, Nolan now—behind him.

Ach, why had he let himself fall so hard for her? He'd known she pined for another. She'd been upfront with him from the beginning. Friendly always, but keeping a distance. He'd hoped that he could change her mind, in time.

And Lord forgive him, when broken, and bitter, Nolan had come home, he'd hoped that final weight would drop the balance in his favor.

Obviously not.

"*Gå*!" He snapped the reins on the horse's rump. "*Gå*!"

His horse complied with the command and stretched out, taking the road with ground-eating strides.

The wind cooled his face. His *sjalusi*, not so much.

Giving the horse its head, he closed his eyes and entreated the heavens to help him lay these ugly emotions to rest.

Perhaps leaving was his answer. He could start a mill in some other town far from here.

But no. That was not what he wanted. Wyldhaven was a good place with good people. There was plenty of work and good roads to deliver his boards. He'd even recently purchased the nearby lot so he could start a lumber yard beside the mill.

He let his mount slow to a canter. Drew in a long breath.

An acrid waft of smoke hung on the air.

With a frown, he slowed the horse again, this time to a walk. Spun in a circle to search for where the smoke might be coming from.

There! From just over the rise. If he hadn't been so much in his own thoughts, he would have noticed it before now. He clucked to the horse, urging it to the top of the hill.

Below in the valley, smoke billowed from the barn on the Nolan spread! A terrified whinny pierced the air.

The horses! "*Gå*!" He urged his mount over the embankment and across the fields. His horse did not like moving toward the smoke, but Taulby kept a firm rein and when they stopped in the yard, he wrapped the reins around a corral post.

Smoke spilled from the top of the barn roof as he approached. Inside, the horses continued to scream.

Taulby shoved open the rolling doors and rushed inside. The hay in the loft burned, but here on the lower part of the barn, he could still see through the haze.

How many animals here?

The first stall held a cow, he opened the door. The creature barreled out and thundered past him.

The two horses were next. The first one needed no prodding, but the second one's eyes were wide with terror and it only bobbed its head and bounced off its front hooves when he opened the stall door.

Overhead the floorboards of the loft crackled and started to glow. A rope hung on a nearby hook and he quickly looped it around the horse's neck. But sparks were falling from the ceiling now and, crazed with fear, the horse only circled her stall. It wanted nothing to do with leaving the barn.

Taulby whipped off his shirt and draped it over the horse's eyes. "Out we must go, ja? Just a short way to safety, little horse."

He was thankful when she stepped out at the tug he gave to the rope. He rushed her to the entrance and slapped her rump, letting her run with his shirt and all. He paused in the doorway, hands propped on his knees and assessed the interior once more.

Was that the last of the animals?

A bark from the back of the barn suddenly registered. A dog? He hadn't known the Nolans had a dog.

The smoke was thicker now. He assessed the loft. The whole floor was aflame. He hated to even think it, but he should leave the dog. He'd done what he could.

Another yip was followed by a terrified squeal.

Ach. He must try. He must be fast.

Taking a big gulp of air, he rushed back into the orange glow of the barn. He searched the dim light for the dog. Where was it?

No more yipping sounded to offer a direction.

He passed all the stalls and still hadn't seen it. His lungs burned for air, begged him to breathe. But the smoke was so thick now he would choke if he tried. His eyes burned, streaming tears. It took every effort to keep them open. He raised one arm by his eyes, but it did not help.

He must return outside. He started for the door, but a waft of smoke, momentarily cleared the air and there! A white spotted lump of fur lay at the base of one of the pillars.

He rushed to it, lungs shooting pain now. Spots drifted before his eyes.

Jinx! The dog was tied to the post with a rope. Taulby fought to untie the knots with fumbling fingers but they were tight, and on instinct he inhaled. The smoke gagged him into a choking cough that doubled him over and only made the burning worse. Tears blurred his vision.

He swiped at his eyes and tugged at the knots again.

The rope would not come free! The dog was limp. Likely already dead. But this was Jinx. He couldn't just leave Zoe's dog to burn in the barn.

The collar!

He held his breath one more time. Concentrated through the agony. The clasp came free! He hauled the dog into his arms and stumbled from the barn, only making it a few steps before he crashed to his knees and lay the dog in the dust at his feet.

He coughed and hacked and coughed some more.

Something stung his arm and then the sting turned into a blaze of pain. He slapped at it, brushing off the ember that had drifted from the sky.

With another cough, Taulby sank into the dust next to the dog.

The crackle of flames faded into the distance as blackness crept across his vision.

Ewan cleared his throat, snapping Zoe's focus from Taulby's retreating form to the waiting line of guests. Ewan's eyes twinkled and Zoe felt her lips pinch tighter.

She thrust out a hand. "Thanks for coming, Ewan."

He bowed over her hand. "My pleasure, Mrs. Nolan."

The words were like a jolt of lightning to Zoe's chest. Mrs. Nolan! She could have floated off the porch right then and there, but the pain in her shin kept her grounded.

The rest of the attendees passed in a blur of handshakes and hugs and well wishes. And by the time Belle arrived to fetch them to the head table, Zoe could have cried with thankfulness to be off her aching leg.

Was this what Wash felt every day? Likely worse!

No wonder his personality seemed to have changed since he'd returned home. She would have to do her best to tiptoe around his sharp edges and enjoy the times when she caught a glimpse of the man she'd once known and fallen in love with.

She'd already learned her first lesson. Never make mention of his weakness.

She could handle that!

She'd been hopeful that she could talk him into trying that surgery that she'd heard Dr. Polson speaking to him about. But now she might need to wait for the right time to bring it up.

That might be better anyhow because she wasn't sure how they would afford it. She would know on Monday whether she would be allowed to retain her job. If not, she would have to find some sort of job since Wash wasn't able to work at all at present.

She pushed the worry away for another day and made sure her relieved sigh wasn't audible when she and Wash sank into their seats. Belle had thoughtfully prepared plates for them, but it was the tall glass of water that Zoe reached for first. She drained nearly the whole thing.

Wash leaned close. "I'm sorry, Zo. I shouldn't have snapped at you like I did."

"I forgive you." She set her glass down and placed her hand on top of his where it rested between them on the table. She angled slightly to get a better look at his face. "We'll get this figured out, Wash. We just have to remember that we love each other, and all will be well. I only want the best for you—you know that, right?"

He nodded, a slight crimp in his brow. "Yes. And I want the same for you."

She gave a firm dip of her chin. "Good. I'm sure we'll have times that we step on each other's toes, but when we do, we simply need to remember that we each only want the best for the other."

Wash lifted her hand and pressed a kiss against her knuckles, seemingly happy to let the subject drop. "Do you need more water?"

She snatched up her glass before he could do it. "I believe I do. I'll be right back."

She hurried from the table lest he insist that he ought to be the one to get it for her.

The food table with the pitcher of water was in the shade of the large oak that sat at the back of the church. When she arrived at the table, no one remained in the vicinity. With a quick glance around, she plunked her glass onto the end of the table and stepped behind the church and farther into the shade. Leaning carefully against the church wall, she bent and hoisted her skirt to look at her shin.

A wince scrunched her face. A long red scrape stretched the length of the bony part of her shin, and it was already turning purple and yellow around the edges. She would be feeling that for a few days.

"Mrs. Nolan? Is all well?"

Zoe snapped her head up, tossing her skirt down as she spun to face Dr. Polson. He stood near the food table with an empty plate in one hand and a spoon filled with Mrs. Griffin's mashed potatoes in the other.

She waved a hand. "It's nothing, I'm sure. I bumped my leg when Wash and I fell and was just checking to see how bad it was."

The man put his plate and spoon down. "Let me have a look, if you don't mind." He motioned that she should step into the sanctuary through the back door.

"It's really noth—"

"Come, Mrs. Nolan. I'd feel better if you allowed me to assess it. You don't want to start out your married life with an injury that might worsen over time."

That was true enough. Zoe relented and motioned him forward.

But he shook his head. "Meet me in the back of the church, if you please. I'll fetch your husband."

Zoe's eyes shot wide. "Doctor Polson?"

He paused. Turned back to face her. "Yes?"

Zoe scrambled to think. Of course propriety dictated that someone else be present. But it couldn't be Wash! Gracious! This was turning into a full-blown ordeal. And she really had only wanted to make sure it wasn't bleeding.

The doctor was still waiting for her to speak. "Could you please get my mother instead? Wash has been standing for an awfully long time."

She tucked her lip between her teeth. Would he buy her reasoning?

"Of course. That's very true. And right thoughtful of you. I'll get your mother."

Zoe blew a puff of relief as she tugged open the door at the back of the church. It led her in at the side of the pulpit and she immediately felt the cool of the sanctuary envelope her. She made her way down the aisle to the small bench that sat against the partition at the back of the room and sank onto it.

Tipping her head against the partition wall, she closed her eyes and willed away the throbbing in her leg.

It was only a moment before she heard Ma and Dr. Polson bustle into the entry.

"Zoe?" Ma rushed past the partition and hurried to her side. "Doctor Polson says you've been hurt?"

Zoe straightened, irritation surging through her. "It's nothing, really. I just needed to look at it for a moment to make sure it was okay, and Doctor Polson saw me. I'm fine." She couldn't help the look of irritation she pinned on the doctor, even if it only took her a moment to school her features.

He cleared his throat and squatted before her. "I'm sure you are right, Mrs. Nolan, but it is always better to be certain."

With a huff, Zoe hoisted her hem just far enough for him to get a look at the injury.

"Oh, Zoe." Ma covered her mouth with her fingers.

"I'm fine, Ma. Honest. I just scraped my leg against a pew when we fell."

"Hmmm." Dr. Polson's fingers were surprisingly gentle as he prodded her leg. She braced for additional pain that never came. His fingers were cool and assured, and then he sat back and lifted his gaze to hers. "You are certainly going to have a whopper of a bruise, but I don't think anything is broken. Thank you, ma'am, for allowing me to take a look. I think we'll all feel better now that we know you'll be fine."

It was his use of "ma'am" that set her back against the bench. "Yes. Thank you."

He stood. "As soon as you get home, if you can put a cool cloth on it, that will help. Keep dipping the cloth in cold water and replacing it on the injury for about twenty minutes a couple times a day and that will aid with the healing and the pain."

She returned her hem to the floor. "Thank you."

He stepped back. "Right. Well, I'll leave you two alone now. Good day." With that, he hurried away.

Ma sank onto the bench beside her. "It was kind of him to fetch me and take a look. I'm glad you are all right. I could hardly fathom what had happened when you both fell the way you did!" Ma shook her head and pulled a face.

Her look of aghast shock struck something funny in Zoe. She imagined the scene that had taken place just down the aisle, from the perspective of those watching. One minute she and Wash had been celebrating their marriage with an exuberant walk down the aisle and the next they'd been on the floor.

A giggle spurted past her lips. She clapped a hand to her mouth.

Ma's lips pinched in irritation, and she cocked one brow, but a sparkle lit her eyes and she had to twist her lips to one side in the signature way she had when she was trying not to smile.

Zoe desperately tried to control herself, but her humor spilled from her in a snort. And then another. And then a thin wheezing mewl.

"Oh, Zoe, do stop! It was awful!" Ma looked away but her shoulders were shaking with laughter.

And then they were both draped across each other, laughing like two donkeys in an alfalfa patch. Zoe started to slide off the bench and had to brace herself with her injured leg, which caused her to gasp in pain and sent them into another gale of laughter.

Finally, Ma straightened and tugged at her waistcoat. She smoothed her hands over her skirt and then over her hair, as though to assess how much damage their laughter had done.

Zoe dabbed at the tears beneath her eyes and sat up straighter. She angled Ma a look.

Ma's gaze had lost all of its humor, and concern had filled it instead. "You're certain you're all right?"

"Yes. It hurts. But I'll be fine. And Ma?"

"Yes?"

"Please don't say anything to Wash. He feels terrible enough to have fallen, I don't want to add to his burden by letting him know that I got hurt."

Ma's brows went up. "That large of a bruise might be a bit difficult to hide . . . well, later . . ." She looked away with an uneasy sound in the back of her throat.

Zoe felt heat slam through her. She jerked her focus to the now wilting lilacs tied at the end of every other bench.

Hopefully, when the time came, Wash wouldn't be focused on her shins and wouldn't notice.

She fanned her cheeks with one hand. Heavens! It was hotter in here all of a sudden than the mill's boiler-room! "I guess I'll just have to deal with that when the time comes." Gracious. She was *not* having this conversation with her mother. She jumped to her feet. "For now, I'd better get back to our table."

Ma stood. She pulled Zoe into a hug. "I'm glad you're okay."

A tightness threatened to constrict Zoe's lungs. "Thanks, Ma. I'll be fine." She might be fine, but she certainly was going to miss getting to see her family every day.

As she stepped out the back door of the church and finally refilled her water glass, weariness registered. Bone deep weariness. But fast on its heels was the recollection of Ma's intimation.

No matter how tired she was, this day was far from over. And the mere consideration of what the evening ahead held sent a surge of heat through her.

Mercy.

She fanned her cheeks.

She ought to have picked a cooler day to get married.

She once more sought the shade of the old oak behind the building and leaned against the coolness of the wall, willing her pounding pulse to ease.

Wash fidgeted in his chair, trying and failing to find a position that eased the torment in his leg. An agonizing cramp zinged through his calf, and before he thought better of it, he leaned down to press his thumbs into the pulsing throb.

From the next table over, Mrs. Hines glanced his way, one of her brows winging upward.

He probably was quite a sight in his Sunday suit, sweating in the sun like a pig on a spit, and face contorted in pain. He only allowed himself a couple moments of the massage and then straightened. It hadn't helped much. He thrust his leg beneath the table and pressed his heel away from himself as he lifted the leg. Sometimes that offered enough of a stretch to ease the cramps.

Not today.

He resisted a wince. Where was Zoe, anyhow? She'd been gone an awful long time to fetch a glass of water.

Guilt nudged him. He ought to have gotten it for her. Likely her delay was only because she'd been held up in a conversation with someone. But not near the food tables, because she wasn't over there. So where—

"Fire! Fire, I say!"

Wash snapped his focus to the horse and rider barreling up the hill toward the churchyard. The horse was lathered, the rider continuing to yell words that were unintelligible from this distance.

Men leapt to their feet, each concerned for their spreads, no doubt. A fire at this time of year could put a small farm or ranch under for good.

Reluctantly, he stood to join the men. Thankful that he could balance on his good leg and had the table to lean on.

The rider hauled his horse to a stop and leapt to the ground. "Where's Butch Nolan?"

Horror whipped through Wash. The man wanted Pa?

Fire . . .

No.

Just like that, he plunked into his chair again.

Please, God, no.

Pa stepped forward from his place down the table. "I-I'm Butch Nolan." He fiddled uncertainly with his hat. Pa's uncertainty filled Wash with a wave of despair.

The rider wiped sweat from his forehead onto his sleeve. "Sorry to say, but there is a raging fire out at your place. The barn and several outbuildings are ablaze!"

Several outbuildings . . . the words swirled through him with nauseating horror. Was his cabin on fire? All of Zoe's things! All the things her ma had spent money on to provide for them. Wash scrubbed a palm over his face.

Pa turned a little pale. His jaw dropped, but for a moment he didn't move. Then he braced himself with a sideways step. "The animals?"

The man shook his head. "Don't know."

Sheriff Reagan was by Pa's side in an instant. He settled one hand against Pa's shoulder. "Listen, everyone. Hate to break up the party, but we are needed at the Nolan spread. Everyone gather as many buckets as you have and meet us there as soon as you can!"

With that, he and several men rushed off, mounted up, and rode away.

Pa was already striding toward the wagon. "Let's go, boys!"

Wash fumbled for his cane as Grant and Lincoln sprinted for the wagon. Jackson took Maude's hand and hurried her toward the buckboard as well.

As quickly as his cane and cramped leg would allow, Wash rushed after them. Then he froze and spun to search the crowd.

Where was Zoe?

She appeared suddenly by his side. "I'm here. What do we do?"

He nudged her toward where his family waited, and when they reached the wagon, he paused by the open tailgate and offered her his hand. "We'll figure that out when we get there."

She accepted his help and climbed aboard. He hauled himself up beside her, thankful to be able to stretch out a bit in the bed of the wagon.

"Ha!" Pa snapped the reins against the team's rumps. "Ha! Ha!"

With a lurch, they barreled out of the churchyard.

Wash bent over his legs and pressed his forehead as close to his knees as he could, thankful for the ease of pain in his leg, but terrified of what they would find on reaching home.

As they careened around a corner, Zoe gripped the side of the wagon bed to keep her balance on the bale of hay that she'd sunk onto when Wash helped her aboard.

They'd been able to see the smoke for miles now. Her stomach churned. This was all her fault. If she hadn't insisted that Wash marry her, the Nolans would have been home and could have prevented the fire.

Wash had sunk onto the floor of the wagon beside her, pressed his head to his knees and had hardly moved since.

Worry over his obvious pain crimped her stomach.

But another thought had been plaguing her all the way from the church.

Jinx was at the Nolan spread. Papa Harrow had given him to Wash last night and insisted that he and Jackson take him to their place. He was Zoe's dog, after all, and she would be living at the Nolans' now. But . . .

Her heart ached and she refused to ponder what might be happening. Was the dog locked in Wash's house? Was Wash's house one of the buildings on fire?

When the wagon topped out on the hill above the Nolan spread and she saw the inferno below, she clapped one hand to her mouth.

She pressed her other hand to her aching heart. "Oh, dear Jesus."

Wash lifted his head, arms clasped around his slightly bent knees. He didn't utter a word, only stared at the patchwork of burning buildings. Everything seemed to be ablaze. Everything except the main house. That was something to be thankful for, she supposed.

Mr. Nolan hauled the team to a stop, already yelling orders at his sons. "Jackson, we'll need a strong man at the well. You man the crank. Lincoln, Grant, you boys are going to have to be strong men today. Strong and fast with the buckets, understand? We have to wet the roof of the house so it doesn't catch."

Even as he said the words, Zoe watched an orange glowing ember drift on the wind toward the house.

The Nolan family bailed from the wagon and Zoe shot out a hand to stop Maude. "Blankets, Maude. As many as you can bring from inside."

Maude looked relieved to have a task. She gave a short nod and dashed for the house. Behind their wagon, others were coming to a halt now.

"Zoe!" Wash called. He pointed to the place between the house and the barn near the corral.

Zoe's heart crashed in her chest. "Is that—Taulby!" Hoisting the skirt of her wedding dress, she sprinted to where her friend lay in the dirt beside—"Oh no! Jinx!"

Zoe fell on her knees beside Taulby. Was he dead? She reached for his shoulder. "Taulby?"

He winced and moaned at her touch and that was when she noticed that he was shirtless and burned in several places. Embers were falling all around them like rain! They had to get him moved!

Zoe looked around. "Wash?"

A wagon rolled to a stop beside her. Wash was on the driver's bench. And thankfully, Sheriff Callahan and Marshal Holloway were right behind him. They leapt from the wagon bed.

"Here! He's here!"

Her shout was unneeded, for the men were already by Taulby's side, using their strength to get him on his feet.

"I am good," she heard him say to the sheriff. But his words were accompanied by a hiss of pain.

Relieved that Taulby was getting help, Zoe scrambled to Jinx. The dog lay on his side, and mercifully his chest was moving as he breathed in and out. When she fell to her knees beside him, he lifted his head and his tail thumped a happy greeting. "Oh Jinx! Were you in that barn?" She stroked a hand over his head, fondling one soft ear. The dog flopped his head back onto the dusty hard-packed dirt and an ember fell near his head. They needed to get away from this area! "I need some help here! Please! Someone—"

"I've got him, Zo."

To her surprise, Wash stopped by her side and crouched to heft the dog into his arms. He winced and grunted, but was able to stand, and limped toward the wagon.

Zoe stuck fast by his side.

Marshall Holloway draped Taulby with his jacket, while Sheriff Callahan climbed over the back onto the driver's bench, looking impatient to drive them away from the burning barn.

Maude was suddenly by her side with a huge armful of blankets. "Zoe. What did you want these for?"

Zoe was torn. Her attention bounced from Taulby, who sat against the side of the buckboard, racked with a cough, to the dog Wash was just laying into the bed of the wagon, to the blankets in Maude's arms.

She made a snap decision. "Jinx, stay with Taulby. Good dog. Marshal and Wash, I need your help."

Taulby gave her a nod of understanding. He reached a hand to stroke the dog. He would take care of Jinx.

Marshal Holloway leapt from the back of the wagon and stopped by her side. "What is it?"

Zoe took one of the blankets from Maude. "We need to soak these and drape them on the roof."

"Good thinking." The marshal hurried with Maude to where Jackson hauled bucket after bucket from the depths of the well.

Butch Nolan already had a bucket brigade pouring water onto the roof of the house. At that moment, Zoe registered the burning cabin down the road.

Wash's burning cabin!

Her gaze flew to his.

His lips pinched into a grim line. "I'm sorry, Zoe."

Unable to live without his touch for even a moment longer, she stepped to his side and wrapped her arms around him. "It's me who should be sorry, Wash. If I hadn't forced you to marry me, you all would have been here and—"

He set her from himself with a firm grip and bent until he could look into her eyes. "This is not your fault. Hear me? Not your fault."

There was such a fierceness in his countenance that she tilted her head. "What is it?"

He shook his head and pulled her back into his arms. They both stood in the chaos and took in the scene.

Finally, Wash said, "Something happened here. I'm not sure what. But buildings don't just randomly start on fire like this. The barn is almost gone, so the fire likely started there. But if a fire blazed through from the barn, it would have caught the house before reaching my cabin. Something isn't right."

A chill slipped down Zoe's spine.

A loud splintering sound spun them to watch as the roof of the barn collapsed and fell in on itself. A cascade of flames shot in every direction!

As if by mutual agreement, they both let each other go and hurried to take up a wet gunnysack from the stack that Sheriff Callahan had placed near the well. Together, they beat out flames that popped to life in the grass around the barn. Many others who had attended the wedding were doing the same.

What had Wash meant? That someone had set these fires on purpose?

She shuddered and took stock of those gathered.

Who would do something like that?

Harlan stood on the hill, well back in the trees beside his men.

Ted had just ridden up with the supplies that Harlan had sent him to Cle Elum to pick up. He'd wanted him gone for this job. After all, the man was the newest of his crew and he'd been subtly suggesting that Harlan look for different property ever since he'd joined them. Harlan had felt it best to have him out of the way while they pulled this particular job.

Now Ted stood beside him, eyes wide as he stared down at the burning spread. "What did you do, boss?"

Harlan bit off a chew of tobacco as he watched the townsfolk scattered like ants across the little valley, beating out the last vestiges of the flames.

Their planning and execution had been perfect. Not everything had gone exactly to plan, but pretty close—well except the man who had showed up and rescued the animals. But that was a small defeat.

He tucked away his tobacco and trained his field glasses on the property.

The barn, gone. The partially built cabin in the distance, gone. The smaller cabin that had sat closer to the main house, gone. The only thing that remained was the main house because the torch they'd thrown there had somehow failed to ignite. But that was okay. In fact, it was perfect because it would give him a place to live while rebuilding the place.

With all the other buildings gone, old Butch Nolan would be needing funds from the bank for certain. And once Olann denied him, he would be so discouraged that he would give up the spread. Served the man right.

Harlan's grin broadened.

He only wished that he could reveal himself to the man. But the time for that would come. Harlan sucked his teeth and drew in a lungful of air to calm the roil of anger that surged.

Yes. The last thing that Butch Nolan ever saw on this earth would be his smiling face.

He couldn't wait to see the look in the man's eyes!

Chapter Ten

Zoe leaned against the rail of the Nolans' front porch. She was exhausted. The last of the flames seemed to have been snuffed, and now that the danger had passed, as if by mutual agreement, the townsfolk had clustered in the front yard and on the porch.

Taulby sat on the other end of the porch, leaning against the house. His head was tipped back, and his eyes closed, or she might have approached to ask how he was feeling. Jinx lay on a small rug beside him and when the dog caught her eye, his tail thumped, but other than that he made no movement.

She blew out a sigh. Earlier, Doc had examined the dog and didn't feel he had too much damage. He'd said his lungs sounded good and felt that though he wasn't currently his rambunctious self, Jinx would likely recover. Zoe hoped he was right. Either way, she owed her dog's life to Taulby's brave and quick thinking!

She looked down at herself. The wedding dress that she and Mrs. Holloway had fretted so over, was a positive ruin of soot and ashes. She'd also burned a hole in the bottom of one of her slippers—she knew because earlier a rock had gotten stuck in it and she'd had to take it off to remove the pebble. The hole was likely from stepping on a coal. And at some point part of her hem had—she bent for a closer inspection—melted?

Aghast, her jaw dropped. She released the material. Straightened.

If her dress had caught fire that would have been . . . well, she couldn't quite decide whether to laugh or cry at the thought.

Beside her, Wash dropped onto the top step. He groaned audibly as he leaned forward to scrub at the muscle of the calf on his injured leg.

She sank down beside him. "I'm so sorry. Is there anything I can do?"

Grimacing, he shook his head, continuing to punish the muscle.

Dr. Griffin was suddenly before them. In one hand he held a glass of water, in the other a vial that contained a deep brown liquid. He held out a vial to Wash. "Drink this. All of it. And I'm not taking no for an answer. You've positively brutalized yourself today, son."

It shouted evidence of the truth Doc spoke when Wash didn't argue, but simply took the small bottle and gulped the contents. He grimaced and shook his head as he thrust the empty bottle back toward Doc.

Doc traded him for the water glass and Wash guzzled the whole glass in one long gulp.

Doc leaned forward to squeeze Wash's shoulder. "You'll be feeling better in a few minutes. Just sit still and rest for at least thirty minutes. Doctor's orders, huh?"

"You'll get no argument from me today," Wash said.

They'd been sitting quietly for a few minutes when a conversation caught Zoe's attention. Sheriff Reagan approached the marshal and Mr. Nolan. He held a long brand of wood in one hand. One end was charred black while the other end was hardly burnt at all.

Zoe's stomach dropped. She darted a look at Wash, but there was no need to speak because she could tell by the look on his face that he'd already seen it too.

She looked back at the firebrand. "Is that what I think it is?"

Before Wash could reply, the sheriff held up one hand. "Could I have everyone's attention, please?" He thrust the stick up for those gathered to see. "I found this near the barn, and the marshal found a similar one near Wash's cabin. We found this one here near the back of the house. How it didn't catch, is simply a miracle—that's the only explanation." He tossed the torches into a pile near his feet. "I think we all know what that means. I just want to urge you all to be careful and vigilant around your places. If someone burned one spread, they won't hesitate to burn another. Of course we have no idea what might have motivated this, and will be investigating. I'm just asking that you folks be aware."

"We all know who was the first on the scene!" Wash's sudden shout made Zoe jump, even as her husband turned to look placidly at Taulby, where he sat on the other end of the porch. "Why don't we ask him why he would do such a thing?"

Zoe's hand shot out. "Wash no! Taulby would never—" Her words cut off at the sharp look Wash turned on her.

A muscle pulsed in his jaw. "We arrived to find him passed out and burnt and half dressed." His words sounded a little thick and slurred. His voice turned soft, meant for Zoe's ears alone. "We know he cares about you. And everyone in town knows how much you love that dog. What if he was starting the fire and heard Jinx in there and went in to save him and got hurt in the process."

Zoe shook her head. "No! Taulby would never doing something like this. Never."

"Not even for a little revenge on me for marrying you?"

Zoe leapt to her feet. "No. Not even for that!" She took note of Ma and Papa sharing a frown before she tossed a glance at Taulby and felt a churn of sorrow at the look of horror and betrayal on his face.

All of the Wyldhaven townsfolk stared at him.

He shook his head. "Is not so." He swept a gesture toward his horse still tied at the corral. "I left the wedding and a ride I took, ja? Because of the smoke, I came to the top of the hill and the flames I saw. The horses they squeal and the dog he bark. And I—I—" He motioned to the barn. "In I go. Saved the cow and the horses. One horse was fearing, and so my shirt I used to cover the eyes. Then out it came with me. The dog still is crying, so back in I go, and nearly did not find him in the smoke." One meaty broad hand fell to rest gently against Jinx's head. "After that . . ." He shrugged. "I don't remember. But—" His glittering gaze drilled into Wash. "The fire I did not start."

Wash hung his head. Scrubbed one palm over his cheek. Held his silence.

Zoe closed her eyes. He owed the man an apology. But she was too tired to fight about it. She simply wanted to clean up and get some sleep. But she and Wash didn't even have a bed to sleep in. Wash's cabin had burned into a pile of ashes.

Tears pricked her eyes. All her worldly possessions had been in that little cabin. She was ever so thankful that she'd decided to leave her books in the schoolhouse until a decision was made about her position. She might not have any clean clothes to wear, but she could borrow something from Belle or Ma. It would have been much worse to lose all her precious books. Some of them would have taken months to replace, not to mention the expense of getting them shipped here.

Zoe realized that a thick silence still hung over those gathered. People shuffled, likely silently contemplating Wash's accusation. Every once in a while someone would glare in Taulby's direction.

Her hand shot into the air before she could think better of it. "I have something to say!"

All eyes fell on her.

"We all know Taulby. Wash has been out of town and so he doesn't know the kind of man Taulby is. But those of us who know him, know he wouldn't do something like this!" Zoe narrowed a look on Ewan McGinty. "Ewan, when the alehouse roof sprung a leak last fall and you couldn't afford to fix it, what happened?"

Ewan's focus drifted to Taulby. "Ecklund gave me half off on shingles."

Zoe lifted her hand in agreement. "That's right, he did. And Sheriff, when the town council needed new logs to corduroy Main Street, who lent his teams and his men to help with the hauling and the work?"

The sheriff gave her a nod of encouragement. "Taulby Ecklund did."

"He helped us fix the porch on one of our bunkhouses," Liora Rodante called. "Just showed up one day and fixed it for us and wouldn't take a penny for it!"

Zoe exhaled, long and slow, as relief coursed through her.

Sheriff Callahan raised his voice. "We'll conduct a thorough investigation and will follow the evidence. But as of this moment, I don't see any indication that Ecklund had anything to do with this, other than to be a hero."

Wash's head hung low enough that his forehead rested on his knees.

Zoe's heart went out to him. He had spoken in haste. Perhaps out of jealousy. He would need to fix his mistake. But now was not the time. He needed to rest and get off his leg. She stepped to his side and touched his shoulder. "Come, Wash. Let's go to Ma and Papa's place to stay tonight. Tomorrow will be another day."

He nodded without lifting his head. He rocked a little and Zoe got the impression he didn't know he was doing it but was in so much pain that it was all he could comprehend in that moment.

Zoe looked around, wondering who might be able to give them a ride. Papa and Ma had only brought the carriage. And with them on the front bench, and Aidan, Belle, and the twins in the back, there was no room for her and Wash. Especially not when Wash would need to stretch out his leg.

Kane stepped to Zoe's side. "Please allow me to give you and Wash a ride?"

Relief surged through her. "Thank you, Kane. That is a big help." She glanced down at Wash, who still hadn't moved. She wasn't sure where Kane's wagon was, but with as weak as he currently looked, she didn't think Wash could walk to it. "If you don't mind, could you—"

Kane held up one hand. "I'll bring the wagon as close as I can."

"Thank you."

As Kane strode away, Ma squeezed Zoe's hand. Zoe hadn't even heard her approach but was relieved to find her there. She wanted to cling to Ma as though she were life itself, because she was suddenly overwhelmed with a terrible dislike for the man she had married today. And the emotion made her irritated with herself. Still . . .

The Wash Nolan that she'd married this afternoon, was not the Wash Nolan that she'd fallen in love with as a young schoolgirl! How could he have called Taulby out like that, and in front of everyone too, when the man had heroically saved the stock and Jinx?

Zoe tugged Ma a few steps away and spoke so only she could hear. "What have I gotten myself into, Ma?" Could her mother see the terror, horror, and despair churning inside her? Why was she ever so impulsive and unable to see the consequences of her choices until it was too late?

"Oh, Zoe." Ma drew her into a quick hug before setting her back to arm's length. Her chin nudged up in that way she had of reminding her children to face life head on. Her brows arched and her lips pressed together. Moisture glistened in her eyes, but she blinked hard, and no tears fell. Her grip firmed around Zoe's shoulders, and she gave her a gentle shake. "No one is at their best after this day. Let's just get home, get some rest, and face the future tomorrow, hmm?"

The problem was, Zoe wasn't sure she wanted to face her future. Would Wash constantly embarrass her with his meanness? What if he never again returned to the gentle and kind man who would have gone out of his way to help anyone? The one who had been deputized at seventeen because of his impeccable reputation for responsibility? The one who had escorted her to Seattle and been so kind to Aidan even when her brother had knocked him and his heirloom pocket watch into Wyldhaven Creek?

She shivered at the memory, pushing away her worries as Kane pulled his wagon to a stop. Ma was right. For now they just needed to rest. Tomorrow she could ponder how to broach the subject with Wash.

"Come, Jinx." She patted her leg and was happy to see that, with a wag of his tail, the dog complied. He even jumped into the back of Kane's wagon without the need of help.

Washington Nolan, however, didn't seem to be faring so well.

Kane and Deputy Joe both took an arm and led her unsteady husband to the wagon, but even with the two of them hefting him, it was almost more than they could do to get him into the bed.

"Tired," Wash muttered.

Doc stopped by Zoe's side and handed her a brown bottle. "The laudanum dose I gave him was pretty strong. He likely won't be good for much this evening. But don't be too hard on him. I have a feeling that some of what he said was caused by a full day of severe pain. It has a tendency to wear on a man until he snaps, and I'd say today was much too demanding for someone with his . . . injury."

Zoe looked down at the bottle. "Does he take this every day?"

Doc shook his head. "My no. In fact, he's refused every time I've offered any. I was a little surprised that he accepted it today."

Her worried gaze traveled to where Wash lay in the wagon next to Jinx. He must have been in a great deal of pain indeed, to have accepted it, then.

Zoe woke at home in her own bed and blinked at the pine-board ceiling. For one blissful moment the horrors of yesterday were far from her mind and then everything came crashing back.

She sat upright, clutching the blankets to her, and leaned to look at the floor.

Wash was still there, one arm thrown over his brow, eyes closed. He breathed deep and slow.

Wash hadn't spoken for the whole ride from his father's spread to their cabin the night before. When they'd arrived, Papa had helped him to her room. Ma had given them extra blankets and a pillow. Zoe had gone to clean up, leaving Wash sitting on the side of her bed, head hanging and hands propped on either side of himself as though he needed them for the balance. And when she'd returned, she'd found him sound asleep on the floor with the extra blanket and pillow, soot still marring his face.

Her heart had softened, if only marginally. How exhausted must he have been to have fallen asleep so quickly and with only her woven rag rug between himself and the floor? The medicine Doc had given him must have played a part in that.

She supposed her bed was too narrow for two, and it had made her more comfortable to have him on the floor anyhow. It would have been some awkward to sleep pressed up next to a man she was suddenly unsure that she even liked. By this evening they would need to come up with a different solution, however, because it wasn't fair to ask Wash to continue to sleep on the floor.

He hadn't even removed any of his clothes, except his boots, belt, and jacket, which he'd set on the floor beside him.

The stench of smoke still clung to her hair, and she was desperate for a bath, but obviously with her husband currently taking up the space where the tub normally went, she would have to pass on that luxury for a while longer.

Her husband . . .

What had she done?

She rose, wincing at the sharp pain in her leg. A glance revealed that the purple had spread in a swath nearly the width and length of her hand. Cool water would hopefully help the pain. She hadn't yet had a chance to obey that particular instruction from Dr. Polson.

She tiptoed to the dressing partition, thankful that Belle had thoughtfully handed her a skirt and blouse the evening before. She slipped them on and tucked the shirt into the skirt. Taking her towel and bathing cover from their hooks, she peeked around the partition. Wash was still sound asleep. She hated to simply leave him there on the floor, but Ma would need help with breakfast, and church would start in just a few hours. Would Wash come with her today?

After she washed in the creek, maybe she would try to wake him and see.

Near the door, she paused to look back at him. With his features relaxed in slumber, she took in the sweep of his firm stubbled cheeks, and the broad width of his brow that balanced the strength of his jawline. A tendril of attraction curled through her, and she felt once again the love she'd carried for this man for so many years.

The doorknob was cool beneath her fingers for a brief moment as she hurried from the room.

The good book said that each day had enough trouble of its own, and today's were already starting to pile up around her.

Wash opened his eyes the moment the door clicked shut. He sat up, suppressing a groan. He'd needed the sleep, and had slept hard, but he never wanted to pass another night with only a thin pad between himself and the hard floorboards again. And he'd broken his promise to himself. A promise that he would never indulge in a doctor's laudanum concoction again.

He worked his mouth. Something tasted like pounded nails, and his tongue felt thick. A smoky odor drew his attention to the fact that his first order of business ought to be a bath. It would have to be in the creek because he didn't want to burden the Harrows any more than he already had, especially not on a Sunday morning.

At least the aches and pains of sleeping on the floor somewhat masked the sharper ache in his leg.

He smirked as he rotated one arm to restore circulation.

At thoughts of yesterday's fire, the smirk faded.

And then another memory washed over him like a tidal wave. The sharp accusation he'd leveled against Taulby Ecklund.

The way the townsfolk had immediately jumped to the man's defense with Zoe as their leader.

Guilt and sorrow slipped in to fill the gaps.

Why had he done that? What had made him speak so to a man who had only been trying to help?

In the cold light of morning, he knew that Taulby hadn't set that fire. He also knew that he'd spoken in haste, something he'd always endeavored not to do. He could blame the pain, but that would be a rationalization. The truth was a lot more complicated. Sure he'd been in pain, but he'd also felt an irrational jaundice toward Taulby. Perhaps because of the way Zoe had flown to the man's side when they'd seen him lying there in the dirt in front of the burning barn. It was indeed irrational, because Zoe had turned down Taulby's proposal and come to him with one of her own. Yet it had hung with him all evening as he'd fought the fire in his best suit while the pain in his leg had amplified in the vice of his injury.

He owed Taulby an apology. He'd known it last night, but the medicine Doc had given him had taken effect rather quickly and he'd hardly been able to think to string two words together.

Surprisingly, with as much pain as he'd been in yesterday, this morning his leg felt as good as it ever did.

He climbed to his feet and padded out into the main room. Mrs. Harrow was cooking breakfast at the kitchen stove.

He gave her a nod. "Morning. Please don't hold breakfast for me. I need a quick wash in the creek."

"All right, but—"

He waited, but she must have changed her mind about whatever she'd been about to say.

She waved him on. "Never mind. You've plenty of time before breakfast is ready. I still have to put this in the oven to bake for a while."

He nodded and thanked her, half wondering where Zoe had gotten to as he made his way out the door. He caught a whiff of himself on a bit of a breeze. Ugh. Probably better that she didn't get too near him until he'd visited the creek anyhow.

In the mornings, he could almost feel like he might one day get his strength and his life back, but when he remembered the dreadful agony of the night before, reality returned to firm root.

He thought of what Dr. Polson had said about another surgery. If only he thought it might help, he would do it in a blink. But what could Polson do that the two cavalry surgeons hadn't been able to do? It was a futile hope.

He rounded the end of the barn and took the path through the trees toward the little Wyldhaven Creek pool he knew lay just beyond the next rise. How many times had they all swam there as kids? He and Kin had pulled their fair share of trout from that swimming hole in the cool of a dawn morning when the water skippers were lively and the birds were launching into chorus.

Before the creek there was an old tree that had been damaged when it was young and the trunk had bent into a near perfect bench before it curled toward the sky once more. He was already yanking his shirt over his head when he came around the corner, and didn't see the clothes until he was nearly to the bench.

He froze, his gaze darting toward the creek that lay on the other side of the cattails, and then back to the skirt and blouse draped carefully over the trunk.

Drat, someone had already beat him here. Was it Belle or—"Zo!"

She emerged on the path between the cattails with a scrap of toweling clutched in front of her as she worked with one end to dry her hair. She froze. "Wash!"

He didn't move. Couldn't have moved if he tried.

She wore a long bathing cover that clung to her in ways that made his jaw go slack and his heart beat from the region of his throat.

Zoe's scrutiny zipped over his bare chest, paused on the hand that clutched his shirt, and then dropped to the path. Her face filled with the prettiest crimson and she tucked one lip between her teeth.

He couldn't stop a grin. "I was just heading for a dip myself. But I think this view is much better than a cold plunge into the creek." Much better indeed.

A small smile tugged at one side of her mouth, but she didn't lift her gaze to his.

He suddenly realized that even though he had every right to be here with his wife, she was uncomfortable, and he wasn't being much of a gentleman.

He stepped to one side, giving her a clear path to the tree that held her clothes. "I'll just mosey on down to the creek and meet you inside in a few minutes."

She pressed her lips together with a shy nod. But as he passed her, she looked up. "Wash?"

"Yeah?" Her eyes were Forget-Me-Nots. Her hair a cascade of flame. He swallowed. Focused on the tip of his boot. Reminded himself that just yesterday he'd promised himself there would be no children until he could figure out an income.

"Will you come to church with me today?"

There was so much emotion in the words that his focus darted back to her. Hope and pleading and . . . concern?

Of course, he'd been missing services a lot recently. Actually . . . when was the last time he'd attended? Maybe more than a lot. It was always such a relief to wake and be pain free for a few blissful hours—sometimes only moments—that he'd sort of gotten into the habit of doing as little as possible so as not to ignite the beast any earlier than it decided to wake on its own. But she was right—skipping weekly services wasn't a good habit that he'd fallen into.

"Sure, Zo."

Her smile was so immediate and full of joy that it made him want to please her always. He relished it. The way it crinkled the corners of her eyes. Bunched her cheeks. Revealed her straight white teeth.

All too soon, she tucked her chin, angling him a shy glance. "We'd best get a move on, if we're to be on time."

"Right. I'll just—" He motioned to the water and started toward the creek but couldn't help but watch her over his shoulder as she headed for her clothes. The way that bathing gown—

Something slapped him in the cheek and then a cold gush filled his boot. He snapped his attention to the fore. Drat! He'd wandered from the path and right into the cattails.

His boot made a sucking noise as he dragged it from the muddy water.

Behind him, Zoe giggled.

"Not fair, woman!"

She only giggled again.

Lord help him, but he needed that cold plunge in the creek!

Chapter Eleven

Taulby Ecklund lay on his stomach on his bed, unable to bring himself to move. He'd only fitfully slept as each movement ignited the burns on his back. It was Sunday morning, and he ought to dress for services, but this once it wouldn't hurt to miss.

This morning he did not want to face the suspicious glances of the townsfolk.

He drifted back to sleep, and woke a few hours later when a pounding knock threatened to beat down his door.

"Coming, I am. Coming!" He winced his way through sitting up and gingerly tugged on a shirt, not bothering to tuck it into his trousers.

He couldn't have been more surprised when he opened the door to find Wash Nolan standing on his porch, leaning on his cane.

Taulby glanced toward the stairs that led up from the mill to his front door. The man had navigated the climb? He must desire to level another accusation.

Taulby folded his arms, wishing the action didn't shoot pain across his shoulder. "Ja?"

Wash cleared his throat and fiddled with his walking stick. "I've come to apologize. I know you had nothing to do with setting that fire. I don't know what made me say that. Thank you for saving our stock, and Zoe's dog." He lifted his gaze, and Taulby saw only sincerity.

He relaxed. "This I accept. Thank you."

Nolan tilted his head. "How are you feeling today? I knocked and knocked. You okay?"

Taulby waved a hand. "Sleep well, I did not. Then when awake I am supposed to be, the sleep it comes." He offered a sheepish smile. He wanted to dislike this man who had stolen his Zoe from him, but he had to admire a man who had faced his own shortcomings and reached out to try to make it right.

A look of understanding rose in Nolan's eyes. "Pain is like that. It sneaks up on you at odd moments and takes you unaware."

Sudden realization filled Taulby. Since returning home, Nolan had hardly been seen around town. But yesterday he had stood through his wedding, fallen on his face in front of everyone, pulling the woman he loved down with him, and still had the fortitude to face everyone in the greeting line. Then after all of that, at his father's spread he'd spent the rest of the day fighting the fire. He must have been in severe pain the evening before when he'd blurted what he had.

Taulby, stepped back, holding the door wider. "Pain can also make us say things that normally we wouldn't, ja?"

Wash pressed his lips together. Shook his head. Remained on the porch. "It's not a good excuse."

"This I understand." He motioned for the man to enter. "Coffee?"

Wash smiled. "Maybe some other time?" He swung his cane toward the street below. "Zoe's family is waiting on me."

Taulby tamped down his *sjalusi*. "Ja. Another time, then."

Wash touched his cane to the brim of his hat and then thumped his way toward the stairs.

The door had only been closed for a few moments when another knock came.

Had the man forgotten to say something? He opened the door and blinked.

On his porch stood a woman that he hadn't seen before. Honey-blond hair looped in a thick braid around her head like a crown. Large gray eyes assessed him unreservedly. The handle of a basket rested on one of her arms.

"Hello." She smiled softly, warmly.

The color of her eyes brought to mind the gentle lapping waves of a fjord, and her soft voice was as welcome as the first bite of a krumkake melting on his tongue. Homesickness gripped him. However, she obviously was lost, and in the wrong place. He felt his brow slump. "How is it I can help you?"

A hint of amusement filled her expression. "I hear there is a miller that lives in here? I'm on orders from my great-uncle to find him and nurse him." She assessed Taulby from head to toe. "But you don't seem like you are injured—and no one mentioned that this miller would be so grumpy. So perhaps I have the wrong house?"

He frowned. He felt a bit off-kilter. "Who are you?"

She fiddled with the basket. "My name is Anja Johansen. I am the niece of Mr. Heath. I've been taking care of him for a few months now. I've seen you about town."

"I see." He shuffled his feet, unable to decide what had brought her to his door.

She thrust out a pale thin hand. "Please, forgive me. My uncle, he has sent me with a salve" —she hefted the basket—"to treat your burns. So perhaps you could summon the less grumpy version of yourself before we start?"

Taulby couldn't help a smirk.

Her eyes glittered. "Ah! I knew he was hiding in there somewhere."

That brought a chuckle. “For this, I apologize. You have not caught me on my best day.”

She tilted her head. “I understand. And I’d like to help with that.”

That would explain why she was here, then. Yet . . . “The doctor, he will in the morning be here. I will be fine.”

She flapped a hand, and to his surprise, stepped right toward him. On instinct, he backed up and she strode past him. “The doctors know nothing of the old country ways. I may have been born and raised here in America, but my gran, she was Uncle Zeb’s sister, and if anyone knew how to treat a burn, it was her.” She smiled. “I’ve mixed up a batch of her balm. You’ll be feeling better in no time. Now, the burns?” She skimmed him. “They are where?”

The top of her head barely reached his chin, but he had a feeling that she could—and would—barrel over him without hesitation, if needed.

He felt peculiar. Like someone had just taken one of his legs, and then demanded that he balance on a bucket. “Most are on my back. One on my shoulder.”

“Good. Off with your shirt, then. Off!” She dropped her basket on his small table and thrust out a hand waiting for his shirt.

“Uh, on the porch would be better, ja?”

She plunked her hands on her hips. “If the tongues of Wyldhaven are fitted with two hinges, Mr. Ecklund, they will flap no matter what we do, right? Perhaps even more so if we stand on the porch. I’ve no fear of you.” She tilted her head. “Have you fear of me?” A twinkle filled those gray eyes, lighting them with a glint of mischief.

With a huff, he tugged his shirt over his head, attempting and failing to keep his face impassive as the material pulled free from the burns. “’Twas only your reputation I thought of.”

She snapped his shirt and folded it with deft hands. "The good Lord is the keeper of my reputation. Now," her assessment drifted over the front of him, and a tinge of pink touched her cheeks. "No burns here. Turn." She made a little sound in the back of her throat and gave an impatient gesture for him to spin.

He did so, wondering why his crazy heart was beating so rapidly.

Anja Johansen had never been more thankful to have a man's attention fixed away from her. There was something unsettling and yet, oh so attractive about the way this man had watched her.

And the moment she'd seen him with his shirt off, she'd known he was right. They should have taken this onto the porch, because she'd never felt this curl of attraction for any of her other patients. Did the man single-handedly lift all the wood in his mill? Because surely such muscles were built with many hours of hard labor.

She forced her gaze to the basket on the table and willed away the coil of nervous energy lodged in her stomach as she lifted out the jar of ointment. "I'll rub this on the burns and then place a bandage over it. Your burns will feel better in no time."

Had she said that already? She clamped her teeth over her lip to keep herself from continuing to blather nonsense. The man would think she had nothing but air between her ears. Besides, if town gossip could be believed, he'd only recently asked the schoolteacher to marry him, only she'd up and married someone else. The last thing he was likely thinking of was moving on with someone he barely knew.

Carefully, she applied the ointment to his back, refusing the temptation to let herself linger over the task.

The top of his shoulder was too high for her to see it properly. She nudged a chair with her boot, turning it to face him. "Sit, please, so I can reach your shoulder."

He complied, and now they were once again face to face.

When she bent to apply the salve, he looked at her. "How long have you in Wyldhaven been?"

Thank heavens, the task of spreading the salve was complete. She stood, breathing a little easier when she could put some space between them, but now she needed to wrap him with the bandages. "A few months. My uncle rarely leaves his house these days. This means that I don't either."

"Does no one give you a time off?"

She shook her head. "There is only me."

His direct scrutiny unsettled her, adding to her dilemma. She studied the bandage in her hands. Normally, she would just march up to her patient, wrap her arms around them, and place and unroll the bandage as needed. But in this case that seemed, well, maybe a bit too . . . risky. Dangerous. Tempting. Any of those words could apply.

His focus dropped to the bandage. "This you need to wrap around me, ja?"

She nodded, hoping he couldn't see the way he affected her.

A sly grin nudged up one corner of his mouth. He stood and spread his arms to the side, never taking his gaze off her. "Much better I think is this doctoring of yours than what I get from Doctor Griffin."

She pressed her lips together, feeling the warmth that his teasing brought to her face.

Fine. If he could tease her, she could pretend that it didn't concern her. She stepped behind him and nudged the chair out of the way. Reaching beneath his arm, she pressed one end of the bandage to his chest. "Hold this here."

If she was a little disappointed that he took the end of the strip carefully so as not to touch her, well, he didn't need to know that. She withdrew her hand as soon as he had a hold of the bandage and rolled it around him as efficiently and quickly as possible. It was easier standing at his back, not only because she could see the burns, but because he couldn't watch her.

With the task done, she blew out a huff of relief and hefted her basket. She withdrew the tin of herbs from inside. "Use this to make a tea." She kept her attention on the tin, trying not to notice too much the way his stomach muscles created ridges as he thrust his arms into the sleeves of his shirt. "B-boil th-the water. Put two teaspoons in a pot and let it, you know . . . soak for five minutes." Why had she suddenly seemed to have lost her grasp of the English language? "Then drink it."

He accepted the tin, his shirt still unmercifully unbuttoned. "I don't rub it on the burns?"

Her gaze flashed to his. "What?"

He was laughing at her!

"What else would I do with a tea but drink it?"

She couldn't resist a chuckle at her own expense. "Well, yes, I supposed that last instruction was unnecessary. Just be sure to let the herbs in the tin steep in the hot water. Five minutes." And with that jabber of utter repetitive nonsense she had better take her leave. She snatched up the basket. "Good afternoon to you, Mr. Ecklund."

"Miss Johansen?" His words stopped her on the threshold.

"Yes?" She angled her head so he would know she was listening, but couldn't quite bring herself to meet his mesmerizing perusal again.

"I feel that my bandages, they may need replacing soon, ja?"

Hearing the teasing in his tone, she suppressed a smile. "I will return tomorrow, but perhaps we should meet on the porch?"

He chuckled. "This, I think, is a good idea." He fiddled with the tin of herbs. "Until tomorrow then?"

She dipped a quick curtsy. "Until tomorrow."

And as she hurried down the mill steps, Anja Johansen couldn't help but wonder if her life had somehow been irrevocably changed.

Chapter Twelve

Their Sunday afternoon had passed in a quiet fashion after Wash had insisted after services that he needed a moment to speak to Taulby. Zoe had stayed in the wagon with her family, but she'd wished upon a wish that she could have been a little bird on the rail so she could have overheard their conversation.

Wash hadn't explained anything, but when he'd returned to the wagon, he'd seemed more at ease.

Since it was the Lord's Day, Butch had told them at church not to come out to the ranch. He'd said Monday would be soon enough for them to begin to see what they needed to do.

The marshal had agreed, offering that the extra hours would give the heat of the fires time to die down anyhow. Poor Wash had spent another night on her thin rug. Zoe had offered him the bed, but he wouldn't hear of it and had flopped onto the floor before she could even offer that he could sleep on her quilt for some extra padding. Then once he'd been on the floor, he'd said he was fine when she made the offer. She'd slept about as well as a Thanksgiving Eve turkey.

So now on Monday morning, as she and her family rode with Wash toward his father's spread, she found herself ever so thankful that she'd given her students the week off. She carefully covered a huge yawn.

When they topped out on the rise, several Wyldhaven families were already on the road heading down to Butch's spread. The Callahans, Holloways, and Rodantes were there, each with their children in their wagons. The Griffins too, with Rose and their two girls on the back bench. Parson Clay, Aurora, Kin, Cora, and Tommy fell into the line directly behind them, and Kane pulled onto the road with his siblings after that.

Zoe settled a hand on Wash's arm. It was wonderful to live in such a caring and giving town.

Wash covered her hand with his own and gave a nod of acknowledgment.

As all the families pulled their wagons to a stop beneath the large maple on the far side of the Nolans' yard, Zoe was surprised when Wash hopped from the wagon and made his way to the middle of the yard. He waited a moment until the townsfolk had come down from their wagons and gotten their children gathered on a blanket with Rose Pottinger in the back of the Griffins' buckboard.

Then he raised his voice. "If I could have a moment?"

Zoe clasped her hands, holding her breath. What was he up to? Would he embarrass her once again?

The gathering quieted by turns as each faced Wash.

He fiddled with his cane for a moment, waiting for everyone to quiet and pay attention. Finally, he lifted his gaze to Zoe. For one long moment he watched her, his eyes softened and turned glassy, and then he tore his focus to the head of his cane.

He jostled it in his hand and then lifted his focus to those gathered, blinking rapidly a few times. "First, I want to say thank you for gathering here to support us today." He pressed his lips together, clearly attempting to compose himself.

Zoe pressed one hand to her chest and took a step, but that was as far as she made it. Just as surely as she'd been overwhelmed with dislike for his actions the other night, she was overwhelmed with love for him right now.

He pressed on. "I need you all to know that I've apologized to Taulby Ecklund. I misspoke the other night. I should not have accused him of . . . this." He motioned to the ash heap that had once been the Nolans' barn. "And now, I want to apologize to you all. I've not been at my best and I just—" He broke off with a deep frown, staring off into the distance as though it were too painful to see any disappointment in their expressions.

Zoe strode forward before she could think better of it. She stopped by his side, and looped her arm with his, looking up at him. When he looked down, she gave him a nod of support and what she hoped was an encouraging smile.

Wash swept the gathering with another look, intently pausing to meet each person's scrutiny. "I just needed each of you to know that I'm sorry for the way I acted and thank you for being here despite my shortcomings."

"That's what friend's do." Kin spoke from the back of the group, where he stood with his arm draped around his wife's shoulders.

"It is, indeed." Cora gave Wash a gentle smile.

"Right. Well, thank you." Wash raised a hand toward his father. "Pa? You want to wrangle us all into a semblance of order?"

Butch stepped up beside Zoe and Wash, his hat clutched in his hands. "Like Wash says, we're mighty obliged to each of you for being here today. This spread . . ." He glanced around at the land and the house. "Well, it's been in our family since my pa bought it from the original owner over forty years ago now. Actually . . ." He grinned. "That's not quite right. Pa bought this place from a man who'd won it in a card game. That man didn't want the place, but needed the money. Pa was looking for a place to settle, and I'm certainly glad that the good Lord directed us to this part of the country." He sniffed, fiddling with his hat as he cleared emotion from his throat. "Today, well, I'm not quite sure where to start . . ." He glanced at Wash and reached out to settle a fatherly hand on Zoe's shoulder. Her heart expanded with love for this wonderful family. "My boy, he needs a place for him and his wife. But without the barn . . ." He shook his head.

"We'll do both." Marshal Holloway stepped forward.

Butch cleared his throat again. "Thing is . . . I don't rightly have the funds to—"

"I'll pay for Zoe's and my cabin, Pa."

Zoe darted her husband a look. They had the money for that? She wasn't even sure if she was going to have a job after today.

Butch too leveled them with a questioning look. Wash gave his father a nod of reassurance. "I have some money saved up from my time in the cavalry. We'll be fine."

A measure of reassurance whipped through her. That at least was a relief.

Jackson spoke then. "Mr. Ecklund has asked me to extend his offer of half off on any lumber we need. And of course Maude and I will pay our own way too, Pa."

Butch blinked hard. His lower lip trembled, and he fiddled with his hat some more. "Well then, we'll be all right, won't we, boys?" He gave an emphatic dip of his chin. "Yes. We'll be all right. With Ecklund's generous offer, I'll have enough set by to purchase the timber for the barn. And I'm sure Olann will grant me a small loan that will cover the costs of, nails, new tack, and the needed hardware."

Relief cascaded through Zoe.

She leaned hard into Wash's side, relishing the warmth of his arm wrapped around her shoulders.

The people of Wyldhaven hadn't let them down. They were all going to be just fine.

While the townsfolk set to clearing the ash and soot from the barn and cabin foundations, Wash rode with Pa to the bank.

Pa pulled the wagon to a stop in front of the bank, and Wash started to get down, but then noticed Pa wasn't moving, so he sank back onto the bench beside him. He waited a moment, but when Pa didn't speak, he asked, "What is it?"

Pa's jaw worked from side to side. "Ain't never taken out a loan before. Never needed one. Always made do until we could afford to buy what we wanted."

Wash dropped a hand on his father's shoulder. "Don't worry. With your reputation for hard work, Olann won't deny you. And we'll get the loan paid off in the next few months. Meantime, we can slaughter one of the pigs, or an extra cow."

Pa shook his head. "Don't have 'em."

"What?"

Pa's shoulders drooped. "I haven't wanted to burden you, but something ain't been right out at the place for several months. We been losing stock right and left. Fences cut. Cattle killed. That sort of thing."

Wash collapsed against the back of the wagon bench. Had he been so much in his own world that his family hadn't felt comfortable coming to him with their troubles? He'd always been the one Pa leaned on for help. Pain lodged in his chest. He couldn't continue in the way he'd been going. He didn't like himself very much right now. The trouble was . . . he didn't know how to repair the man he became when the pain overwhelmed him.

Realizing Pa was still sitting quietly by his side, he offered, "Well, the boys and I can do some extra fishing and trapping to make up meals. Then we won't need to buy any meat."

A smile quirked Pa's lips. "That fishing will be mighty hard on you, won't it, son?"

Wash grinned despite the heavy feeling in his chest. "We all have to make sacrifices."

Instead of laughing as he'd expected him to, Pa sniffed. Blinked hard. "You've already made plenty of sacrifices. Ain't right that I should ask you to make more. You've been the best son a man could—" Pa's voice broke, clipping off his words.

Guilt crashed through him. He looked away. Dropped his hand. "Maybe not so much lately. As evidenced by the fact that you didn't feel you could come to me with the problems."

Pa shook his head emphatically. "Don't you talk like that. With what you've been through . . . Well, a lesser man would have turned to dust by now. And the problems—" He flapped a hand. "They started before you came back. Little things at first. A cut fence. A caved-in drainage ditch. I didn't think much of them at first, but then they kept happening consistently. And then the sow was killed. Shot and simply left in the forest where she'd been foraging. Wolves had gotten to her by the time I found her so there wasn't much evidence left, but I could see the bullet hole in her skull." He sucked his teeth. "By that time, though, you were home, and you were more important."

"Did you report any of this to the law?"

Pa waved his hand again. "Didn't seem right to bother them with my paltry troubles when they have so much more important things to deal with each day. What matters is that you're bouncing back. I'm right proud of you for finally stepping up to create a family with that little gal that you've loved for so many years."

Wash angled him a sharp look. "You knew?"

Pa laughed. "Son, the whole of Wyldhaven knew!"

Wash smiled. "Guess you might be right about that."

"You're a good man, son. A man she'll be proud to love for all the years to come."

Wash clamped his teeth together. He wasn't so sure about Zoe being proud to love him. His sharp words about Taulby came to mind. But he'd taken ownership of his failure there and done what he could to repair the damage. It was the best he could do.

He felt like dust most days, recently. Like Job sitting on his ash heap, scraping his sores with a broken scrap of pottery. And yet somehow he knew deep down inside that God would take care of them. "God will see us through, Pa. Not sure how, but He will."

"You're right. He always does." Pa tapped Wash's knee with one fist. "Let's go inside."

Wash agreed and by the time he got down from the wagon and reached the bank's door, Pa was already striding inside.

Mr. Olann stood behind the counter just ahead. When he noted their arrival, he reached to tug at his necktie stretching his neck like he was suddenly uncomfortable and preparing himself for a task.

An uneasy feeling filled the pit of Wash's stomach. His cane tap tapped across the bank's wooden floors to where he paused next to Pa at the teller window.

"How can I help you today?" Olann asked.

Pa loosed a sigh and glanced at Wash. Wash jutted his chin to encourage him to get on with it.

"You may have heard that we had a bad fire out at our place the other day?"

Olann fidgeted. Stretched his neck again. Swallowed hard.

Wash frowned.

"I heard. I'm terribly sorry."

Pa folded his arms and leaned into his heels, a sure sign that he was uncomfortable being here. "Thank you. As you might guess, with needing to rebuild so much at once, I'll need a small loan."

"How small?" Olann didn't seem to want to meet Pa's gaze.

Had the man's face paled? He sure was acting mighty dodgy.

Pa dug into his shirt pocket and laid a list on the counter, pushing it under the bars to the banker. "Made a list of the things we'll need from the mercantile. As you can see, it's not so much. I'm certain I can have it paid back in the next six months."

Olann's hand trembled when he picked up the list and looked it over.

Wash folded his arms, unable to release his frown. What was happening here? This should be a safe bet. No question Pa was good for the small amount they were asking for. The most expensive things on the list were the extra tack, harnesses, and saddles. Thankfully, their main wagon, and team, had been with them at the wedding. He wasn't sure how much Pa had asked for, but knowing Pa, he planned to make do with everything they didn't absolutely need.

Olann shoved the list toward Pa and snatched his hand back. He shuffled uneasily.

Trembling . . . uneasy . . . Wash was suddenly on the alert. Was there someone behind the counter holding a gun on Olann?

His hand dropped to his pistol on instinct. But when he rose to his tiptoes and pressed close to the bars, he couldn't see anyone.

Olann frowned at him.

Wash merely returned to his position by his father's side, still puzzling over what might be happening here.

Olann tugged at his tie again. "I'm sorry, Nolan, but I can't offer you a loan at this time."

Pa simply stood still looking at the banker for a moment. "What?"

"You heard me. It's out of the question. Please see yourselves out."

Pa looked over at him, a look of incredulity on his face.

Wash snatched Pa's list and looked it over. Milk pails, nails, a few screws and hinges to hang the stall doors. A few bags of oats, which would be thin feeding for the horses over the next few months, but they could turn them out to pasture more. The tack and one saddle. All told, Pa had only asked for a loan of one hundred and twenty-five dollars. It was a paltry sum, especially considering there were three families to call on for the repayment, and in light of the vast amount they'd recently lost. Why, his savings alone could cover this amount. It wouldn't leave him and Zoe with anything to build their cabin, but . . .

Wash thrust the list back at Pa. He made sure Olann could clearly see the glitter of ire in his eyes as he spoke. "You have a good day, Mr. Olann. I hope it treats you kinder than you have treated us."

With that, he nudged Pa toward the boardwalk, letting his cane thump out his irritation loud and clear.

On the boardwalk, Pa's shoulders slumped. "Now what?"

Wash drew in a long steady breath to calm the tympanic beating of his pulse. "I have enough Pa. We don't need the bank. Let's go to the mercantile."

"You're sure?"

He nodded.

And as he hauled himself back onto the wagon bench, he couldn't help but consider that if he hadn't gotten shot, and that by a rich irresponsible kid, he never would have been sent the stipends each month that had allowed him to save up what he had.

He frowned at the sky. Rubbed the ache in his calf.

Had God used his injury to prepare the funds that He'd known they would need, come this very day?

Wash shook his head. It was too much for him to wrap his thoughts around at the moment.

Chapter Thirteen

Zoe was covered in soot when she heard Wash and his pa return with the wagon from town. Her hands were nearly black, and Belle's poor skirt might never recover, but she was quite proud of the little pile of things she'd been able to salvage. Two cast-iron pans, one milk pail that would need a good scrubbing, and several pieces of melted metal that she presumed had once been the silverware. It certainly couldn't be used for an eating utensil now, but perhaps they could sell the silver to the assayers to offset the cost of a new set. She'd also saved a few of the canning jars, though many of them had exploded in the heat of the fire. She likely wouldn't trust the ones she'd saved for canning again, but every kitchen needed a few jars for this and that. Herbs and tea or coffee. They would be perfect for dried goods like beans and grains too—after she gave them a good wash.

Sadly, none of their clothes had survived. And neither had anything else, really. The little pile of things at her feet were the only things she'd salvaged.

Wash was leaning heavily on his cane when he approached. "Didn't find any unburned papers, by chance, did you?"

She shook her head. "Afraid not." When he twisted his face in discouragement, she pressed, "Why?"

He thrust out a hand in frustration. "All my papers to prove I was injured while enlisted were in there." After a moment to inhale and then exhale, he added, “It shouldn’t be a problem. I’ll just have to get new ones issued.”

Zoe looped her arm with his, looking up at him. “It’s not like they’ll be able to deny that it happened.”

He glanced down at her and humor crinkled the corners of his eyes. That was not what she’d expected. She pulled back slightly, a bit of unease touching her. “What is it?”

Wash leaned close. “You’ve just got a bit of . . .” He pressed his thumb at something on her cheek. “Oh, that didn’t help. One moment.” His hand cupped her cheek, and his thumb rubbed a little harder, but after a moment, he stopped with a grin. “Never mind. You can wash it off later.”

Zoe giggled. “I’m sure I’m quite a sight.”

“You sure are.” Wash’s low words sent a wave of warmth straight through her for his tone hadn’t indicated that he minded what he was looking at in the least.

“Were you able to get everything we will need in town?”

Wash sighed. “I need to talk to you about that.”

“What is it?”

“Mr. Olann refused to give Pa the loan.”

“He didn’t! Why, everyone knows what a hard worker your father is.”

“I know.” Wash looked grim. “Something isn’t right. But that’s not the worst of it, Zo.”

She waited, not wanting to press him to share more than he wanted to.

He looked down at her. Reached to sweep one of her stray locks behind her ear. “I had to give Pa my money to get the things to rebuild the barn. We don’t have the money to rebuild our cabin.”

“Oh.” Relief zipped through her. Was that it? “That’s not a problem. We can stay on at Ma and Papa’s place until we can build our own.”

He winced a little.

And she grinned up at him. "We'll get the bed situation sorted out. Mine's a bit small and it might be cramped, but it has to be better than the floor. Besides . . ." She glanced around to make sure no one was within hearing distance, then lowered her voice to be doubly sure her next words were private. "It might not be so bad, right?"

She felt heat sweep through her at her temerity and when Wash's brows shot up and his throat worked, she bit her lower lip to hold back a giggle.

"There's something else we should talk about, Zoe."

"Oh?"

"Hey you two lovebirds, quit staring at each other like lightning just struck and get to work!" Jackson's laugh floated to them from the other side of the ash heap that had once been Wash's cabin. He was reclaiming the rocks that had made up the chimney.

Wash tossed his brother an irritated glance.

Zoe's giggle spurted free.

Looking back at her, he tapped her nose. "We can finish this conversation later."

Before he could walk away, Zoe shot out one hand to clamp his arm.

"What?"

She hesitated. Would he be upset with her for saying what was on her mind? Maybe she ought to rethink her words, but it was a little late now that she'd stopped him. She pressed forward. "Be careful today, huh? Don't overdo?"

Holding her breath, she worried her lower lip. Would he take that as her calling him an invalid? Be upset with her like he had been right after the wedding?

She watched him as he looked over the busy work taking place all across the valley. The group up by Jackson's place was already sweeping off the foundation. That home hadn't been much more than a few logs notched together. Down by the barn, several men were hefting a large beam that seemed to have been spared from most of the damage. A few others were stacking together a few still-usable boards. Others were sifting through the rubble for anything metal that might still be salvageable.

Zoe knew that work like this would be hard for him with an injury such as his.

After a long moment, Wash lowered his gaze to hers. "Doctor Polson wants to do another surgery."

Zoe's heart gave a thump. He must not remember that she'd overheard that conversation. Was he considering it? Everything she'd heard about Dr. Polson was that he was a talented doctor. But even a talented doctor couldn't fix what was damaged beyond repair.

The question, of course, was that none of them knew whether that pertained to Wash or not.

But she wanted him to try. Not for her sake, but for his own. If there was even a chance that he could have less pain in his future, shouldn't he take it?

"And what do you think?"

Wash shook his head. "I don't know. I've already had two surgeries. Not sure if you knew that."

"No. I didn't know that."

Wash fiddled with his cane. "Second surgeon said it was the best he could do and that I would just have to live with the pain for the rest of my life." His brow crimped.

Zoe laid a hand on his arm. "But you hope that he was wrong, right?"

He blew a sound of frustration. "I *wish* I could hope he was wrong."

"Then let me hope for you." Zoe stepped around until she stood directly in front of him. She took both his hands in hers. "Doctor Polson only recently went through his training. Doctors are learning new things all the time. Maybe he knows some things that those other doctors don't. And maybe he can help you more. Isn't it worth the possibility? Not for me, or anyone else, but for you, Wash. Only for you."

He looked down at her, uncertainty in his gaze. "I'm not sure, Zoe. I'm really not." She felt the warmth of his fingers on her cheek as he stroked another strand of her hair behind her ear. "What I do know is that I want to provide for you, and I can't see a way to do that in my current condition." His thumb trailed gentle caresses against her cheek. "But when I think about facing another surgery . . ." He shook his head. "I'm just not sure."

"You two working or canoodling over there?" Jackson groused teasingly.

Wash's good nature crinkled the corners of his eyes. He hefted his cane a couple of times in one hand. His words remained low, for her ears alone. "If I did have the surgery maybe I could put this to good use beating that no-good brother of mine?"

Zoe smiled. But she wasn't ready to let their conversation end. "I think you should let Dr. Polson try to help you. It can't make you worse, right? I mean, there will likely be a bit of time you'll need to recover from the surgery, but after that, well, if it doesn't help, you'll be right back to how you are now."

Wash pressed his lips together grimly. "Surgeries cost money, though, Zoe."

She hummed her agreement as she squeezed his arm. "Let's pray about it. If the Lord wants you to have that surgery, He can provide the funds, right?"

Wash waggled his head. "All right. We'll pray about it."

Zoe smiled. "Good. Now, we better get to work before Jackson comes over here, snatches your cane, and starts beating *us* with it."

Wash laughed. "I wouldn't put it past him." He pointed to the large maple. "I'll be over there seeing what I can salvage of the tack they are piling up in the Rodantes' wagon. Do you need water or anything?"

Zoe shook her head. "I'll come get some in a bit."

As he walked away, she lifted her gaze to the sky overhead. *Lord, please, I want Wash to try this one last surgery. Please, I'm begging You, provide the funds to allow that to happen.*

Charlotte sat beside Reagan as they pulled the wagon away from their cabin. She'd wondered this morning if she would make it to the meeting because she'd woken with a bit of lightheadedness. However, it had seemed to pass after she'd had some breakfast. She must have simply needed to get some food in her stomach. She had been rushing around a lot lately and probably hadn't been eating well enough. She felt fine now.

Isaiah would stay at home to plant some apple and cherry trees. Reagan had told him he could go fishing, but only after his chores were done. He was whistling a tuneless song while he dug a hole near the drive as they passed by.

Charlotte called for him to enjoy his day, then glanced back at him as the wagon continued on down the road. "Do you think we have him working too hard? I don't want him to resent us later."

Reagan shook his head. "A boy needs to work to stay out of trouble. He gets plenty of time off. Why, he'll have those trees planted inside half an hour and then be off to his favorite fishing hole. He'll probably spend three hours lying in the grass beside his pole with one of those books of his before he gets bored and hungry and shows up back home for more food." He angled her a look filled with humor.

Charlotte laughed. "I didn't think there was going to be any stew left for the two of us last night, as full as he filled his bowl."

"And then he went back for seconds."

"And thirds, after you were called away! What was the issue last night, by the way?"

Reagan waved a hand. "Just a bit of a ruckus down to McGinty's. Sent one of the men home and told McGinty not to serve the other one any more drinks."

Charlotte fiddled with her gloves in her lap. "Have you decided how you are going to vote today?" She didn't look at him. Was afraid to see the answer in his face. But she did feel the look he angled her all the way to her churning middle.

They hadn't talked about this yet. And perhaps on the way to the schoolboard meeting was a little late to be bringing it up, but she wanted to know what to expect from him before they went into the meeting.

"Get on, now!" Reagan snapped the reins to the team's rumps to urge them up an incline. To her he said, "You afraid I'm going to consign poor Zoe and Wash to having no income?"

Charlotte shifted on the squeaking seat. "Well, you have always supported me in the little work that I've done, but I've also been able to stay at home while doing it. I just wondered your thoughts is all."

Reagan reached over and took her hand. "I don't consider your work 'little,' Charlie. I've appreciated every penny you've worked so hard to contribute to our family. Lord knows that when I decided to become a sheriff, I had no thoughts about pay or providing for a family. Everything you've done has been a huge help—even if it does sting a little that you can bring in more by making pies part time for Dixie's than I do by working my tail off to keep our town safe and peaceful."

Charlotte leaned across the bench to plant a kiss on her husband's lips. "You've kept everyone in line so that customers are comfortable coming into town, which has allowed Dixie's to be prosperous. And that allows me to make the money that I do. A peaceful town is good for everyone."

Reagan squeezed her hand. "I'm not going to vote no to Zoe keeping her job."

Charlotte felt herself relax a little. "Good. But . . ." She slumped against the back of the bench. "I'm afraid that the other members of our board will not be so forward thinking."

Beside her, Reagan gave a sly smile. "You just leave that up to me, Charlie. You just leave that up to me."

Charlotte eyed him. "What do you have up your sleeve?"

Reagan grinned. "You'll see."

Chapter Fourteen

It was several hours before Zoe realized just how thirsty she was and stopped to join Wash near the wagons. She arrived as Deputy Joe set a bucket of clear water that he had just pulled from the depths of the Nolans' well onto the stump upended for that purpose. After he took a long drink, he wiped his forehead with his bandanna and offered an apology to Wash, saying he was needed in town for a matter pertaining to the law.

Wash gave him a nod of understanding.

As the deputy departed, Zoe couldn't help but wonder why he was needed in town. But knowing it was none of her concern, she took up the dipper. The water was cool and sweet, and she drank long and deep—so deep that some of the water sloshed over the edge of the dipper to drizzle down her chin.

Wash, who had paused his work to watch her, smiled.

She held the dipper away in embarrassment as she wiped her chin.

He gave the dipper a jut of his chin. "Drink some more. You likely took too long to break for water."

Zoe complied without hesitation. Finally, she tossed the dipper back into the bucket with a satisfied hum. "My, this shade does feel lovely."

Wash's jaw bunched and he bent his head over the two pieces of leather he was working on splicing together.

She reached out a hand. "I didn't mean to imply anything by that."

"I know."

Zoe felt at a loss as to what to say. He was unhappy with his circumstances—and who wouldn't be? Yet he was here, working. Many in his position would still be hiding away on the excuse that they were incapable of helping with something like this.

She studied the pile of reins and harnesses by him. On one side were several that were already mended and neatly looped together in organized stacks. On the other side were a few remaining pieces that he was still working on.

He lifted his gaze to hers. "Heard anything about the decision of the school board yet?"

"Oh my." She smacked a hand over the sudden churning in her middle. "With all the chaos, I'd completely forgotten that they were meeting today. No. I haven't heard anything."

He bent back to his task. "Sorry. Didn't mean to cause you angst."

"No. No. It's fine." She angled a glance to where the sun peeked through the branches of the old maple. "They are likely meeting right now."

"Guess we'll know soon enough, then."

Zoe studied the top of his head. "And what do you want them to decide, Wash? Do you want them to allow me to keep my job? Or would you rather I stayed home?"

He straightened. Looked off at the work taking place at the barn for a long moment. Then turned his gray-green eyes back to her. "I wish that I could provide for you, Zoe, so that you could stay home and only have the burden of our home and maybe one day" —he cleared his throat and lowered his gaze— "well, maybe one day some children."

Zoe felt her heart warm at the thought.

"But our situation just doesn't make that feasible. Not until . . . Well, not at this time. So yes, I'm hoping that you can keep your job, Zoe. But you have to promise me that you won't overdo. You work too hard as it is. I don't want you killing yourself on account of doing more than you can handle."

She shook her head. "I promise I'll be careful. And maybe this" —she swept a hand to the fire-ravaged valley— "is a blessing in disguise. If we are living at Ma's, the upkeep of the place is already humming along. We each have our own chores that we do. That will allow me to work and not have to come home and do more than I've already been doing."

Wash's shoulders sagged. "I don't want to be a burden to your parents."

"They won't see it as a burden. Besides, it will just be for a short time. The Lord is going to provide for us, and we'll soon have our own place and have a firmer foundation under us. You'll see."

Wash didn't quite look convinced, but he said, "You always were one for a positive outlook. But, yeah, Lord willing."

"Yes. Lord willing." She motioned back to the small pile of kitchen items that she'd gathered. "I'm going to take the jars and things down to the main house to wash them now."

"All right."

She couldn't help but notice how his countenance dimmed as she walked away. Had she made things worse by trying to encourage him? By trying to assess where he stood on their situation? That was the last thing she'd wanted to do.

In truth, she'd made things worse from the moment that she'd asked him to marry her! She sighed. She hadn't wanted to increase his burden. Only to make him realize just how much she loved him.

Well there was no going back now. And soon enough they would learn whether she still had a job. A pang of uncertainty swirled in her stomach.

She closed her eyes. *Father, please, help me to lay this to rest in Your very capable hands. I didn't intend to cause more trouble for him when I asked him to marry me. But somehow, that's all I've seemed to do in the past few days. With the fire and now his concerns about providing for us . . .*

With a sigh, she turned to her task.

As she gathered the pans, jars, milk pails, and melted silver into a small wheelbarrow, Zoe tried not to think about what might be happening at the schoolboard meeting right that very minute.

She failed miserably.

Charlotte sank into her seat at the table in the back of the schoolhouse.

Mrs. Hines had commissioned Dixie to bring tea and cookies, and Charlotte smiled over the fact that she would make a little money because of providing the cookies for the meeting through Dixie's.

Dixie had thoughtfully included one of her favorite raspberry leaf teas as well, and Charlotte prepared a cup, adding a spoonful of sugar and taking two of the apple spice oatmeal cookies that were also favorites.

She smiled. It seemed that Dixie had known that today would be difficult for her.

Mrs. Hines clanged her teaspoon against her cup to draw everyone's attention. "I think it's time we called this meeting to order."

Charlotte was surprised when Reagan sank into the seat beside her, dropped his hat on the table, folded his hands, and offered loudly, "Yes. I think we should. But before we start, I have a short story to tell."

Charlotte almost choked on the bite of cookie she'd just taken. He had a story?

As the Olanns and Jerry Hines found their seats, Mrs. Hines frowned. "A what?"

"Just a little bit of fiction that I think you'll all enjoy."

She looked uncertain as she delicately stirred her tea. "I don't think now is the time for—"

"Indulge me."

Mrs. Hines pinched her lips in aggravation. "Very well. You may proceed."

"Thank you." Reagan scratched his forehead with his thumbnail for a moment as he stared at the table before him.

Charlotte set her cookie down. No telling what he was up to, and she didn't want to choke again.

"Sheriff?" Mrs. Hines prodded.

"There once was a barnyard guarded by a watchdog." Reagan lifted a probing look on both Jerry and Merle.

Mrs. Hines sputtered. "A barnyard?"

Reagan drummed his thumbs on the table and didn't miss a beat. "The watchdog wasn't the only occupant of the barnyard, of course. There were cattle and goats and chickens. Even a pig or two."

Charlotte's brows arched, for she would dare to say that Reagan's glance had flickered off of Mrs. Hines on that last sentence.

The woman must have noted it too. Her chin jutted into the air and her gaze narrowed in that signature way she had of looking down her nose at people.

"Of course all the critters in the barnyard had to eat each day." Reagan hurried on. "And Felix the Fox, well, he was in charge of the feed store. Felix, he liked pretty pebbles. And so every day the cows and goats and chickens and pigs would bring their pretty pebbles to Felix in exchange for a bag of feed." Reagan paused to take a sip of coffee, and no one said a word. "But Felix, he had to use some of those pebbles in order to get more feed to sell to the barnyard. And he really liked his pebbles! One day, though, one day, he got an idea. If he could figure out a way to make the feed that he gave to the animals smaller, then he wouldn't have to spend so many of his pebbles to get more grain. But he didn't want the farm animals to know that he was giving them less. He knew he had to be subtle, or he was going to have a whole mess of uproar on his hands. The chickens would be clucking, the cows mooing . . ." Reagan waved a hand. "You get the idea."

Charlotte almost giggled when the Olanns and the Hinses both bobbed their heads like wonderstruck school children hearing a book being read to them for the first time.

"So Felix the Fox, he had a friend. His friend was . . ." Reagan swirled his hand as he searched for a name. "We'll call him Walter the Wolf. Well when Walter heard what Felix wanted to do, he knew just how to help him.

"'Felix,' he said, 'I know just what to do. But if I help you, in exchange, you have to do something for me!'

"'I'll do anything you want,' said Felix.

"'All right,' says Walter. 'You sell your feed based on weight, right? So all you have to do is hollow out your weight. Just a little each week.'

"'That's brilliant!' said Felix. 'The animals will think they are getting the same amount of feed. And if I do it a little at a time, they'll never notice that they are getting less.'"

From the place where he sat next to Charlotte, Jerry Hines was suddenly squirming like a schoolboy in need of the necessary.

She looked over at him. He was intensely focused on prodding at the grain of the table in front of him.

Her jaw went a little slack. Was Jerry the fox in Reagan's story?

But it seemed Reagan's story wasn't finished.

"Well Felix was mightily pleased with this solution to saving his pebbles. But he hadn't forgotten that Wally wanted something in exchange for his idea. 'So what is it you want in exchange?' asked Felix.

"Wally slyly folded his wolf arms and replied, 'You give me three-quarters of the pebbles you save, and I won't tell the watchdog what you're doing!'"

Charlotte couldn't withhold a gasp as her gaze flew to Mr. Olann. The man's fist was gripped so tightly on the table that his knuckles were white. Another glance at Jerry revealed that he had gone unnaturally still and was looking more than a little peaked. They hadn't, surely!

Both the men's wives were bouncing looks between them and each other in surprised horror. It seemed everyone had caught on to the real meaning of Reagan's story.

Reagan drummed the table for another moment. His face remained impassive, friendly even, but Charlotte didn't miss the telltale anger that hardened his jawline when his teeth clamped together. "This scheme went on for some time, but one thing that both the fox and the wolf forgot to consider was that the watchdog always finds out what's going on in his barnyard." Reagan sank rather cavalierly against the back of his chair and offered the room a cheeky grin. "Right. Well that's my story. I think we can get on with voting over whether Zoe gets to keep her job as the schoolmarm. I think it would be most unchristian of us to take that young couple's main income from them. I vote that we allow her to remain on as Wyldhaven's schoolteacher." He raised one hand. "Anyone else?"

Charlotte blinked a couple of times, feeling like she was still running to catch up with all that had just happened. But her hand shot into the air. "Yes. I do too."

They both turned to look at Jerry. Shoulders still slumped, he seemed awfully focused on his thumbs that were twiddling before him. "Yes. Zoe can keep her job."

Mrs. Hines sputtered and sputtered some more. Her gaze zipped between her defeated husband and Reagan's unwavering grin. "I—Well—I—Well, yes. I think that would be the most charitable thing to do."

Charlotte eased against her chair in relief even as both the Olanns quickly agreed as well.

Zoe was going to be so relieved to have maintained her job!

But Charlotte couldn't stop a little shiver of concern over what Reagan's story might mean for the future of Wyldhaven. Why, their little town wouldn't survive without a mercantile. And though the bank was new, it sure had made financial matters a lot easier since it had come to town.

"Wonderful!" Reagan thrust back his chair and stood, taking up his hat and motioning for her to join him. "If you'll excuse me, I have some business to attend to. And we need to ride out to the Nolans' to give Zoe the good news. Shall we, Charlie?"

She stood, but not before snatching up the remainder of the cookies on her plate that she hadn't yet had a chance to eat. She'd worked hard to bake those to perfection and didn't want to see them to go to waste. "Yes. Thank you, dear. Would you like some cookies before we leave?"

"Why yes! I think I would." Reagan maintained his cheerful attitude as he took up four cookies and stuffed one of them into his mouth whole.

He held the door for Charlotte and then waved to the two couples still seated in stunned silence at the table.

And then they were on the walk and Charlotte was staring at him in disbelief. "Was all of that true?"

Reagan's face immediately hardened into frustration. He took a moment to swallow the cookie, then offered, "I was hoping I was wrong. Most of it was conjecture and suspicion. But now I have some legwork to do. You think you'd be fine to ride out to the Nolans' alone? I need to visit the mercantile before Jerry and Priscilla have time to get there."

Charlotte went up on her tiptoes and gave him a kiss. "Enjoy your cookies, and be careful, hmmm? The most important thing to Isaiah and me is that you come home safely."

Reagan paused by their wagon and held out a hand to help her to the seat. "I will. See you at home this evening."

"Where I will expect a full explanation." She took up the reins.

He smiled. "I'll know more by then."

She clucked to the team. "See you later, then." She headed the team out of town, and as she turned the corner at the end of the street, she looked back to see him already heading into the mercantile with Deputy Joe and Marshal Zane by his side.

She shook her head with a smile. He'd had that whole thing planned!

How long had he known?

Chapter Fifteen

Reagan paused on the boardwalk in front of the mercantile as Joe and Zane pulled up in Joe's wagon and hopped down.

"Is it true?" Zane asked. In one hand he gripped the neck of a heavy gunnysack.

Reagan waggled his head. "They were squirming worse than two dogs with fleas, but of course that's not proof."

Zane's shoulders slumped as he pushed open the door to the mercantile. "Well, I guess we'll know soon enough."

Reagan motioned for Joe to go before him and then followed the men inside. He lowered his voice. "We'll know about the weights, but what troubles me is how we'll make the connection to Merle." A glance around the interior revealed that it was currently unoccupied. "At least the store is empty. Thank the Lord for small favors."

"Jerry's not so hardened that he won't talk." Joe strode for the counter and pushed through the swinging gate that divided the front of the store from the area behind. Zane was right on his heels. He clunked his gunnysack onto the floor and started to open it.

"Excuse me? May I help you?" They all froze as Mrs. King glided into sight from behind the curtained-off back area behind the register. She must have been tasked with watching the store during the board meeting. She had a newspaper in one hand—which she'd likely been using to occupy her time what with no customers in the store at the moment. When she plunked her hands on her hips, the paper fanned out, bringing to mind the ruffled tailfeathers of an angry hen.

Reagan gave himself a shake. He'd apparently been telling too many barnyard stories of late. He stepped forward and held open the gate. "This is a legal matter, Mrs. King. I'm going to have to ask you to vacate the premises. The store is closed for now."

"It's what?!" Her mouth gaped big enough to resemble a bass.

At least that wasn't a barnyard critter. He hid his humor with a cough.

Zane released the mouth of the gunnysack and straightened. He took the paper from her and set it on the counter. Then grasped her gently by one arm. "Right this way if you please, Mrs. King. How is Ben doing these days? Been a while since I chatted with him."

"Why he's . . . Well, he's fine—" She held her skirts with one hand while craning her neck to see over her shoulder what he and Joe were doing near the counter.

But in his genteel southern manner, Zane kept right on walking. "That's real good to hear, ma'am. Here we are." He opened the door for her and gently propelled her onto the walk. "You have a good day now." With that, Zane pulled the door shut with a decided click.

She cupped both hands to her eyes and pressed her face to the glass, peering in at them. They all three simply looked back, waiting her out. Finally with a little flounce, she marched off down the walk.

Reagan couldn't help a grin. "News will be all over town inside five minutes."

Zane brushed past him, retrieved his sack, and plunked it on the counter. He pointed Joe toward the scale that Jerry used to weigh out everything from nails to coffee for his patrons. "Best we hurry then. We need our proof so we can arrest Jerry and get him talking."

Reagan gripped the back of his neck as a thought struck him. "You don't think Merle would . . ."

Both lawmen lifted their gazes to his.

"What? Kill Jerry?" Joe shook his head. "He might be a crook. But I don't think he's a killer."

"Neither do I," Zane concurred.

Reagan motioned for them to get on with it. "Well, the sooner we have him behind bars, the sooner he'll be protected. So let's get on with it."

Zane reached into his gunnysack. He pulled out a flat, heavy weight and read the amount stamped on the front. "One pound. Ready?" He looked to Joe.

Joe fished around in the basket of weights that Jerry kept beside his scale and hefted the one that should be a match. "Ready."

Both men set the weights on each side of the scale.

Reagan stepped closer to make sure he got a good look. If both weights weighed the same, the scale should balance. However, the scale quickly clunked down on Zane's side, revealing that his weight was quite a bit heavier than the other.

Reagan sighed. He turned his back to the counter and hung his head. "Blazes! I was hoping I was wrong about this."

"Sorry, boss, me too," Joe said.

"All right, well, let's see the others." Reagan leaned his elbows on the counter, feeling the weight of the world growing heavier and heavier as one by one Jerry's weights proved that they were lighter than they should be.

With the final weights measured, he straightened, adjusted his hat, and gave his men a nod. "Joe, you're with me. Zane, if you don't mind, catalog just how much each weight is off by and bring me a list? Mark our good weights and Jerry's bad ones so that there's no question later from the judge as to whose weights were whose."

Zane concurred with a nod. "Will do."

Reagan felt just about as low as he'd ever felt in his entire life as he left the mercantile with Joe on his heels to arrest Jerry Hines. The man had a son only a little older than Isaiah!

The day had been long. Very long.

Zoe's back ached, unused to the manual labor she'd subjected herself to today. First she'd been bent over rubble, and then she'd been bent over a washbasin. Even though Maude had helped her with quite a bit of the washing, her back screamed as she placed the last jar on the drying rack and pressed her fists into the offended muscles.

Maude took up the jar and dried it with a towel. She smiled. "One of my least favorite chores is standing bent over that low sink."

Zoe flapped a hand and grabbed the plug in the bottom of the basin. "I simply do too much sitting at my desk at the schoolhouse. A little manual labor is good for me. Thank you for your help."

"Of course." Maude set the last jar beside the others on the table and puffed out a breath. "It's not much of a salvage, is it?"

Zoe suddenly felt tears prick the backs of her eyes. Her voice choked off when she offered, "No. It's not much at all."

She would not think about the fact that she'd lost all her worldly possessions!

Her vision blurred with tears.

She would not think about how much money Ma had spent so that she and Wash could be well set up to start their own home.

After drying her hands, she lifted the hem of her apron and pressed it to her eyes.

She would *not* think about the fact that she might not have an income any longer or how they would go about recouping anything if that were the case.

A sob caught her unaware.

She kept the apron pressed to her face and attempted but failed to corral another outcry. "Sorry." She was blubbering worse than little Helen Trivet during math class!

"Hey, it's okay to cry." Maude slung an arm around her shoulders and tilted her head against Zoe's. "I don't know what I would have done if Jackson and I had lost everything on the same day we got married."

"It's just a lot to take in, you know?" She desperately needed to blow her nose. Lowering her apron, she searched the kitchen but there was nothing to use. She sniffed instead. Dashed some more tears from beneath her eyes. "I mean, there we were at the wedding and Wash fell and I could tell he was so embarrassed."

Maude tisked. "He handled it beautifully. You both did. I was right proud of you!"

The comfort of Maude's arm was like an open invitation for all the emotions she'd been bottling up for the past two days. "And then we hadn't even left the churchyard yet, and we heard about the fire, and it was such a long day—fighting the flames and Wash yelling at Taulby." Zoe flapped a hand to brush away that line of thought. "Then we had to go to Ma and Papa's. And I have a tiny bed and Wash was so tired that he fell asleep on the floor and then yesterday . . . Well, Wash did come to church and that was wonderful, and he did go and apologize to Taulby, and that was wonderful too."

"I heard. I'm glad he did that. We all knew Taulby couldn't have set that fire. Come, let's sit at the table and have some tea." Maude pushed the salvaged items away from one corner of the table and pulled out a chair, patting it to indicate Zoe should sit.

She did, gratefully. The muscles in her back eased with one last rebellion. She propped her head on one hand, uncaring that her posture must be terrible, or that she continued to drip tears onto the tabletop.

Maude slid a steaming cup of tea into her line of vision. "Sugar?" She nudged the sugar bowl closer.

Zoe took up the spoon and added two heaping teaspoons to her cup. If Ma were here, she would chastise her for her rudeness. Sugar was expensive. But today she needed the comfort of a good, sweet tea. Especially if she were going to work up the courage to ask the question plaguing her. It certainly wasn't something she would be comfortable asking Ma. And Belle, well, Belle wouldn't know the answer to this particular question. But Maude was recently married herself, and to Wash's brother. Surely she would know . . .

Zoe lifted her focus to her friend across the corner of the table. "I have a question."

Maude sipped her tea quietly, looking at her over the rim of the cup. "All right."

Zoe's eyes felt gritty and puffy. Her face blazed hot. She lowered her focus to the steam drifting up from her cup. "When you married Jackson did he—Well, did he—You see, Wash hasn't . . . Oh my." She flapped a hand at her heated cheeks. "Hasn't touched me since the ceremony and . . ." She surveilled Maude once more, needing to see the truth on her face when she answered. "I'm just worried that I might have pushed him into something he didn't want and now . . . Well, was that how it was with you and Jackson?"

Maude's cheeks immediately blazed crimson. She plunked her cup into her saucer and turned her attention out the window.

Zoe's shoulders fell. So that would be a no. "I see." She turned her cup on its saucer until Maude's hand covered hers.

"Our circumstances were different, Zoe. And I've seen more life in Wash over the past week than I did the whole months he was home before that. Also, if there's one thing I know about the Nolan men, it's that no one can force them to do anything they don't want to do. You said yourself that the last few days have been far from the norm. Give things time to settle and I'm sure . . . It will all work itself out."

"You're right of course. Things have been far from normal in the past week."

Maude tilted her head. "There's something I wanted to offer."

Zoe lifted her gaze to hers. "Oh?"

She motioned toward the back of the house. "There's Wash's old room and it still has a bed, bureau, and wardrobe. The bed is good-sized and we'd be more than happy to have you both here at the house. Lincoln has been sleeping in there since Wash left, but his old bed is still in Grant's room and . . ." She lifted one shoulder. "I just thought it might be better than your room at your Ma and Papa's place."

"Thank you. That's very thoughtful. I'd hate to put Linc out of his room. However . . ." She frowned, thinking of Wash's frown when she'd mentioned them staying in her room back home. Thinking of how narrow her small bed was. "Let me talk to Wash and see what he says?"

Maude agreed just as the sound of a wagon pulling into the yard could be heard.

Zoe caught a glimpse of Charlotte out the window. She leapt to her feet. "Oh, if Charlotte's here, that means the board meeting is over." She tugged nervously at the ties of her apron and then hung it on the hook in the kitchen. "If you'll pardon me?"

Maude shooed her on her way. "Of course."

Zoe flew onto the porch, hands wringing. "What did they decide?"

Charlotte was already walking toward her, arms outstretched. "You get to keep your job, Zoe."

Zoe fell into her embrace, tears already flowing again. "Oh, thank you! Thank You, Jesus!"

Charlotte's warm arms enveloped her. "There, Zoe. All's well. All's well."

And for the first time that day, Zoe felt like perhaps that might be true.

The coffee Jerry had consumed before the start of the schoolboard meeting had turned sour in his stomach the moment he'd registered the meaning of the sheriff's story.

Horror and fear and dread and embarrassment vied for preeminence.

The sheriff and Charlotte had been gone for several moments now, and neither the Olanns nor Priscilla had spoken. They had all remained in their seats, staring into their cups, and processing, he supposed, what had just happened.

And then as if the dam of her anger finally broke, Priscilla leapt to her feet. "What have you done, Jerry?"

He couldn't meet her gaze. He was numb. Unsure where to go or what to do. Was his crime a hanging offense?

At the thought of a noose settling around his neck, he leapt for the schoolhouse door, hearing the clatter and crash of his cup behind him. He lost his coffee over the side of the porch. When he was once more able to stand upright, he turned, wiping his mouth, to find Priscilla behind him, fists propped on her hips. Her beauty was her saving grace, for she had been shrewish from almost the first moment that he'd met her.

"Well?"

Defeat weighed down his shoulders. "I did it for you."

Her eyes narrowed.

"You came from such a wealthy family, and I never felt like you were happy with what I had to offer. Do you think that grand piano in the parlor was cheap? Or the walnut suite in the dining room?"

"You're an idiot, Jerry!" Priscilla snatched off her feather hat and whacked him with it!

One of the feathers slapped him in the eye. "Ow!" He cowered beneath curled arms.

She whacked him again! "Do you think I wouldn't have stayed with you if we had a homemade dining table or a smaller piano?"

Sudden anger seeped in to take the place of his nausea. He straightened and snatched her hat. Took a step toward her. "Would you have?"

She blinked at him. Dropped her gaze to her hat crumpled in his fist and then returned her focus to his face. Her mouth opened, but no word emerged.

"Would you?!"

Her chin trembled. "I-I don't know."

He thrust her hat against her chest. "And *that's* why I did it."

Tears filled her eyes as she fiddled with the crumpled feathers. "What are we going to do now?" Her chin trembled.

A tremor worked through him as well. His mind was blank. What *were* they going to do? He'd never thought ahead to what might happen if he got caught. How had the sheriff figured it out, anyway?

That didn't matter now. What did matter was that if they didn't act quickly, he was going to be arrested. The sheriff had known all the details.

A thrumming rhythm of guilt and fear echoed in his ears. Beads of sweat dotted his brow.

There was only one thing to do and that was to make their escape while they still could. "Where's David?"

Priscilla's shoulders hunched. She looked across the creek toward the town. "Off with the boys somewhere, I would imagine."

Jerry took her by the shoulders. "Prissy, we're going to get through this, but I need you to trust me, understand?"

She tucked her lower lip between her teeth, looking unconvinced.

"The sheriff won't come after you. At least not yet."

She gasped. "What do you mean not yet? I had no idea what you were doing!"

He flapped a hand to shush her. "They will still want to ask you some questions. But they'll want to arrest me first. I'm not sure why he didn't arrest me on the spot, but maybe that was a mercy. Find David. Find him as quickly as you can and then meet me at the fork in the road that leads to Cle Elum? Don't go back to the store for anything, hear me?"

Her teary eyes widened a little, but she acknowledged his instructions with a nod.

He squeezed her shoulders. "Good. Take the carriage and go. Quickly now."

She dashed at her tears and gave him another nod before settling her hat atop her head, lifting her chin, and gliding down the schoolhouse steps to their waiting carriage.

Jerry rolled his eyes. She looked like she was descending into a royal ballroom, not off to find his son so they could make their escape from the law!

But he had no time to focus on his wife's idiosyncrasies right now. After a quick perusal of the area to make sure no lawmen were hiding nearby, Jerry dashed off the porch and into the brush that ran parallel to the creek. He was going to have to get his feet wet. He couldn't risk taking the bridge into town in broad daylight!

Why, oh why hadn't he listened to his conscience and refused to work with Olann when the man had made his suggestions all those months ago?

He hurried far enough down the creek to avoid being seen if anyone was on the bridge. To his favor, the creek wound through several curves not too far from the bridge, so he didn't have to jog too far. After wading through the creek, he climbed the embankment and dashed across the open lot next to the post office. After that, he ran behind the stores until he reached his own. He paused at the back of the mercantile and peered around the corner toward Main Street.

No one was there.

His scrutiny fixed on the large hydrangea at the back corner of the lot. Could he risk it? The area seemed empty. But he knew Sheriff Callahan. He only had moments. The man was probably already searching the town for him.

He ran for the bush and dropped to his knees, his trembling fingers sinking into the dirt.

He tossed a glance over his shoulder. Still clear.

Why hadn't he thought to bury the box behind the bush instead of on this side where he would be seen if anyone stepped down the alley from Main Street?

Each handful of soil dug painfully into the skin beneath his nails and felt like a weight upon his conscience.

He hesitated for the briefest of moments. Maybe he should simply turn himself in?

His neck prickled and he swallowed convulsively at the imaginary feel of hemp against his skin.

No! He couldn't risk it.

He could simply leave the tin. They would have nothing, but they could start over.

He shook his head. Priscilla would never speak to him again if he did that.

Only a few minutes more. The last place Sheriff Callahan would think to look for him would be here in his own back yard, right? Especially since he'd left him at the schoolhouse.

With renewed fervor, Jerry ignored the small rocks cutting into his skin and kept clawing at the dirt.

As soon as he retrieved the box, he would make his escape.

Chapter Sixteen

Merle Olann looked at his wife as the Hineses dashed from the room.

Betsy fiddled with the lace at her collar. "What have you done, Merle?" Weariness cloaked the words.

He rose. "Nothing that they have proof of."

She narrowed her eyes, standing with him. "You don't think Jerry will talk?"

A wave of his hand dismissed the idea. "They'll have to catch him first." And he was going to ensure that didn't happen, but Betsy didn't need to know that. He reached over and took her hand. "Please don't worry. I have everything under control. I was careful with the accounting and they'll have a very hard time proving I had any part in this. Why don't you run on home and pack a bag, hmmm? Carmen has the week off from school. You and the children can jaunt over to Seattle for a few days."

That ought to give him time to settle everything here without her underfoot.

She narrowed her eyes and pinched her lips. "I'm not a fool, Merle."

"I know you're not. Which is why you are going to take the children to Seattle like I said." He let the ring of his authority remind her where she stood. "Unless of course you would like to leave Carmen here with me?"

As he'd known she would, she broke eye contact. Studied her fidgeting fingers. "No. It's fine, of course, Merle. You're so thoughtful to give us a little time away."

Satisfied, he straightened his vest. Checked his pocket watch. Perfect. Just enough time to get them to the station for the evening departure. "Be quick. We have an hour and fifteen minutes."

Betsy nodded. "Yes, dear."

Beyond her shoulder, through the window, he saw Priscilla Hines drive by in a carriage. Alone.

Interesting.

Betsy's feet dragged a little as she left the school, but he couldn't worry about her now. He first had to avoid the law, and then he had to catch up to Jerry.

Where would he have gone?

Wash had finished with the harnesses and sat in the shade of the maple feeling every bit as useless as he was.

His heart had skipped a beat when Charlotte pulled into the yard, but now he felt himself relax a little as she smiled and threw her arms around Zoe. They spoke for a moment and then Zoe dashed excitedly back into the house.

Charlotte placed one hand to her forehead and swayed slightly.

Wash frowned and was just leaning to the side to climb down from the wagon to see if she needed help, when she straightened, tugged at her sleeves and walked toward the group of women who were helping to sort things by the barn.

He eased back to his seat. She must be fine. Perhaps it was just her joy at having good news for Zoe that had made her seem woozy for a moment.

Based on their interaction, it was certainly joyous news!

He rolled his shoulders to release the tension he suddenly realized was cramping his neck. They would at least have a little more income than his disability pay. That thought brought a frown. He'd been getting regular offerings from Clint Royce's father after Clint had accidentally shot him in the leg. Not that he'd asked for them. But the family was of means and Mr. Royce had promised to continue supporting him.

But since he'd come home, leaving his forwarding address with the infirmary where he'd been receiving care after his injury, he'd received not one payment.

Not that he felt the man owed him anything. It just seemed odd that the payments had stopped so suddenly just as he'd left California. And if Mr. Royce was still sending the money, well, that meant that the doctor who'd kept him medicated out of his senses wasn't forwarding the funds.

Perhaps he should have Kin look into it for him.

Jackson stopped by the wagon. "Hey. Got time to slaughter a few chickens? Pa wants to put them on to roast so we can feed everyone lunch as a thank-you for all their help today."

Wash nodded, relieved to have something to do. Plucking feathers wouldn't be too taxing on his leg.

Jax thumped the wagon with the side of his fist. "Thanks. I'll get a good hot fire going in the smoke house."

Wash's mouth watered at just the thought. One of his favorites of his Pa's meals was his specially roasted and smoked hens with potatoes baked right in the coals of the fire. "Put some corn on to soak, too. We can boil that up."

Jax pumped his brows. "I'm fairly salivating just thinking about it. Pluck fast."

Wash chuckled. "I always could pluck faster than you."

Jackson wrinkled his nose. "That's a point I'll just have to concede. I'll have Maude put the pot of boiled water on the stump out the back door."

"Thanks." Wash worked his way down from the wagon bench, hopping for one moment on his good leg until his crippled one got used to the new position and quit screaming so loudly. Who was he kidding. His leg had been screaming like a banshee all week long.

He clenched his teeth. Thought again about Dr. Polson's offer of a surgery.

As he hobbled his way toward the chicken coop, he angled a look at the sky. *Lord, I promised Zoe I would pray about that surgery. You know that it's a burden to me not to be able to provide for Zoe. And a surgery will surely cost a lot of money. I need some real direction before I wade into something like that.*

The chicken coop loomed before him, diverting his thoughts from prayer. He eyed the cluster of clucking hens and rolled his eyes. He was slow. Chickens were fast. How was he ever going to catch enough of them to feed the crowd of people that had arrived to help with their work today?

His answer arrived in the form of Zoe, who dashed around the house calling his name. He turned to look at her and was struck by her beauty all over again.

Her face was glowing brighter than the sun. "I get to keep my job."

He smiled. He already knew that, but he was genuinely happy for her. "I'm glad, Zo. The kids will be too." He reached out an arm and relished the way she settled her head right beneath his chin.

She wrapped her arms about him and released a happy sigh. "God's going to take care of us, Wash."

He swallowed. Blinked a few times. This was a good woman he'd gotten who didn't mind heading off to work to support him.

Standing there in the back yard of Pa's place by the chicken coop, he promised himself that he would do everything in his power to one day be able to support her instead of the other way around.

And that was the answer to his prayer, wasn't it? If he were ever going to be able to do that, he had to at least try the surgery. For the past week he'd been gutting out the pain, but he couldn't fathom trying to do this for the rest of his life. If the surgery helped him, he would be that much closer to figuring out what job he could do.

"Zo?"

"Yeah?" She remained settled in his arms.

He pressed his lips into the hair just above her ear. Today he could barely catch a hint of the lavender smell he liked on her so much. Today, she smelled like smoke and hard work and somehow that made her all the more attractive. Best he get on with the conversation before he got too sidetracked. "I think I want to try that surgery."

She jolted back to look up at him. "You do?!" Happiness lit her eyes. "But just a bit ago, you said—"

"I know what I said. I just . . . It scares me a little, you know? I don't want my hopes to get built up and then have the surgery not create an improvement, or worse yet, cause further injury."

Zoe reached to touch his face. "You are the bravest of men, Wash. You've walked through the valley of the shadow of death and I'm so proud of the man you remain despite it all."

His throat hitched with a tight emotion. "I wouldn't say I've been living much in a way to be proud of lately."

Her hands remained around his face. "Wash Nolan, you sell yourself short. I know you've been in a lot of pain and worried over how your injury will affect your future—our future." She released him and instead settled her palms against his chest. "We can talk to Dr. Polson and find out the risks before we decide further. How about that?"

He worried his lower lip. Why hadn't he thought of that? "Yes. That sounds like a good idea."

"How about we go into town after lunch? I believe Mondays are his days in the new town office he talked Doc into setting up."

Wash's stomach clenched. This was all happening very fast. But he supposed the sooner he got it over with, the sooner he would know what the future held. And there was no winning in a fight with her. "Okay."

"Wonderful." She looked around. "Why are you standing here by the coop?"

He quirked her a smile. "Want to help me wrangle some hens to slaughter?"

Her face fell as she turned a look on the red hens scratching at the leftover vegetables that likely Maude had tossed them earlier. "Oh, dear. I do so hate picking out the ones for the pot. It hurts my heart."

Wash tugged her to him and pressed a kiss to her temple. "You've such a soft heart."

She looked up at him again. "Is that a bad thing?"

He shook his head. "Not in the least." He felt such a love fill him, such a wonder that despite his reclusive anger, the Lord had brought this woman into his life. He touched her face, lowered his lips to hers, but only allowed himself the briefest of kisses. She was too much of a temptation and there were still too many questions about their future.

Releasing her, he stepped back. "I'll ask Maude."

Zoe's expression filled with relief. "Oh, thank you!"

He chuckled and waved to her over his shoulder as he made his way to the back door of the kitchen.

Harlan stood on the hill with his binoculars pressed to his eyes.

He cursed. "Why are all those people down there helping them?!"

No one answered.

He looked at Ted. "You certain that Olann denied them the loan?"

Ted bobbed his head. "He sure did. But apparently the oldest son had some money set aside. And what with all the townsfolk pitching in to help, I don't see's how they are planning to go anywhere anytime soon." At Harlan's cowing look, Ted ducked his head. "Sorry, boss."

Harlan watched the activity in the valley for a few more moments and finally registered that Ted's feet kept shuffling. "What is it, Ted?" he snapped.

"I got further bad news, I'm afraid, boss."

Harlan lowered his field glasses and turned to assess the look on Ted's face. "Well?"

Ted sucked his teeth. Grimaced. "Heard that the banker is in some bit of trouble with the law."

Harlan's heart gave a stutter. "Over my deal with him?"

Ted's eyes widened. "Oh no. I don't think they know about that yet. It was some situation he had going with the mercantile owner."

Harlan's dread mounted with each passing word. But it was one word that struck him straight in the chest and bored in like a barbed arrow. "What do you mean they don't know about me 'yet'?"

Ted lifted one shoulder. "Word is that Olann will soon face some serious scrutiny over his dealings at the bank." He scratched his neck. "You think he might have written anything down about your little . . . *deal*?"

Harlan's blood ran cold. "He wouldn't have done that, if he were smart."

Ted lifted one shoulder amiably. "Sure, boss. Only I was thinking." He jutted his chin toward the small spread in the valley. "Nolan down there is on friendly terms with the law in these parts and it wouldn't take more than a word or two from him to have them pondering why Olann would deny a man like him a loan. I mean, he's a sure bet—"

Harlan raised a hand for silence, glowering at Ted.

Ted gave him a nod of recognition that he'd heard enough. He shuffled away to slump against a tree trunk in the shade.

Harlan raised his glasses to his eyes again, but now all he could think about was the lump of apprehension in his gut.

He wanted that place down there for Maisie. Well, and because it ought to be his anyway. But now it looked like he might not get it.

He ground his teeth. No.

He would get it. He just had to figure out a way.

Maybe it was time for that confrontation with Butch Nolan after all.

Wash was just plunging the last of the chickens into the scalding water when Zoe came back around the side of the house with a garbage pail. She pitched in and started scooping the feathers into the bucket.

She'd been there for several moments when he realized that she hadn't said anything the whole time. Certainly not like her.

"Thanks." He watched her face.

She tucked her bottom lip between her teeth but only nodded and kept picking up feathers.

"What is it, Zo?" He shook a handful of damp feathers from his hand and set to work plucking the last bird.

She hesitated, mouth clamped. Gave him an uncertain look. Pink stained her cheeks.

Well, now she really had his curiosity up. He arched a brow.

"I forgot to mention something to you earlier."

"Okay?"

"Maude, well, she offered that we could move in here to the main house and have your old room."

Ah. It would certainly be a more comfortable bed than her floor had been the past two nights. But the thought of sharing a bed with her and yet not, well . . . He coughed. Focused on the bird. "What are your thoughts?"

She picked up several feathers before she finally offered. "Well, it would be a site more comfortable than my room back home. But I hate to ask Linc to give up his room."

Wash frowned. Considered. "These are trying times. We all have to make sacrifices to help each other in times such as these."

"Yes. I understand that. What do you think?"

He chuckled. "I think it's a better option than me continuing to sleep on the floor in your room."

Her face flamed. "Yes." She kept her focus shyly on her task.

Hang but she was going to be a temptation he was going to have a hard time resisting. He'd let her talk him into marrying her. But the line had to be drawn there. She would be able to care for herself if something happened to him and he couldn't leave her with anything. But he didn't want to bring a child into the picture until he was certain he could provide for them.

He cleared his throat. "I'll talk to Linc."

"Do you think he'll mind terribly?"

Linc would hate it. But he would do it for them. "He'll be fine," Wash reassured her.

Chapter Seventeen

Reagan stepped out of the empty schoolhouse and paused next to Joe on the porch. He scanned the town across the creek, discouragement and frustration with himself warring for top place in his emotions.

"Guess we should have known they'd make a run for it," Joe offered.

"Yeah. I guess I thought I knew better than I did. I thought he would be man enough to face his crimes and deal with the consequences."

"You figured out how we are going to catch Olann yet?"

Irritation welled up inside him. He shook his head. "Working on it. I have a feeling he's some smarter than Jerry and will be harder to nail down."

Joe dipped his chin and adjusted his Stetson. "Several of the town boys have been playing baseball recently in that flat field by Grady Gulch out toward our place."

"Yeah, good thinking. Jerry wouldn't leave town without David. I at least know him that much! You head out there and see if you can find him. Meanwhile, I'm going back to his mercantile and then if he's not there I'll ask around town to see if anyone has seen which direction he might have gone."

"Sounds good." They trotted down the porch steps and Joe mounted up beside him. "I'll meet you back at the jailhouse in say . . . an hour?"

Reagan reined his mount toward town. "I'll leave you a note if I can't be there. Ha!" His horse's hooves clattered across the Wyldhaven Creek bridge with Joe's right behind him.

Joe angled for the road out of town at a gallop, and Reagan pulled up in front of the mercantile, meeting Zane just emerging with the two bags of weights.

Zane glanced toward the schoolhouse. "Made a run for it, huh?"

"Yep. I was just checking to see if he may have come back here."

Zane shook his head. "Not inside, and I just checked around back a few minutes ago to make sure there weren't any extra weights back there. Didn't see anyone. Let me drop these in the jailhouse" —he hefted the burlap bags— "and I'll help you search."

Reagan was at a loss as to where to start. But they should split up to cover more ground. "Zane!" he called.

The marshal paused on the other side of the street and turned to look at him.

"Start down at the livery. I'll start on the north end of town."

Zane waved his acknowledgment and hurried to deposit his bags in the jailhouse as Reagan headed toward the mill on the banks of the creek.

Wash caught up to Lincoln after lunch. His brother had inhaled his food and then escaped to his room—Wash's old room—as soon as he finished. He was already leaning against his headboard, engrossed in a book, when Wash tapped on the door. Pa wouldn't let him lounge in his room for long, but Linc was a student at heart and always snatched every minute he could to immerse himself in study of one form or another.

Lincoln looked up. Muttered something inaudible. Dropped his book onto the bedside table and adjusted the pillow behind his back to a more comfortable position.

"What're you reading?"

Linc narrowed his eyes. "Book about animal husbandry. Might as well ask me what you're here to ask and not beat the wheat with a needle."

Wash couldn't withhold a smile. "I'm here to ask if you'd mind moving back in with Grant for a bit so that Zoe and I can have this room?"

Linc sighed. "That's what I figured would happen."

Wash propped himself against the doorframe to take a little of the weight off his leg. "I know it's not ideal, but we're all facing challenges after the fire. Zoe and I need a place to stay, but we won't be here long. It's temporary, I promise."

Lincoln crossed his arms, irritation evident. "I can't believe I have to bunk with Grant again. His snoring could keep the cow in the barn awake—I mean, you know, providing we still had a barn. She's probably thankful to have the barn burnt down so that she can have a few peaceful nights of sleep out in the pasture!"

Amusement crinkled Wash's eyes. "Just consider it an adventure. Think of all the stories you'll have about surviving Grant's snores! And don't forget about his smelly feet." He gave his brother a wink.

Lincoln rolled his eyes, but a smirk tugged at his lips. "Oh, joy. I can't wait to add that to my list of thrilling feats—no pun intended." Humor over his own wit notched up the side of his mouth.

Wash laughed outright. He hoped his brother would one day understand his appreciation. "Thank you for understanding, Linc. It means a lot."

Lincoln grumbled under his breath but gave a reluctant nod of acknowledgment. "Yeah, yeah. Just get your cabin built quick, okay? Otherwise, you'll be left standing at my funeral having to acquiesce to your culpability in my demise." He arched a hand through the air. "Here lies Lincoln Nolan, killed by the stench of his brother's sweaty feet."

Wash laughed again. If his brother didn't become an orator of some sort, the world would be missing out on a great talent.

He promised to find a more permanent solution as soon as possible.

With begrudging acceptance, Linc stood from the bed and began gathering his belongings. "Might as well get it over with, I suppose."

Wash clapped him on the shoulder. "Thanks, Linc."

With that task concluded, he resisted the temptation to fall onto the bed himself and lose his pain in a good long nap. He needed to find Zoe and ease her mind over where they would stay tonight and of course they were heading into town to talk to Dr. Polson in a few minutes.

He was already dreading the jostling trip in the wagon.

After Betsy had left earlier to go pack for herself and the children, Merle had fled from the schoolhouse and hidden beneath the Wyldhaven Creek bridge. It was low and cramped, but experience had taught him that no one would expect a man like him to choose a place like that to hide—which of course was what made it the perfect hiding place.

Even though he hadn't been under the bridge for long, he hadn't been able to get high enough on the embankment to get out of the water, and now he was soaked and irritated and Jerry had a good head start.

But Merle would have to give the sheriff credit. He'd returned to the school in record time with his deputy—even if he was disappointed to find neither of them there.

Now, he and his deputy had just thundered across the bridge heading back to town and Merle felt he could risk leaving his hiding place.

As he'd sat beneath the bridge, he had plenty of time to ponder. He felt certain that Jerry would want a nest egg to help his family start over. Certain, also, that the man wouldn't leave town without it. The only question remained, where had he hidden it and how long would it take him to retrieve it?

It was imperative that Merle find him before the law did.

Priscilla had ridden away in the carriage alone, for he'd seen her from the schoolhouse window while he and Betsy were still speaking. That meant that Jerry had gone somewhere on foot, and Merle would bet his life savings that the idiot had his nest egg somewhere on his own property.

It was at least a place to start his search. And Lord help Jerry, if he actually was there. Merle only hoped that he could summon some of the skills he'd had to hone in prison. He hadn't been that man since he'd come to Wyldhaven. And honestly, he had no desire to be that man, even now. But Jerry and his lack of finesse were forcing his hand. How *had* the sheriff got wind of their scheme, anyhow? It was near perfect and had been humming along for months now.

Whatever had put him onto them didn't matter. All that mattered was that Merle needed to be long gone before the law arrived to find Jerry deceased.

The sun hovered over the mountains to the west when he poked his head from beneath the bridge and assessed the area. No one nearby.

Perfect.

Now he just had to make sure Jerry escaped a chat with the law.

He felt for the matches in his shirt pocket and was pleased to find that they'd been high enough to avoid the soaking that much of the rest of him had taken.

Keeping as low as he could so that the creek-side brush would keep him hidden from town, he hurried once more toward the schoolhouse porch.

Reagan searched from building to building along both sides of Main Street, making his way south. It felt like a futile effort. He should have arrested Jerry on the spot, but he had always hesitated to ruin a man's reputation on hearsay alone. He'd wanted to verify his suspicions with evidence before dragging Jerry into the jail.

Wyldhaven was a small town and news like that would travel like an unruly horse heading for the barn.

It was easy to second guess himself, however, now that he had the evidence.

Dixie had just allowed him to search in each room of the boardinghouse, the dining room, and the kitchen. No sign of Jerry hiding out anywhere in Dixie's place. He'd already searched the post office. That meant the alehouse was next.

McGinty gave him a nod from where he stood wiping down the bar when Reagan entered. "Sheriff."

Reagan searched the faces of each man in the room. Jerry wasn't here. Merle either. After taking a look behind the bar, he pointed toward the stairs. "You seen Jerry or Merle come in here?" Much as Reagan disliked it, Ewan's girls upstairs kept pretty busy with men coming and going.

Ewan shook his head. "Nah. Neither of them are in here."

"Need to take a look in your rooms upstairs, anyhow."

Ewan tossed down his rag. "Come on now, Sheriff. You know having the law snooping around is terrible for business."

Reagan narrowed his eyes. "I don't much care if your place goes out of business or not, Ewan." He started up to the second floor.

Ewan grunted his frustration and called, "The girls is on a break, anyhow. Just knock and go easy like on the hinges."

Reagan only glowered before he lost sight of him as he reached the second level. Not long ago, he'd been looking for a perpetrator and had needed to kick in some of Ewan's doors, which his girls kept locked when they were . . . busy.

Tonight however, a knock seemed sufficient. Each of the women opened their respective doors and allowed him to look around the interior and under the beds and in the wardrobes. As Ewan had said, there were no men in the rooms.

No Jerry. No Merle.

After leaving the last room, he paused on the landing. Ewan used to rent these rooms to respectable citizens like Doc and Joe, but it seemed that the women made him more money.

One of them sidled up to him and dallied a finger on his shoulder. "You should stop by sometime when you're not on duty, Sheriff. We could make it worth your time."

The other women tittered seductively.

His cue to depart. Reagan strode for the stairs without responding. What was the woman's name? Edith . . . ? Edin . . . ? Edwina!

He descended and gave Ewan a wave before bursting onto the boardwalk once more.

His gaze landed on the mercantile across the street. It was the next building on his route. He was tempted to skip it since Zane had said only a few minutes before that he hadn't seen

Jerry there, but a sweep wasn't much good if he didn't do it in a proper fashion.

He stepped off the boardwalk.

"Fire! Sheriff look!" Dixie Griffin stood on the boardwalk in front of her diner pointing toward the schoolhouse.

Smoke spewed upward from the building!

From behind the church, Merle Olann watched with satisfaction as townsfolk streamed toward the schoolhouse with buckets and urgency.

Seeing the sheriff and the marshal among them was just what he'd been hoping for.

Kin burst from inside his office on the next lot over and Merle ducked out of sight behind the large tree until he sprinted past.

"Buckets!" someone yelled. "Bring buckets."

As soon as the way was clear, Merle hurried down the brushy hill that led to the back of the buildings on the near side of Main Street. He slipped and slid on the steep grassy slope, but when he arrived behind the mercantile he wasn't disappointed. For standing wide-eyed in his own backyard staring toward the column of smoke streaming into the sky, was Jerry Hines.

His hands were caked in dirt, and in one he gripped a large dirty tin that likely once held coffee. There was zero chance that was what it contained now.

"Jerry!" Merle whispered.

Jerry gasped and spun to face him.

Merle motioned for him to follow. "We have to get out of town! I set the fire to lure the sheriff away from his search. We only have moments. Come now."

Jerry pointed to the smoke. "That was you?!"

Merle's impatience surged. "Yes. Now come on!" He waved, trying to tamp down panic.

Jerry seemed to give himself a shake and finally surged into motion. Thankfully! Because obviously he couldn't shoot him here or anywhere nearby where the sound of the shot would carry into town.

"Wait!" Jerry exclaimed as they ran behind the buildings toward the livery. "Was it you who set fire to the Nolan spread?"

Merle's gut hitched. "No! Of course not." He wouldn't mention that he had a very strong suspicion about who actually had set that fire. "I only started the porch on fire at the schoolhouse to give us time to escape. Hurry!"

All he had to do was get Jerry far enough out of town. Then he'd be home free.

Chapter Eighteen

Zoe sat on the seat of the wagon beside Wash as they trundled along the road toward Wyldhaven. Mr. Nolan had caught up with them just as they were leaving the spread and asked to join them. While they were at Dr. Polson's, he planned to purchase a few more things they would need for the reconstruction from the mill.

Many of the townsfolk had dispersed after lunch anyhow, so Butch wasn't necessarily needed out at the spread.

Wash had seemed relieved when his pa asked if he could join them and had quietly passed him the reins. He'd been quiet for most of the way into town, his hands gripping the seat until his knuckles turned white, and Zoe had a feeling that he was in quite a bit of discomfort.

Her concern mounted. *Please, Lord, please let Doctor Polson be able to help Wash heal through another surgery. And if that's not possible then I know that nothing is impossible for You. With one word, You could make him well again. I don't understand why You don't always just do that for us. But help us to be faithful and keep trusting You, even through the hard times.*

They topped out on the rise above Wyldhaven and Zoe gasped at the sight that greeted them. The schoolhouse was on fire!

"No! Not another one!" Her school!

Wash took her hand, his fingers warm and comforting around hers.

"Ha!" Butch slapped the reins against the horses and the wagon lurched forward.

Townsfolk streamed toward the schoolhouse, several of them already forming a brigade from the creek to the school. Butch hauled the team to a stop beside the boardinghouse.

Zoe scrambled down. "What happened?" she asked Dixie, who was standing at her door, giving pails and bowls of every sort to those running by.

Dixie shook her head. "I don't know. I just stepped out a moment ago and saw the smoke."

Old Bill Giddens tottered by with a heavy coil of hose over his shoulder. "Someone fetch the pump from the livery!"

No one seemed to be paying him any mind, each too focused on their own tasks.

Wash started toward the livery with his cane. But Zoe placed a hand on his shoulder. "I'll get it." She lifted her skirts and took off at a run for the other end of the street, too late realizing that Wash might consider her desire to help an insult.

She surged into the livery and into the little compartment beside the tack room.

The town had invested in an iron forge pump on a barrow a few years ago after hearing about the great Seattle fire that had burned down much of the heart of that city. The pump could be rolled with ease to any building in town. They'd also invested in a long length of hose to go with it, which was what Bill had been carrying a moment ago.

Zoe grabbed the handles and trundled the pump out of the livery. Heavens! It was heavier than she'd expected it to be. She supposed with its brass and solid steel construction, she should have expected that.

The handles dug into her palms. Her lungs burned and her hands rebelled against the pain. But she had to save the school! She leaned into the work. "Come on, Zoe, push!"

Merle Olann and Jerry Hines suddenly burst into sight in the livery yard.

"Oh, hello, could you help me with—"

The men ignored her and kept running in the opposite direction of the fire.

Zoe hesitated and looked after them for a moment. "Well, that was rude!" She gave herself a shake and resumed pushing the heavy pump up the slight incline of Main Street.

Ewan McGinty appeared by her side. "I'll take this, little lady."

Zoe gladly gave him the task. "Oh, thank you."

He rushed ahead of her.

By the time she reached the creek, the men already had the hose hooked up and Taulby had the pump handle worked into a blur. Blessed water sizzled against the few remaining flames that she could now see had thankfully only destroyed part of the porch. That at least wouldn't be too hard to repair. And it looked like they would soon have it snuffed out completely.

Wash called to her from the place where he was holding the suction hose into the deepest part of the creek. "You okay?"

She gulped several lungsful of air as she strode to him, taking in the flurry of work. "Yes! It was just some heavier than I expected it to be."

"Thank you." His words were spoken quietly.

She looked at him. His lips were pressed into a grim line. He obviously had realized that he wouldn't have been able to bring the pump.

She slipped her hand onto his shoulder. "Ewan helped me. It's fine. Unlike Mr. Hines and Mr. Olann! They ran right past me and didn't even pause."

"What did you say?" Sheriff Callahan, who'd been standing nearby waiting for his turn at the pump, whirled to face her. "You saw Jerry and Merle?"

Zoe was taken aback by the venom in his tone. She gestured toward the livery. "I was just coming out and they ran past me, heading out of town. Didn't even pause."

"Zane! With me!" The sheriff called, already running in that direction.

Zoe watched the lawmen, perplexed as they all raced down the street. "What was that about?"

Wash lifted a shoulder. "You got me."

Merle knew the moment that Zoe called to them that his time was up. If he wanted to save his bank—and maybe his marriage, yet again—the sheriff could not speak to Jerry. The man was weak. It would only take him five minutes in a cell before he would be blathering everything. If he did that, Merle would soon be in the cell with him. And Betsy would leave him for certain this time.

He needed to act now because if Zoe happened to mention that she'd seen them, the law would be on them in moments!

So not a shot then. It would have to be something quieter. And out of sight.

As Zoe resumed pushing the pump up the street, Merle thumped Jerry on his shoulder. "In here!" He angled toward the livery and ducked into the shadows of the interior.

He bent and propped his hands on his knees like he needed oxygen. But he was busy searching for any sort of weapon. There was a pitchfork. He grimaced. Jerry wasn't tall, but he was beefy. Did he have the strength to thrust him through? The tines were dulled with years of use. Plus, he could get spattered with blood and that would be hard to explain away. Not the pitchfork, then.

There! A pile of old horseshoes.

"What are we doing?" Jerry asked. "We need to keep going! I have to meet my wife and boy in just a few minutes."

Merle waved him onward. "I just needed a moment to catch my breath. Thought we could cut through here. Keep going!"

Jerry frowned down at him where he remained propped on his knees. "Everything all right?"

"Fine. Fine. I'm right behind you." He would need to be fast.

As Jerry started for the far side of the livery and the door that would take them out the other side, Merle reached carefully for one of the horseshoes. He picked it up carefully so that it didn't clank against the others.

Jerry reached the sliding doors and inched them open, peering out to make sure no one was on the other side. With his attention focused away, it was the perfect opportunity.

Willing himself to be quick, Merle gripped one side of the horseshoe in his hand and ran at Jerry's back. With all his might, he sprang forward and swung at the side of Jerry's head.

There was a hollow thud and a zip of sharp pain ricocheted through Merle's hand. Instinctively, he dropped the horseshoe. It jangled to a stop a few paces away.

"Ow!" Jerry whirled on him. His tin fell and bounced with a clatter. "Why you!" Anger glimmering in his eyes, Jerry raised a meaty fist and took a step toward him.

Merle ducked beneath his arms and retreated. He'd swung hard! How was the man still standing?

"What did you—" Jerry toppled like a felled tree right in the middle of the livery's aisle.

"You cut through there. I'll go around this side." The yell came from just outside!

Merle fell into a crouch, panic threatening to steal his faculties.

Marshal Holloway! And whoever was with him would be coming in here within seconds.

With the marshal apparently skirting around one side of the livery, Merle was trapped. He dove for the nearest stall—thankfully it was empty at the moment. Merle sank into the darkness of one corner and willed himself to stop shaking.

Reagan slowed as he entered the danger of the livery. Lots of places for a crook to hide in here. Would either Jerry or Merle hurt him? After all, they'd been part of the same community for at least several years now.

He stepped immediately to the side of the door so that he wouldn't be outlined against the light and an easy target for anyone who might want to make him one.

The doors at the other end of the livery were parted slightly and in the light streaming through the crack, he caught a glimpse of a head full of red hair. His teeth clenched. "Jerry, are you all right?" Despite his concern, he remained where he was. He would do Jerry no good if he rushed ahead and got himself hurt while trying to help him.

Whoever had felled him, must have done it recently, because Zoe had just seen him with Merle Olann only moments earlier. He tried to resist jumping to the obvious conclusion that Merle had done this. The man deserved to be considered innocent until proven guilty.

He ground his teeth. Maybe.

Easing forward, he checked the tack room. "Zane!" he yelled. "In here! Careful!"

As he checked the first stall, the doors at the far end of the livery slid open a little more. Reagan was thankful for the extra light. The stall was empty. He motioned for Zane to check Jerry as he eased to the next stall.

Zane bent to feel for a pulse. "Soft and thready, but he still has a pulse."

A sound like a sharp inhale came from the stall nearest to Zane.

Reagan and Zane met each other's gaze. Reagan motioned for him to hold steady a moment. He needed to quickly check each stall. That sound could have been a trap of some sort.

Zane gave him a nod, falling into a crouch and quietly drawing his gun.

As quickly and quietly as he could, Reagan cleared each stall until he and Zane were standing on either side of the door to the last stall.

"Merle Olann?" Reagan called. "You in there? You come on out now and the first thing I better see is your empty hands coming through that door." So much for assuming the man innocent until proven guilty.

Jerry moaned loudly from his spot on the wood-chip-covered ground.

For one long moment after that there was silence.

"Merle? If Zane or I have to come in after you, we're going to come in shooting, understand? Happy as I would be to put some holes in your hide about now, old Bill won't be happy with me if I put holes in the walls of his livery, and I'd like to stay on his good side."

Zane thunked his pistol against the stall wall. "I, on the other hand, would be happy to put some bullet holes in Bill's walls if I could get a rat in the process, Merle!"

"Don't shoot!"

Reagan gave Zane a wink. "Come on out real slow, Merle. Real slow."

Trembling hands came into view. "I don't have a weapon. Don't shoot."

Reagan slapped a cuff onto the nearest wrist and spun him till his hand was behind him. "On your knees. Zane, call Polson."

Zane waited only until Reagan had both of Merle's hands cuffed behind him, and then he sprinted for the doctor.

Seeing that the fire was under control and there was nothing more they could do here, and feeling his pain mounting with each moment, Wash rose, leaving the hose in the creek. "Zoe? Shall we head down to Doctor Polson's place?" He reached a hand toward his wife. She likely needed a distraction from the near destruction of her schoolhouse anyhow.

She'd been whimpering a little, still stood gaping at the school with discouragement in her eyes. After a long moment, she replied, "Yes. I suppose we should."

Wash threaded his fingers with hers as they started to walk. "Don't worry. The men will have the porch repaired in no time." Likely Ecklund would even have the lumber already on hand. "Where is this clinic of Polson's?" It really showed how isolated he'd been keeping himself when he didn't know something as important as that!

Zoe motioned distractedly. "Over on Second, just past Jacinda's dress shop. It's just strange, don't you think?" She glanced over her shoulder at the burnt porch. "Two fires within a couple days of each other?"

Wash leaned heavily on his cane with each step, willing himself to breathe through each stab through his knee. All the way to the other end of Second was a long way to walk. "It does at that. Let's cut through here." He thrust his cane toward the alley that cut between the alehouse and the sheriff's office to

Second Street. "Sheriff Callahan has always done a good job of keeping us safe. I'm sure that he'll get it all figured—"

"Wash!" Pa called from down the street.

Both he and Zoe paused in the entrance to the alley and turned to face him.

"Ecklund says we can have six-by-twelves for the same price as the four-by-twelves. What do you think?"

Wash tilted his head in thought. It felt good to have Pa asking for his opinion again. He hadn't done that for a long time. "That one beam we salvaged was a four-by. So maybe the ridge beam can be larger, but keep the other side beam the smaller size?"

Pa concurred. "Yes. Good thinking. I'll do—" His words cut off abruptly as his gaze widened on something just behind Wash and Zoe.

Wash frowned, turning to see what it was.

A man stood on the alehouse porch, hands propped on his hips as he glowered down the street at Pa. "Nolan," he snapped. "Been a long time." He spat a stream of tobacco that landed in the dust near Wash's cane.

Wash looked back at Pa. He knew this man?

Pa strode closer, motioning for Wash and Zoe to come toward him.

Wash nudged Zoe, his pulse kicking up at the glitter of caution shining in Pa's eyes. When they reached him, Pa stepped forward as though to shield them from the man.

"Harlan White. Never thought I'd see you 'round these parts again." There was no welcome in the words.

White spat another stream of tobacco. "Surprise!"

Pa never took his eyes off the man as he asked, "You have something to do with the fire?"

White's gaze drifted lazily to the schoolhouse. "Nope. Been right here in the alehouse all morning. The barman will testify to that."

"That's not the fire I was referring to and you know it," Pa snapped.

The man smirked. "Now, would I do something like that?" He laid a sun-spotted hand against his chest. "I'm downright offended that you would think so!"

"We own that land fair and square." Pa snapped. "We want no quarrel with you."

Something hardened in the stranger's eyes. "Well now. We don't always get what we want, now do we?"

With that, he turned and slammed back into the alehouse.

"Pa?" Wash asked. "What was that all about?"

Pa's whole demeanor seemed to sag with weariness. "We need to talk to the sheriff."

Just as they started toward the sheriff's office, Reagan, Zane and a prisoner appeared at the far end of the street.

Wash's brows shot up and, beside him, Zoe gasped.

Pa asked, "Is that Olann?"

"It is." What in the world had the banker done to get himself arrested?

Pa headed down the street at a rapid clip and Wash did his best to keep up. Zoe was uncommonly quiet as she walked beside him.

He looked over at her. "You all right?"

She flapped a hand. "I just feel as though the world has gone completely crazy, you know?"

He settled his free hand at her back as they passed the alehouse. He glanced up to see the stranger glowering at them through the window as they walked by.

Wash couldn't quite comprehend it. Zoe was right. The world had gone completely hooves over horns in the past few days.

Zoe could hardly believe all that had happened in the last few days. And now on top of it all there was a stranger making subtle threats against Butch!

And Mr. Olann? Arrested? The lawmen were taking the banker into the jailhouse now.

What in the world could that be about?

"Sheriff, I need to speak with you." Butch led them into the sheriff's small office.

Reagan was already locking Mr. Olann into one of the two cells that took up the back third of the room. "Can it wait, Butch? I'm kind of in the middle of something here." The cell door clanged shut and the key turned with a metallic finality.

Mr. Olann sank onto the edge of the cell's cot and rested his head in his hands.

The sheriff's office was much too small for the five of them plus the desk and wood stove. Zoe stepped further into the corner of the room, allowing Butch and Wash to take the space in front of her.

Marshal Zane and the sheriff stood behind the desk.

"'Fraid it can't wait, Sheriff. It has to do with the fires out at my place."

Movement at the corner of her eye caught Zoe's attention. Mr. Olann's head had snapped up! He was listening with great interest now.

"I got a story," Butch persisted. "I promise I'll make it as short as possible."

Reagan sighed and folded his arms. "Fine. Let's have it."

Leaning into his heels, Butch hooked his thumbs into his back pockets. “Before I came to Wyldhaven, my family—Pa, brothers, and I—lived over in the Idaho Territory, you know, before it became a state. That was back when the Nez Percé were still battling for their freedom. And I was in the cavalry.”

Zoe felt her jaw go slack. She hadn’t known that Butch had also been in the cavalry!

And by the surprised look that Wash leveled on his father, he hadn’t known either. “Pa! You never told me that!”

Butch scratched at the back of his neck. “I know, son. Those days weren’t my proudest moments. We were asked to do some godawful things in the name of our country.”

Zoe heard more than saw the sheriff hang the cell keys on the hook behind his desk. “And this has something to do with the fire out at your place how?”

“In my unit, there was a man named Harlan White. He reveled in tormenting those Indians, and I couldn’t abide it.” Butch’s weight shifted. He hung his head and Zoe could see a tremor working through his shoulders. “I turned him in for one particularly heinous act.” He cleared his throat and gripped the back of his neck.

Zoe knew they wouldn’t discuss the details in front of her, but she could well imagine any number of scenarios that might have happened to make kind Butch Nolan loathe that stranger so much.

Butch continued. “He was summarily arrested. And while Harlan whiled away his time in a jail cell, his brother, Gregory, lost their family spread in a poker game.”

Silence hung heavy in the room.

“About that time, my pa was done with the dealings in Idaho. Our place was burned out by Indians as they retreated toward the Canadian border. And Pa said it was time to move on. We came further west and by a crazy twist of circumstance, we stopped at a boardinghouse in Cle Elum and in the dining room there, met the gambler who had won the land from Harlan's brother." The floorboards squeaked beneath the shuffling of Butch's boots. "Pa bought our spread from the man."

Zoe let the wall behind her take her weight. "So, Harlan White got out of jail? And you think he started the fires at your place as revenge for you buying the land?"

Butch's shoulders sagged. "It's more than that. I think he's been trying to run us off for months. We've been fighting little things for a long time. Cut fences. Animals killed. Water drainage ditches caved in. That sort of thing."

"Why didn't you come to me?" the sheriff asked.

"I didn't want to bother you, Sheriff. At first it just seemed like a string of bad luck. He's been careful. But when I saw him on the street just now—"

Reagan jolted upright, and between Wash and Butch's shoulder Zoe saw him exchange a glance with Zane. "You just saw him? What's he look like?"

"White bushy hair that's on the long side. Big muttonchop sideburns. Red face," Wash said. "He just went into McGinty's. Claims he's been there all morning."

"Well, I'll go talk to him," the sheriff said. "As you can see, I've got a bit of a situation going here, but I think it's controlled enough that it can be put on hold for a wh—"

"I've got information for you about him, Sheriff."

All eyes turned toward the cell where Mr. Olann was now standing with his hands wrapped around the bars, peering earnestly toward Reagan.

"Oh yeah?"

Olann shifted. "Of course, I'll want my freedom in exchange for this damning—very damning—information."

Reagan didn't look impressed. "You just spill your information and let me decide just how damning it is."

"Oh, no." Olann shook his head. "You've got to offer me something better than that."

Zoe wondered what he'd done. Surely, he must be in a good deal of trouble if he was scrapping so forcefully for his release.

Wash blew out a breath. "Pa, if you'll excuse me, Zoe and I were just headed to speak with Dr. Polson."

Butch stepped to the side of the doorway with a nod of acknowledgment.

Zane moved to join them. "I'll come with you to check on our other prisoner."

Zoe blinked. Someone other than Olann? Why, that had to be Jerry Hines, right? After all, she'd seen the men together only a few minutes ago. She'd known Jerry almost her entire life! What could the man have done to get himself arrested?

And that was when another realization hit her. If Jerry wasn't here in the jailhouse and Zane was talking about visiting him in the clinic, something must have happened to him!

Her gaze settled on Olann before she slipped out the door with Wash and Zane. Likely something to do with that man.

Lord forgive her, but she hadn't liked Mr. Olann since he and his family had moved to town a few years ago!

Chapter Nineteen

Zoe had never been inside the new clinic since it had been built at the end of last year. Dr. Polson had been—and still was—a wonderful addition to Wyldhaven. And Dr. Griffin was even seeming more rested these last few months, since he was having to ride out to the surrounding logging camps less as people learned of the clinic in town.

When they stepped into the main room, Zoe was impressed. The walls were stark white, and everything looked pristine and clean. Several beds lined each wall, and at the back of the room partitions had been erected so that more than one patient could be examined at once. At the far back corner of the room a door led to what Zoe had heard was the dedicated surgery room.

My, how modern Wyldhaven was becoming!

Dr. Polson and Marshal Zane, who was seated by Jerry Hines, were the only other occupants of the room. The doctor worked quietly at a desk opposite the entry, but Jerry sat in a chair against the far wall, one arm handcuffed to the armrest, and the other holding a bloody rag to the side of his head.

Zoe's eyes widened.

Zane stood beside the man with his arms folded over his chest.

Jerry's eyes were closed, and his head lolled a little. He looked awfully pale.

What in the world had happened to him? He'd been running through town when she'd seen him a few minutes ago.

"Did he fall?" The words blurted out before she could think better of them.

Zane shook his head, his lips thinned to a grim line. "No. But he did have a run-in with a hefty horseshoe."

"A horseshoe?!" One hand involuntarily went to her chest. Why that must mean that Mr. Olann . . . "Oh, heavens!"

She was still trying to process all her thoughts when a door to an exam room on the back wall opened and Dr. Griffin and Mrs. Callahan emerged.

Concern tightened Zoe's chest. Her gaze flitted from the injured man to Charlotte and back. What was Charlotte doing here? She'd seemed fine earlier this morning when she'd been out at the spread! Had she been hurt during the whole ordeal with the fire?

Just then, Dr. Griffin and Mrs. Callahan beamed at each other. Dr. Griffin patted Mrs. Callahan's shoulder with neighborly affection. "I'm very happy for you, Charlotte."

"Thank you. I can hardly believe it," she replied.

"Well, I'll be!" Zane's grin nearly split his face.

Charlotte's cheeks blazed as she suddenly seemed to realize she and Dr. Griffin were not the only ones in the room. She looked down and fiddled with her gloves. "Marshal, I'll ask that you allow me to speak to my husband before you go blabbing anything to your wife?" She pegged him with a stern look, though the humor dancing in her eyes probably took any sting from it.

The marshal pressed one hand to his chest. "Why Charlotte, you know I'm the soul of discretion."

"I'm counting on it. Good day to you all." She set about tugging on her gloves.

Dr. Griffin motioned for her to lead the way. "I'll follow you home in my own carriage if it's all right. Just to make sure you get there safely since Reagan is a bit tied up at the moment."

"Thank you." Charlotte gave them a nod as she passed by with Dr. Griffin on her heels, and it was the sheer joy in her eyes that brought a grin to Zoe's lips.

She would bet her bottom dollar that within a few months there would be a little Callahan joining their community.

She looked up to find Wash scrutinizing her. Her joy immediately dissipated, and she lowered her focus to her clasped hands as the outer door clicked shut behind the pair. Would Wash ever be willing to give her such a happiness? She pressed her lips into a thin line. Talking him into having this surgery might be her only hope in that regard.

With Dr. Griffin and Mrs. Callahan now departed, Dr. Polson looked up from where he had been scribbling something in a ledger. His focus settled on the marshal. "He will live. But I'm very concerned about that blow he took. Go easy on him, will you? And I'd like to monitor him for a few more hours, at least. Even overnight, if you think you can allow him that."

The marshal spun his hat through his fingers, his perusal on the patient. "Can he talk?"

"Oh sure. I'm not certain how coherent he'll be but—"

"I'll be co-here-ant." Jerry's words were spoken slowly with a slight slur.

Zoe exchanged a look with Wash.

He lifted one shoulder in a gesture that said he was just as much in the dark here as she was.

Dr. Polson suddenly seemed to notice her and Wash. He rose from his desk, and strode toward them, hand outthrust. "Washington Nolan. I'm so glad to see you here." There was a hopeful note in the words. "Zoe, good to see you." He offered her a nod and a smile before returning his attention to Wash. "How can I help you?"

Wash swallowed and fiddled with the head of his cane. "I've been thinking about your recommendation. Just here to have a chat about that."

"I'm so glad to hear it. Would you be willing to let me take a look at your leg?"

Slowly, Wash agreed. "That'd be fine."

"Wonderful." The doctor motioned toward the partitions at the back of the room. "Your wife can wait here. We should only be a moment."

Wash didn't move. "I'd like her to come with me, if you don't mind."

The doctor didn't miss a beat. "Of course, that's fine. Right fine." He smiled.

Zoe's heart warmed to hear Wash say that he wanted her with him. She fell into step behind the doctor and then moved into the little room with the curtain pushed to one side that he indicated.

The middle of the room held a narrow table with a piece of cloth folded neatly on the near end. There was a wash basin, and one extra chair. The cubicle was narrow with hardly any room to move.

After Wash joined her in the small space, the doctor set to pulling the curtain closed. "I'll just fetch a few instruments and return in a moment. Your britches can go on that chair there."

Zoe couldn't withhold a gasp, but thankfully the doctor had already made his retreat and maybe the sliding of the curtain rings on the rod had disguised the sound of her shock. She and Wash looked at one another, eyes wide, for a moment.

Wash grinned. Whispered, "Sorry about this. I didn't know that he would want me to, ah, you know. But . . . for better or worse, right?" He reached for his belt buckle.

Zoe whipped around to present him with her back. Heavens, were her cheeks as red as they felt? She felt sure they were and only hoped she could regain her composure before the doctor returned. He couldn't have known that they hadn't shared any . . . intimacies yet. "Would you prefer that I step out?" she whispered.

"You're fine, Zo."

His belt clanked against the wood of the chair she'd glimpsed and then she heard the rustle of him settling onto the small table.

Goodness! She most certainly was *not* fine!

Wash bumped her arm with the back of his hand. "You can turn around now."

She hesitated. Preparing herself for what she was about to see. What would his leg look like?

"It's fine, Zo. Honest."

She turned slowly, willing away the embarrassment of seeing him sitting on the table in his shirt and with only that piece of cloth across his lap. Her focus fell to his injured leg, which was the one nearest to her. "Oh, Wash." The words of sympathy were out before she could even think to stop them.

He lifted the leg with a wince. "Yeah, it's a doozy, huh?"

A long scar puckered the skin from his knee all the way to his ankle. Closer to the joint, on the fleshy part of his leg, a large red welt marred the skin. It was the size of her fist! Crooked white slashes and red trenches fissured through the flesh like an explosion. At the center there was a large concave dent where it seemed part of his leg was missing altogether.

No longer embarrassed by his state of undress, she leaned forward and pressed her fingers to the scar. "Wash, I'm so sorry. I had no idea it was this bad."

She lifted her gaze to his.

His eyes held a soft glow that drew her nearer. "I was half afraid the sight of it might send you running."

She shook her head. "Never."

He leaned toward her, hesitantly. Paused just before his lips touched hers. She breathed him in for a moment, hardly able to believe that, after all the months of anguish and missing him, he was finally here. Right here. And her husband. She leaned forward, closed the gap, and pressed her lips to his. She didn't linger long, but when she retreated, and touched his face, she hoped he could read all the emotions she was feeling in her eyes. Love. Sorrow. Horror. But most of all joy to finally have him sharing himself and his hurts with her.

"Thank you, Zo. I—"

"All right, I believe I have everything I need."

Zoe barely had time to step back before the doctor breezed through the curtain. He was all business and immediately focused on Wash's leg, even as he set a few of his tools on the little washstand table on the other side of the cubicle.

"Hmmm." He bent to get a closer examination of Wash's leg. "That was a doozy, wasn't it?"

Zoe pressed her fingers to her lips, still feeling the lingering brush of Wash's lips.

He winked at her above the doctor's back.

"Hmmm." Dr. Polson took Wash by the ankle and lifted his leg to get a better look. He prodded and poked and manipulated the joint until at one point Wash hissed. "Sorry about that, so sorry." But the doctor kept gently palpating the injury. He lifted an instrument that looked for all the world like some type of ruler and began measuring the size of Wash's scars and muttering to himself. Finally, he carefully released the leg to a relaxed position. "It appears the past surgeons were rather . . . haphazard in their approach."

Wash snorted. "Let's just say that cavalry surgeons aren't known for their finesse and gentleness, Doc."

Zoe gripped her husband's hand. She had suspected as much, but to hear it confirmed sent a pang of anger and frustration through her.

Dr. Polson's eyes filled with empathy. "Your injury was severe. Can you tell me please where you feel the most pain?"

Wash lifted his leg gingerly. "Most often in my knee, I guess. Sometimes it feels like someone is thrusting a red-hot branding iron right into my bones. But the muscles cramp something fierce too."

Dr. Polson tilted his head, a light of empathy in his gaze. "As I move your leg, I can feel a slight grating in your joint. Have you felt that before?"

Wash nodded, brows nudging up. "Often. Yes."

The doctor pressed his lips together. "I believe that some of your pain is the result of a bone fragment or two that is still inside your leg."

Zoe felt a little sick at that description. But when Wash's hand tightened against hers, she knew she wouldn't choose to be anywhere else no matter how many gruesome details she might have to overhear.

The doctor was still talking, and she realized that she'd missed some of what he said. "While the road to recovery won't be easy, I strongly believe that a carefully planned surgery can alleviate some of your suffering. It won't be a quick fix, and there will be a recovery period. But with time and careful ministration, I'm hopeful that we can significantly lessen your pain."

Zoe's heart pattered with anticipation.

Wash stared at his knee, and she could tell he was in a bit of a quandary—torn between the desire for relief and the fear of undergoing yet another invasive procedure.

She squeezed his hand, hoping he could feel her support and understanding. "I know how hesitant you are, but Dr. Polson is not a cavalry butcher." She wanted to press him further, but suddenly knew that she could not and resisted the temptation. She felt shame for having wanted to push him into this. With all that he'd been through, he deserved to make this decision himself.

Wash's gaze flickered to Dr. Polson. "You said you're hopeful that there will be less pain. But will there be?"

Dr. Polson waggled his head. "I can't promise you anything. But if those are bone fragments I'm feeling in your joint, I can tell you that removing them will result in a great improvement. As to what else I might be able to fix while I'm in there, well, I won't know that until we do the surgery."

After a moment of contemplation, Wash let out a weary sigh. "If it were your leg, Doc? Tell me honestly. What would you do?"

Dr. Polson set to scrubbing his hands at the wash basin. "Knowing what I know now after a few years in the medical profession? I would do the surgery, without question."

Wash's shoulders slumped under the weight of his decision. "What will the recovery time be?"

The doctor pondered as he dried his hands on a towel. "If there are only minor repairs needed, I would guess about six weeks. That should at least have you back to walking reasonable distances again. If there are more extensive repairs needed, it might be longer. But I can assure you that I'll do everything in my power to make the recovery as easy as possible while at the same time giving you the best results for your years to come."

"Can it make me worse?"

Zoe's heart stuttered and she snapped her focus to the doctor. They had talked of that. Would the doctor have an answer?

Dr. Polson shook his head. "The chances of that are very slim. But we can never say for certain. Any surgery carries risk."

Zoe felt her tension release a little.

Wash exhaled slowly. Turned a look on Zoe. "What do you think?"

She wanted to scream "Yes, yes, yes!" But renewed her resolve to keep silent. This couldn't be up to her. "This must be your decision. I'll support you no matter what you decide."

He hung his head, staring down at the map of trauma on his calf. Finally, he looked up. "All right, Doc. I'll trust your judgment." He raised Zoe's hand to give her knuckles a quick kiss.

Hope surged in Zoe's heart. She squeezed his hand, blinking back tears of happiness. "The Lord is our Shepherd. We shall not want, no matter the outcome. He will always be there for us."

Wash's brow crimped.

But before she could ask him why, the doctor spoke again.

"Wonderful! We'll begin preparations for the surgery right away. Both Doc Griffin and I are slated to be here at the surgery tomorrow afternoon. Shall we say one o'clock?"

Zoe felt the immediate tension in Wash's grip. "That soon?" He swallowed.

"The sooner the better," Dr. Polson replied. He laid a hand on Wash's shoulder. "We'll do everything possible to improve your quality of life."

As they left the office a few minutes later, Zoe's pulse thundered with a mixture of optimism and concern. For the next several hours she needed to guard her emotions and make sure that Wash only saw the optimism!

Chapter Twenty

Zane paced the small clinic trying not to overhear too much of what was going on behind the curtain as he waited for Wash and Zoe to vacate the place before diving into his interrogation. With only the thin curtain partitioning them, he felt it was only fair to allow Jerry as much of his sorry dignity as possible.

As soon as Wash and Zoe left, Zane grabbed a chair and turned it around backward in front of Jerry. "Doc? Mind giving me the room for a bit?"

"Certainly. I'll stop to give the sheriff an update on his condition and then go speak to Dr. Griffin about tomorrow's surgery." The door creaked open, then clicked shut, and his footsteps retreated.

Zane leaned over the back of his chair and checked Jerry's cuff to make sure it wasn't too tight. "Can I get you anything, Jerry?"

Jerry opened his mouth, but before he could speak, a knock sounded on the clinic's front door and then Joe poked his head inside. "Hey, I've got Priscilla and David here. Reagan said I should bring them down to see Jerry."

Zane tamped down his frustration. So much for his interrogation. He rolled his hand in a motion for them to enter. "Come on in." He rose and tugged his chair back from the patient.

Priscilla was the first one through the door when Joe swung it wide. She shrieked so loudly that Zane couldn't stop a wince. He jiggled a finger in his ear as she rushed past.

"Jerry!" She fell to her knees in front of her husband and reached a trembling hand to cup his cheek. "Oh, darling what did he do to you?"

David, who had trailed in quietly behind his stepmother, froze the moment he saw the purple bruise spreading across the side of his father's face. He folded his arms and leaned against the wall nearby.

Jerry tilted his head away from Priscilla's probing fingers. "Don't touch it. I'm fine. I'll be fine."

Priscilla climbed to her feet, fists clenched on her hips. "You tell them everything, you hear me? Everything. Why, he tried to *kill* you!"

Jerry rested his head against the wall and dabbed his rag gingerly to his temple. "If I talk, I'll, well, I don't know what will happen to me, Prissy."

Zane had to give the woman credit. He would have guessed that she would have been a sobbing heap by this point of the conversation.

Instead, she thrust her chin in the air. "Then you make a deal. You're just a little fish, Jerry. You make sure they know how sorry you are. How sorry *we* are." She turned big doe eyes on Zane.

He exchanged a look with Joe. It was true that Jerry's crimes were not as heinous as trying to kill someone, but neither could they simply let a man go when he'd purposely been stealing from his neighbors for who knew how long.

He stepped forward and took her arm. "Mrs. Hines, you take David on home now. I'll come and give you a full report just as soon as Joe and I are done talking to Jerry."

She tugged a hanky from her sleeve and dabbed her eyes. "Thank you, Marshal." She gave another glance at her husband, who had closed his eyes and tilted his head against the wall. She lowered her voice. "He is going to live, right?"

Zane nudged her toward the exit. "The doctor seems to think so, yes."

"Oh, thank the good Lord. David, honey, come on. Let's go home."

With one last worried frown in his father's direction, David followed his stepmother from the room.

Finally alone with their suspect, Joe and Zane both pulled up chairs. Zane straddled his backward, then leaned forward and rested his arms across the back.

Jerry cocked one eye open. "Can I ask a question?"

Zane nudged out his lower lip. "Don't see's how it could hurt."

"How did you all find out?"

Joe leaned into the slats of his chair, stretching his legs out and crossing them at the ankles. "The sheriff likes his coffee, Jerry."

The man frowned. "I don't understand? I never tampered with diluting the coffee—or any other of my products for that matter." He gave Zane a pointed look.

Zane felt a headache tapping at his temples. "You'll forgive us if we aren't awed by your wonderful morality, Jerry."

"You may not have cut your coffee," Joe continued, "but Reagan keeps his coffee in a tin on the little shelf right by the stove in the jailhouse. The same tin that he's used ever since he started working in Wyldhaven."

Jerry frowned. "And?"

Zane exchanged a look with Joe. Jerry wasn't the brightest tool in the shed.

"And . . . the last few pounds of coffee that you sold him, kept falling shorter and shorter of the spot in his tin where he knew a pound should reach."

Jerry rested his head against the rag in his hand with a wince. "Shouldn't have cheated the sheriff. But I didn't want to give him too much by measuring in more."

Zane shook his head, finding it hard to summon up any sympathy for the man. "Tell us how it started."

Jerry gave his head a little shake of regret. "Olann came to me. Because he had access to my accounts at the bank, he could see how much I was spending on foodstuffs. He was mighty friendly at first. Suggesting how much money I could save. I was reluctant, but for months he kept after me. He would drop little hints every time I went in to deposit or withdraw money. And Prissy . . ." He flapped his bloody rag, before readjusting it and pressing it to his head again. "She was never quite satisfied with the life I'd been able to give her here in Wyldhaven." He scrunched his forehead. "I'm not proud of it, but I gave in to the temptation. The weights have those felt patches on the bottom and that made it easy to pry one off, carve out a little of the lead, and then just cover it back over with the felt. The first week I was terrified. But when no one noticed, I carved out a little more the next week. And a little more the week after that. Pretty soon, the savings really started adding up."

"And what did you do with the money?" Zane prodded him.

"Well, at first I bought things for Prissy. A grand piano. A walnut dining suite. Our new carriage. But then Merle came around and threatened that he would tell the law if I didn't pay him half of my savings each month."

Zane glanced at Joe. So they'd been right. That *had* been the man's motivation for encouraging Jerry to cheat his neighbors. A portion of the proceeds. How many other merchants had he compromised in town?

He voiced the question, but Jerry shook his head. "If he did, he never mentioned anything to me about it."

"So when Merle threatened you, what was your response?"

Jerry worked his mouth like he was thirsty. Joe hopped up and poured water into a tin mug from the pitcher on the doctors' desk.

Jerry downed half the glass then handed it back to Joe. "Thanks."

Joe nodded and set it on the floor between Jerry's chair and the bed next to him. "I'll just leave it right here."

Zane tamped down his impatience. "What did you do after his threat, Jerry?"

"Instead of taking it all to the bank, I started putting some into a mason jar in the pantry. And then one day I realized that wasn't very smart, so I took an old coffee tin and buried the money in the back yard under that big old hydrangea." His eyes suddenly widened. "Where is the tin?"

Zane frowned. He looked at Joe, but he shook his head. They looked back at Jerry.

"I had it with me in the livery when Merle . . ." He motioned to his head. "Did this."

Joe rose without a word and headed out. Zane didn't think Merle would have had time to grab it. He'd been cowering in hiding, so they must have come upon the scene fairly quickly. "We likely saved your life, you know that?"

Jerry winced and touched the side of his head. "Yeah. I didn't ever consider that he'd stoop so low."

Zane only pressed his lips together. The man was a fool not to have thought it, but he couldn't bring himself to say it. "Can you think of anything else that you ought to tell me?"

Jerry's eyes closed and his brow furrowed. "Not that I can think of."

"One last question. How long has this been going on?"

Jerry's eyes remained shut. His brow scrunched further. "Nigh on six months now."

Six months! Zane hated that crime had been taking place in their town for such a length of time and none of them had caught on until now. Thank God for Reagan's observant nature and his hankering for coffee—even if he did make it strong enough that it could wade into a swamp and tackle a 'gator!

He let Jerry rest then, and Joe returned only moments later with a dirty coffee tin in his hands. "It had fallen into the shadows behind a bale of hay. You're not going to believe this." He gave the tin a little shake, but it didn't make a sound.

Zane frowned. "Is it empty?"

Joe shook his head. "Oh, no."

He opened the tin and Zane's eyes shot wide at the sight of the tight-packed stacks of one-hundred-dollar bills. He glanced over at Jerry. "You made this much money off your little scheme?"

Jerry worked his jaw back and forth and grimaced as he touched it gingerly with the pads of his fingers. "I do a lot of business."

Zane supposed he did, what with his store being the closest one to many logging camps for miles around. He just hadn't realized that the mercantile kept that busy!

Joe pressed the lid back on the coffee tin. "Not anymore, you don't, Jerry. Not anymore."

As Wash and Zoe left the clinic, Wash directed Zoe across the street. What he really wanted to do was fall into the back of the wagon and take the pressure off his leg, but with the surgery happening tomorrow, he needed to take care of this today.

He pointed with his cane to the path that led up the hill to Kin's law office. "Let's see if Kin is back at work. I don't see him down by the schoolhouse anymore."

Indeed, only a few men remained by the building. And already, Wash could see Taulby tearing some of the burnt boards from the porch. Ewan and Doc Griffin were helping him. The town would have the schoolhouse porch rebuilt in no time.

Zoe's small hand settled into the crook of his arm, and with her walking by his side, he felt like he could face anything that came his way!

"Should we take the wagon up the hill?"

Until she went and said something like that. His spirits sagged. But soon this would all be over.

He hoped.

He quickly quashed the hope so that he wouldn't be disappointed if the surgery did nothing to improve his circumstances. He reminded himself that she hadn't meant to make him feel inadequate with the question. She was only concerned for his wellbeing.

"I'll be fine. Let's just take it slow." He rested his hand over hers. Swallowed. There was something he wanted to bring up anyhow. "Zoe, if something happens to me tomorrow—"

"Wash!" She gasped. "Don't talk like that. Everything is going to be fine." She refused to look at him.

"No. Listen. You heard the doctor. Every surgery has risks. So if something happens to me, you go to Kin. I don't have much, especially now after the fire, but he'll help you get everything settled, understand?"

She dashed at her cheeks. "I don't like to hear you talking like that."

He let his thumb caress her knuckles. "I'm sure it will be fine, Zoe. It's just a precaution. But there would be a widow's pension that comes to you from the cavalry because of my injury."

"Well, I won't want it."

"But I want you to have it." He smiled down at her. "Just promise me you won't use it to build Jinx a palace."

She laughed.

Just what he'd been hoping for.

With a bat of her eyelashes, she said, "But Jinx is such a good dog. He deserves a palace."

Wash winced dramatically. "That's what I was afraid of."

Zoe gave him a tart look as she started up the steps to Kin's office porch. "Well, I guess you'll just have to stick around for years to come to make sure that doesn't happen!"

He gave her a nod, certain she could see the humor dancing in his eyes. "I'll do my best."

The office door opened, and Kin stepped into the doorway. "This is a nice surprise. What brings you two up my way?" He stepped back and gestured for them to join him inside. "Business? Or pleasure?"

"Business, I'm afraid." Wash took off his hat as he stepped into the room and sank into the seat next to Zoe. Kin's office chairs were upholstered in red leather that molded to his body and when he stretched out his leg and propped it on the footstool, he felt like he could happily settle in for a nap right here. He grinned at Kin. "You ever have clients fall asleep in these chairs?"

Kin chuckled as he resumed his place behind the desk. "Can't say that has happened yet."

"I might be the first."

Kin folded his hands on the top of his desk. It was cluttered with all sorts of papers. "You got any whipped cream, Zoe?"

She laughed. "I'm sure we could whisk some up." She glanced over at Wash fondly.

He reached for her hand. "I guess I'd better stay awake if I don't want to find my head slathered in a mound of sticky whipped cream."

Kin let the humor die out. "I presume you came for something serious. What can I help you with?"

Wash shifted in his chair. "When you found me in California and brought me home, was anything mentioned about a man who had been paying me a stipend each month? His son was the one who accidentally shot me."

Kin was already nodding. "Yes. I left instructions that any more money they received should be forwarded to the Wyldhaven bank. And then when we got here, I sent a letter directly to the man informing him of your move. He replied . . ." Kin opened a drawer in his desk and filtered through several files. He pulled out a manilla folder and dropped it on the desktop before him. He flipped through some of the papers and then pulled one from near the middle. "Here." He thrust the letter across the desk toward Wash. "As you can see," Kin continued, "he said he'd be happy to begin sending the money here. I arranged it all with Olann and he said he would begin depositing the money into your account forthwith."

Wash frowned. He returned the missive to Kin. "Maybe the man changed his mind?"

Kin shook his head. "It didn't sound like he planned to do that."

Wash looked at Zoe. She lifted one shoulder. "Mr. Olann did just get arrested for something. Maybe . . . Well, I hate to speak ill of the man."

Kin's brows arched. "Cora's uncle has been arrested?"

Zoe tipped her head toward town as she nodded. "They were just putting him in a cell a few minutes ago when Wash and I were heading over to talk to Dr. Polson."

Kin's gaze darted to Wash. "You going to let him give you that surgery he's been pestering you about?"

"You knew about that?"

Kin shrugged. "The other night in the diner, he was lamenting his inability to convince you."

"Well, I've been convinced."

Kin's brown eyes softened with kindness. "I'm glad. It's been hard for many of us to see you in so much pain."

Wash felt all his hesitancies rise up inside him. "There are no guarantees."

Kin pushed out his lip. Gripped the back of his neck. "I understand that. But even though Polson might not be my favorite person in town—"

Zoe's giggle cut Kin off mid-sentence.

Wash looked over at her, puzzled first by Kin saying he didn't really like the man and then by Zoe laughing about it. "What is it?"

She gave him a wink. "Polson was interested in Cora before Kin returned to town. But Kin somehow managed to win her over."

"Ah!" He'd been away and had missed all that interaction. He gave Kin a knowing shrug. "Taulby Ecklund isn't my favorite person either."

Kin laughed as Zoe smacked Wash's arm. "For shame!"

"Anyhow, as I was saying, I think Polson is a very skilled physician and, from what I've heard, that also carries over into his surgical skills. When is your surgery?"

Wash sighed. "Supposed to be tomorrow."

"Wow. Well, Cora and I will take time to pray this evening that all will go well and that he'll be able to bring as much healing as possible."

It warmed Wash's heart considerably to hear his friend's assurances. It was wonderful to watch him growing and maturing in his relationship with the Lord. Wash gave him a nod. "I appreciate that. Any thoughts for me on where I should start to try to sort out this situation with the money?"

Kin rose from his chair and came around to open the door for them. "You just leave that to me and concentrate on simply healing from your surgery tomorrow, okay? I'll check in with you in a few days to let you know what I find out."

Wash stood and gave his friend a nod. "Thank you. I appreciate it. And if anything happens to me, it all goes to Zoe, got it?"

Zoe made a sound of disgruntlement and smacked him again. "Will you stop that!"

But Kin didn't even crack a smile. His serious gaze bored into Wash's. "I got it, friend. Rest easy."

Wash released a breath. "Thank you."

With that, he settled his hat on his head and navigated the steps down to the path. Tomorrow was an unknown.

Between now and then, he simply wanted to spend as much time with his family as possible. "Let's go home, Zoe."

She nestled her hand in the crook of his arm once more, and he relished the feel of her small warm fingers beneath his own.

Chapter Twenty-one

Harlan knew it had probably been a mistake to step out and confront Butch. He hadn't planned to have his confrontation in broad daylight—especially not right in the middle of town—but when he'd seen the man walking down the street, he hadn't been able to remain in his chair.

Now, however, it was time to get out of town.

He lifted his jacket from where he'd draped it on the back of his chair. "Let's go, men."

Ted stood right away, but the rest of them hesitated, as though waiting for an explanation. When he spoke, they ought to jump! However, he didn't want to draw attention, so he merely turned and marched out the rear door of the saloon—they'd tied their horses at the back so as to be less conspicuous, and right about now, he figured that was a good thing.

His men could have their small moment of rebellion today, however, he couldn't keep tolerating their insubordination if he wanted to maintain control for much longer.

One problem at a time. First, he would get Butch off his land. And then he would decide what to do about his men's lack of respect for his authority!

They mounted up and rode out of town, taking the branch of the Y that led to the west—toward the Nolan spread.

He felt satisfaction as he glimpsed several men across the creek, already rebuilding the schoolhouse porch. Yes. This was a good town. It would be a good place to settle.

Maisie would like it!

Anja arrived at the mill to treat Taulby's burns, only to find him next door at the schoolhouse ripping up burnt porch boards.

She stormed up the steps. Plunked her hands on her hips. "What are you doing?"

Yesterday she'd been quite pleased with the thin film that had formed over his burns. And he'd informed her that the doctor had said she should keep nursing him. Now he was here, undoing all her careful work!

Taulby froze. He knelt by a hole in the porch, with a hammer in his hand and a saw by his side. He looked up at her guiltily. A new board was being measured and marked by the barkeeper.

Taulby motioned to the man. "There was a fire. We are fixing it."

Anja reached out a hand for the board that the barkeeper tried to hand to Taulby. "I can already see blood seeping through your shirt. You're not doing anything except destroying all my nursing of your wounds!"

The barkeeper grinned at each of them in turn, causing Anja's chin to jut higher. Maintaining his grip on the board, he stood and set it to one side. "Taulby, friend, you've been holding out on me."

Anja folded her arms, refusing to acknowledge the wave of warmth that filled her at the sight of Taulby's ears turning pink.

"Not holding out, Ewan." Taulby said. "Just for dear life holding on."

Ewan laughed.

Anja had heard enough. "Up! Up! I have salve for your burns. If, after that, you want to destroy all of my attempts at healing, then you may do so!" Why was she so upset about this? The man owed her nothing.

She pivoted on one heel and marched from the school's porch to wait for him on his own.

A few minutes later, he lumbered up the stairs and paused before her with a contrite look. "I do not wish all your healing to undo, Anja."

She tipped her chin into the air. "Then you should think before you try to be a hero to a woman who chose another!" Realization hit her. So that was why she was so upset about this. She spun away and folded her arms. She hadn't even realized until the words slipped past her betraying lips.

"'Tis well-able, I am, to remember the rejection, and I wasn't trying to impress anyone!" Stone-hard anger chiseled each word.

He'd never spoken crossly to her before! She twirled to face him. Froze.

His head hung and he scuffed a toe at a knot on the porch. His face scrunched into an expression of apology. "I'm sorry, Anja. But the fire I saw from my window. In the house I could not stay. I went to help—for the children. For the town. But not once of Zoe did I think. This I'm surprised to say." He flapped one hand through the air as though to dismiss the subject. "Yet, it is true."

His expression softened.

She released the air trapped in her lungs and stepped toward him. "I shouldn't have said that. I, too, apologize."

His gaze leveled on her. "Say it, you did, however. Why?"

Foolish, Anja! Now she was in it up to her neck! She did not want to lose her friendship with this man over her silly feelings. They had only known one another for a few days and yet when she was with him, she felt as though she had arrived home. It would push him away if he could discern the strength of her feelings. She brushed aside his question and concentrated on pulling the salve from her basket. "You are a friend. I should not like to see you hurt again, that's all. Now, please, off with your shirt. This has already taken too long. Uncle Zeb is home alone."

He studied her as he slowly undid the buttons down the front of his shirt. "Honest, you are not being with me, little Anja."

She snorted. "You think I have time—all day maybe—to wait for you?"

He thinned his lips and slid his shirt down to his elbows, presenting her with his muscled brown shoulders. "Disagreeable you are determined today to be, ja?"

She tucked her lower lip between her teeth and focused on the task at hand, dipping her fingers into the salve jar. "Call it what you want."

He spun toward her so quickly that she didn't have time to retreat before he had gently captured her hand, salve and all, in his. "And if attraction is what I want to call it?" He curled his hand around hers and drew her closer. "*Sjalusi*, even?"

"Nonsense." She couldn't bring herself to meet his gaze. "Me? Jealous?"

He reached up to brush back an escaped strand of her hair. "Ja, Anja. Maybe?"

She closed her eyes. This couldn't be happening. She was in Wyldhaven only to take care of her uncle. Then she would return east. The thought was torture. But she firmed her resolve. She didn't have time for courting, and yet, she could not deny the strong connection between them. "You need time. 'Tis only confusion."

He stroked a hand over her hair once more. "Aye. A great deal of confusion there is, this is true." He released her then and presented her with his back again.

With trembling fingers, she dug out more salve and tried to ignore the flinch of his skin as she began to smooth it over the healing burns.

Reagan had just been stepping out to go over to the saloon and look for this Harlan White to ask him some questions when Dr. Polson arrived on his doorstep to give him a report about Jerry. Then, by the time he'd reached the alehouse, the man hadn't been inside. Edwina, who'd been manning the bar while Ewan was over helping out at the schoolhouse, seemed to know nothing about the man, and since she made Reagan uncomfortable with her forwardness, he'd returned to the jailhouse.

Merle had refused to share what he knew about Harlan White unless Reagan gave him immunity for his crimes. Reagan certainly wasn't ready to make that deal.

He finished his paperwork about the arrests, Jerry's injury imminently prior to his arrest, and the carefully counted money in the tin Joe had found in the livery—fourteen thousand seven hundred dollars. It was a staggering sum that left Reagan's mouth dry, especially considering the fact that he himself made just over one hundred dollars a month now after years of faithfully serving Wyldhaven's citizens.

In a few months of stealing from the town's hardworking citizens, Jerry and Merle had taken over twenty times the amount of Reagan's annual salary—well maybe not quite that much if Jerry really had been holding out on Merle. Joe had quietly informed Reagan that Jerry had claimed as much.

All while Reagan had been doing the paperwork, Merle had sat quietly in his cell—but he had risen to his feet and stared a bit wide-eyed at the stacks of bills as Reagan purposefully counted them slowly. Then he'd cursed and returned to his cot.

For that reason, Reagan figured maybe Jerry had been telling the truth and really had been holding out on Merle.

Merle certainly wasn't happy to realize it only now.

That made Reagan smile a little on the inside.

After letting the banker stew in his juices for a good long while, Reagan finally looked up from the papers on his desk. "You ready to share what you know about this Harlan White?"

Stretched out on his cot, Merle folded his arms and stared at the ceiling. "I'm ready for some dinner."

Reagan propped his boots on the corner of the desk. "Missed lunch, did you? Hard to find time to eat while you are running around starting fires and planning to kill your partner in crime, I suppose."

Merle only huffed.

A knock sounded on the door and Reagan called for them to enter.

Ben King poked his head through the crack. "Got that telegram you needed."

Reagan held out his hand. "Thanks, Ben."

With a nod, the man handed him the paper, gave Merle a cursory curious glance, and then left, pulling the door shut behind him.

Earlier when Reagan had searched the post office, he'd asked King to wire for information on both Jerry and Merle. As he read the response, his brows nudged up. "Well now. This is interesting, Merle. There're a few things you didn't disclose to us a few years ago when the town council agreed to let you start a bank in our town, aren't there?"

Merle sighed. Scrubbed a hand over his face. Made no reply.

"You know the judge in our county doesn't take kindly to repeat offenders, Merle. Not kindly at all." He dropped the telegram on his desk. "However, if you should decide to be forthcoming with regard to another criminal in my jurisdiction, I think I could perhaps persuade the judge to go a little easier on you." He rose. "I'll go get your dinner now."

He would take his time. Maybe the man would be willing to talk when he returned. Reagan stepped out onto his porch and closed the door behind him, leaving Merle alone in his cell.

Belle stepped out of Dixie's Boardinghouse on her last day of work, ready to head for home. She felt downcast and discouraged. Her departure for Seattle loomed on the horizon, and she'd requested all of the next two weeks off so that she could pack and be sure to do some extra things around the house so that Ma wouldn't be left with all that work.

Lord knew the twins and Aidan weren't very helpful most of the time and with Zoe off to her own household now, Belle didn't want Ma to overwork herself.

However, it had been such a topsy turvy day. First the sheriff had come through asking to search the place and Dixie had needed to help him, leaving Belle to manage both the kitchen and the dining room through the lunch rush. Then there had been the fire at the schoolhouse and since Dixie had handed out many of the containers from her kitchen to help put out the flames, there had been a huge amount of cleanup afterward when everyone brought the containers back.

She was very thankful there hadn't been more damage to the school than there was. Also, very thankful to hear that the board had voted to let Zoe keep her job.

But it felt like a chaotic note to leave on. She'd spent additional time cleaning up the kitchen to make sure Dixie didn't have any extra work the next day. And now her feet practically dragged on the way home.

As she entered the shade of the trees near her wildflower field, she decided to take a moment to visit her favorite alcove under the spreading branches of the large tree at the back of the field one more time. It was the place where she'd been putting the finishing touches on a family portrait on the night that her father had died. She'd stayed out all night, hoping to finish it before he passed—and had failed.

It was also the place where, years later, she had desperately painted a portrait of dear Pa for fear that she might one day forget his face. The place where Kane Carver had heard her sobbing and come to see if she was all right. The place where she'd first fallen in love with him.

But now, as she approached the path that cut through the wild lilac and rosebushes, she heard the whuffle of a horse and the jangle of a bit.

She looked up and smiled to see Kane's horse contentedly cropping grass from where he was hobbled in the field.

Kane sat on a stump just beyond the horse, his gaze warm on her face. "Hi." He stood with a smile. "Thought I might have missed you there for a few minutes—okay, more like an hour and a half."

Belle covered her mouth. "You've been waiting for me for an hour and a half?"

He dipped his chin. "I have, and the sight of you makes it worth every moment."

She felt suddenly shy at the blatant compliment that was unlike him. "I'm sorry. It was . . . such a day! I don't even know where to begin to tell you about it. I had to stay late to do some cleaning."

"No matter now that you're here. Do you have a few minutes?"

For him? She had all the time in the world. "I do."

He reached out a hand.

Her heart gave a thump as she settled her fingers into the warmth of his grasp.

He led her through the field to her little hideaway, and when they pushed their way under the tangle of intertwined branches and canes, Belle gasped. "Oh, Kane!"

On the grass, he'd spread a blanket and atop that he'd placed a picnic basket.

"I know you'll be right busy packing and helping at your parents' place over the next week. I wanted to . . . have a little time with you to myself before all that."

She wished she felt the freedom to sidle close to him and give him a kiss. She thought he might welcome it, but wasn't sure she could handle the hurt if he didn't, so she remained where she stood and hoped he could read the appreciation in her eyes.

Her stomach gave a loud rumble, and she slapped a palm over it in embarrassment. "Do forgive me. I didn't have time to eat lunch."

"Well then, we'd best dive in right away." Kane pointed to the blanket for her to sit, and when she did, he immediately joined her and set to pulling plates from the basket. The plates were followed by a small basket of apples, a tin of cold fried chicken, and another of baked potatoes.

He touched one. Grimaced. "I'm afraid they are somewhat colder than I planned them to be."

Belle never remembered feeling happier. "Cold potatoes are lovely. One of my favorite foods." She swept her tongue along the inside of her cheek.

He angled her a look. "I have a feeling, Miss Kastain, that you aren't being completely honest with me."

She couldn't withhold a chuckle. "It will be fine. Life is a wonderful adventure! And if we have to eat cold potatoes sometimes, well, then it just allows us to enjoy the days with warm potatoes all the more!"

He set the tin of potatoes to one side and leaned toward her, planting one arm behind her. “You are a wonder, you know that?”

She held her breath. He was so close she could feel the warmth of him. See the small scar on his chin that prevented his beard from growing there. And the smaller one that lay at the outer corner of his eye.

Kane’s gaze trailed across her forehead and over her cheeks to pause at her lips.

Belle felt her heart stutter in her chest. Her breathing stilled. Her pulse raced.

He leaned forward and brushed her lips with his own, sending a wave of warmth through her. She angled into the contact and settled one hand against his cheek. His lips were soft and warm and gentle. The stubble on his cheek prickled the tips of her fingers.

Her stomach rumbled loudly again.

Kane pulled back with a chuckle and Belle hung her head, tucking her lower lip between her teeth. But it was probably a good thing to have the interruption with their current isolation.

Kane gave her a wink. “The stomach has spoken.” He handed her a plate and held the tin of chicken toward her. After she’d taken a piece, he offered a potato. “Cold potatoes? I hear they are a great aid to adventure.”

“I love adventures!” She offered as she lifted one onto her plate.

After he’d given her an apple, they quietly set about eating. Belle wasn’t sure if she’d ever tasted anything as good as that cold chicken. Even the potato went down easily between bites of apple. She saved the last bite of chicken for the end and savored it as she wiped her fingers on the cloth Kane had provided. “I think that’s the best chicken I’ve ever had.”

"Maude is a wonder in the kitchen and that's certain." Kane reached for the cloth and wiped his own fingers. "Feeling better now?"

Belle rested a hand on her stomach. "I am, thank you very much."

"Good, because I have a question to ask you." His expression sharpened with sudden seriousness. He tossed aside the rag, moved their plates, and shifted until he was leaning on one knee before her. His focus never left her face as he unbuttoned the flap on his shirt pocket and reached inside to pull out a gold ring. With his arms propped against his knee, he held the ring up, angling it back and forth between two fingers.

Her eyes shot wide. She scrambled upright until she, too, was on her knees and resting on her ankles. Her hand trembled as it fluttered to cover her lips. For the longest of moments all she could do was stare at that lovely golden circlet. Finally, she lifted her focus. "I thought you said . . ."

He tilted his head. "I know what I said. But I couldn't stand the thought of sending you off to Seattle and all those fancy men who will be vying for your hand without my ring on your finger. I love you, Belle, and I want you to come home to me and only me."

She wanted to reach for the ring and slide it on her finger. But she made herself stay still, simply enjoying the sight of it for a few moments longer. "Did you speak to Papa?" She couldn't stop the tick of humor that tugged at her lips.

He pumped his brows. "I did."

"And what did he say?"

"He gave us his blessing, but not until after giving me a near attack of angina by pretending that he was unsure."

Belle felt her cheeks bunch. "Have you recovered then, from this attack?"

Humor sparkled in his brown eyes. “I’m not certain yet. It’s still lingering as I wait for an answer.”

She quirked a brow at him. “Mr. Carver . . . A girl cannot answer a question that has not yet been asked.”

His cheeks flushed. “Did I forget to ask a question?”

“You did indeed.”

He leaned toward her. “Belle Kastain, would you do me the honor of becoming my wife?”

She breathed out relief and stretched out her left hand. “The answer to that is a very emphatic yes.”

With happiness glittering in his gaze, Kane slipped the ring onto her finger and then stood, pulling her with him. He kissed her then, slow and steady, with his hands cupped around her cheeks. She relished the caress of his lips, the warmth of his chest beneath her fingers, the lilac-scented air swirling all around them.

After a long moment, he eased back. “I will always look forward to adventures with you, Belle.”

She rested one finger against his chin. “Just promise me one thing?”

His brow crimped as he searched her face. “What’s that?”

“Next time, we’ll have warm potatoes.”

He threw back his head on a laugh, then pulled her to him and settled a kiss against her forehead. “I promise I’ll try to do my best.”

She chuckled. “Well then, that’s all that a girl can ask.” With that, she settled her cheek against the beat of his heart and relished having his arms around her here in this place where she’d first fallen in love with him.

Her heart was filled with anticipation for a lifetime of growing in that love as his wife.

Chapter Twenty-two

By the time Zoe and Wash met Mr. Nolan at the mill and then made it back to the spread, most of the townsfolk who'd been helping with cleanup had headed on to their own places and chores for the evening. Zoe was surprised and grateful at the amount of work that had been completed while they'd been away in town.

The rubble that had once been Wash's cabin had all been cleared away. The stone foundation was still discolored by the fire, but stood clear and clean, ready for their new house.

Much of the rubble at the barn had also been cleared.

She was once again filled with gratitude that they lived in such a supportive community.

Maude had a meal of fried chicken and baked potatoes keeping warm in the warming drawer. As soon as they stepped into the house, she started putting food on the table that was set and ready. Jackson, Grant, and Lincoln all appeared, hunger shining in their eyes.

"'Bout time you all got home," Grant groused.

"A man's work is never done, son," Butch replied, sinking into his seat at the head of the table with a weary sigh.

"Yes, Pa." Grant quietly pulled out his chair, and everyone sat down.

After grace, Maude held the plate of fried chicken to Zoe first. Her eyes crinkled at the corners. "My brother was by earlier and asked me to pack a picnic that he hoped to share with your sister."

Zoe's gaze sharpened on her. "Oh?" She took a piece and handed the platter on to Wash.

Maude nodded. "And from the round circlet that I caught a glimpse of in his shirt pocket, I'm guessing he had a particular question in mind too!"

Zoe's heart soared. "Oh! That would be wonderful!"

Maude's eyes crinkled with joy. "I'm quite pleased, myself. Finally!"

"Finally, indeed," Zoe concurred.

Wash shared the news about Dr. Polson wanting to do a surgery the next day.

Jackson stilled and looked at him. "You're okay with that?"

Wash lifted one shoulder. "He seems to think that he can lessen my pain. If he's right, then I feel I ought to try."

Butch gave Zoe a grateful look as he spoke to his son. "You should. I, for one, am glad you are taking him up on his advice, son. I hope and pray that it will be the solution you need. In fact, I would like for us to pray as a family, if you don't mind." He stretched his hands out to Lincoln and Grant, who sat on either side of him.

Lincoln grumbled as he set down the chicken leg that had already been halfway to his mouth. "We're never gonna get to eat."

After a few chuckles, they all turned serious. And Zoe only felt a little guilt over the fact that when everyone else bowed their heads, she kept her eyes open to relish the sight of this family that she'd so recently joined bonding together as one to petition the Almighty on behalf of the man she loved.

Butch's voice was sincere and deep. Wash's fingers were warm around her own. He swallowed hard and used his shoulder to swipe away a tear that escaped. Jackson and Maude bobbed their heads and murmured some amens in response to Butch's prayer.

Lincoln and Grant were quiet, but kept their heads bowed respectfully.

And most heartening of all was to see Wash's features relax as his father lifted him before the throne. The furrows in his brow eased. The lines of tension around his lips smoothed. And by the time Butch said his "Amen," Wash's grip on her hand had even relaxed.

Zoe sighed in contentment. This was a good family the Lord had allowed her to be a part of.

They ate in silence then, all of them weary from the strain of the past few days.

When plates were empty, Butch placed his serviette on the table and looked between Lincoln and Grant. "Boys, get your evening chores done and then I want you in bed right away tonight. Going to be an early start in the morning. And then we'll all head to town to wait word on Wash's surgery."

"Pa, you don't have to—"

Butch raised his palm. "We won't be anywhere else, son. Nowhere else."

Wash swallowed and blinked hard a few times. "Thanks, Pa."

Zoe rose and helped Maude clear the table. While Wash and Jackson settled beside the chess board, she helped with the dishes.

Her nervousness increased with each dish that she dried.

Tonight would be the first night that she and Wash shared their own room with a real bed—one they could both fit into. And with Wash's surgery happening tomorrow, this might be the only night they would share for some weeks to come. Surely he would respond differently tonight after all the ways they'd connected today? She hoped he would respond differently, though she could see even from her place here in the kitchen that he was in a great deal of pain.

His stance was no longer relaxed, and he kept rubbing his lower leg as he studied the chess board, waiting for Jackson to make his move.

Jackson moved his queen, just as Zoe and Maude entered the living room.

With a grunt of satisfaction, Wash nudged his own queen one space. "Checkmate."

Jackson groaned. "I'm a dunce. I should have seen that."

Maude approached her husband and wrapped her arms around him from behind as she bent to drop a kiss on his cheek. "Come on, dunce of my heart. Let's say our goodnights. I'm tired and tomorrow isn't looking any shorter than today."

Jackson rose, pointing a finger at Wash. He resisted the tug of Maude's hand as she tried to pull him out of the room. "I demand a rematch."

Wash chuckled. "I'm sure there will be plenty of time for that when I'm laid up in bed recovering from surgery."

Jackson pumped a fist and finally gave in to his wife's tugging. He called over his shoulder as they disappeared down the hall, "I'll be whipping you in ten moves by the time you are healed up."

Wash only chuckled.

His gaze collided with Zoe's then and turned serious, thoughtful. "Ready to get some sleep?"

She stepped closer. "I am." Boldly, she stretched her hand toward him. "Coming?"

His brow crimped. He ignored her hand and scrubbed at the hair on the back of his neck. "Last room down the hall on the left. Go ahead and I'll be down in a few minutes." He didn't seem to want to look her way after that.

Zoe's shoulders fell. She dropped her hand. He really didn't want to be with her. Discouragement weighted her feet as she slowly made her way down the hall.

A new toothbrush and new red metal tube of Colgate's Ribbon Dental Cream waited for her on the washstand inside the door. A clean full-length nightgown was laid out on the foot of the bed.

Lord bless Maude's thoughtfulness!

The tears started to flow when she was only halfway into the nightgown. By the time she'd thrown herself onto the bed and scooted as close to the wall as she could—under the covers with her back to the door—she was silently sobbing in earnest.

It was only a few minutes later that Wash tapped lightly on the door and she heard him ease it open.

She gathered her composure and kept her shoulder planted firmly into the feather mattress, pretending to be asleep. If he didn't want to be with her, she would leave him to himself. But just the thought of facing years like this made another sob escape. She tucked her lips between her teeth and scrunched her eyes tight.

Please don't let him have heard that.

Behind her, the sounds of Wash's movements ceased. After a moment he whispered, "Zo? You okay?"

She didn't respond. Let him think that he'd just imagined it.

His belt buckle clanked against the bureau top.

She needed to sniff, but refused to do so. Tears from her top eye pooled into the curve by her nose and spilled over. They joined the tears from her other eye to soak the pillowcase beneath her cheek. It was uncomfortable. Still, she didn't move.

The bed dipped as Wash sank onto his side of the mattress. One by one, his boots hit the floor.

The mattress moved again.

She remained still. Frowned. Quieted her breathing. Tried to hear what he was doing.

And then his voice spoke from just above her ear. “Ah, Zo. You’re tearing my heart out, here.” His hand smoothed the tangles of her hair away from her face.

Her eyes flew open.

He was on one elbow, leaning over her.

He tugged on her shoulder to roll her to her back and then smoothed the hair from the damp side of her face as well.

Confusion swelled through her at the compassion filling his eyes.

He shook his head. “I know what you’re thinking, and you couldn’t be more wrong.”

She narrowed her gaze. “I think you’ve made yourself pretty clear.”

He shook his head again. “No. No, I apparently haven’t.”

Her body betrayed her because while she wanted to remain angry with him, her pulse thrummed with her love for him as he continued to brush his fingers through her hair, thumb the tears from beneath her lashes, and study her with that soft look in his eyes.

He leaned toward her. “You’ve no idea how hard you are to resist.”

She felt tension tug at her brow. Finally, she let herself sniff. “You seem to be doing a fair job of it.”

He made a dismissive sound. “I’m not resisting you because I don’t want to be with you, Zo. In fact, I want it so much that I’m weak with it.” His thumb trembled against her bottom lip.

She reached to cover his hand with her own. “Then why?”

He exhaled sharply and flopped back on his pillow, tugging her with him. “Come here.” He wrapped one arm around her, and she settled her cheek against his chest. He scooped the fingers of his opposite hand into her hair, and simply held her. When he spoke, his voice rumbled in her ear. "Earlier at the doctor's office, you quoted from Psalm twenty-three. 'The Lord is our shepherd. We shall not want,' you said. A few years ago I might have agreed with that sentiment, Zoe. But I'm not certain I understand what that means anymore. The Lord was my shepherd that day that I was simply walking through camp and a new recruit accidentally discharged his weapon into my leg. The Lord was my shepherd through two previous surgeries, neither of which fixed my problem. The Lord has been my shepherd in all the years since, but I still want, Zoe. I don't know how not to! I want to sleep through the night without waking in pain. I want to be a man who can support his family! I want to be able to walk down the aisle with my bride without" —his voice hitched— "falling on my face in front of everyone."

He paused but Zoe sensed that he wasn't finished, so she held her silence and merely listened.

His chest rose and fell beneath her cheek. The sound of a bullfrog chorused through the background. Finally, he continued. "I want to be a father to my children, Zoe. But I'm not guaranteed that will happen. You're not guaranteed that will happen. And I don't want to leave you in a position where you regret—"

"I could never—"

"Just listen." His thumb brushed gently against the skin of her arm. "If something happens to me tomorrow, it will be hard for you. But it would be so much harder if you were left with a child to raise on your own."

She pushed up onto her elbow and glowered into his face. "Nothing is going to happen to you!"

He shook his head. "You don't know that! Haven't you been listening to me?"

She frowned and plucked at a tie on the quilt. "I think the meaning of that verse is not that we'll never have hard times, Wash, but that we realize that God will take care of us through the hard times. We may have wants as in we *wish* that things were different, but if we trust Him through the hard times, we see how all things work together for the good of those who love Him and are called according to His purpose." She pressed a hand to his arm. "Even that Psalm I quoted talks about the valley of the shadow of death. There are hard times, but God will comfort us, provide for us. In the valleys, that might be hard to see, but I believe it is true."

There was ire in the gaze he turned on her. "And you think that I don't?"

She shook her head. "I didn't say that."

He relaxed, tucking one arm beneath his head. "It's so easy to say, Zoe, and so much harder to trust when you are the one flat on your back looking up at a brazen sky. I just want life to be easy for you. Not like—well, not like this." He thrust a frustrated gesture that encompassed his injured leg and then returned his arm to the position behind his head.

"And what if I would want a . . . a son or a daughter, to remember you by?" She felt flames lick her cheeks but refused to break eye contact. "A child, *your* child, would never be a burden, Wash. I would consider it a blessing."

With his near hand, he wrapped a strand of her hair around his finger, caressing it with his thumb. "You say that now. But you can't know that's how you would always feel. Besides, it would be irresponsible of me. A child needs a father. And, selfishly, I wouldn't want my child raised by someone else."

"So I get no say?"

He closed his eyes and tugged her back down. "Not this time. Please, try to understand. We have a long day tomorrow."

Try to understand? Oh she understood! He was completely selfish and uncaring of what she wanted! He was angry with God and taking that grudge out on her! And on top of it all, he felt she wouldn't be capable of raising his child on her own. Not to mention that the chances of her getting with child were slim after only one night together.

Maybe she simply hadn't made herself clear enough. He said she was a temptation. Perhaps she could convince him.

With her lower lip tucked between her teeth, she stroked a hand over the shirt he still wore.

His breath hitched, but other than that, he didn't move.

She eased closer to press a kiss against his cheek.

He angled his eyes toward her but remained stiff.

Next she kissed the stubble of his jaw. The soft corner of his mouth.

In one swift move, he grabbed her hand and rolled toward her so that she was once more on her back as he leaned over her. But instead of holding her hand in a caress, he pressed it tightly to the mattress on the other side of her as though to keep her from touching him. Fire lit his eyes and his chest rose and fell. His focus dropped to her lips. He swallowed hard.

For one moment, she thought she'd won him over.

Then his jaw hardened and his eyes glittered as they returned to hers. "You know, Zo, sometimes a man likes to be the leader in a relationship." He flopped away from her, leaving her with only the view of his broad back. "Go to sleep. Please."

His breaths were ragged and rapid. After a few moments they slowed, and then quieted.

She grew more riled with each breath she listened to him take. They grew longer, deeper, softer.

She lay beside him until the wee hours of the morning, feeling deeply the sting of his continued rejection. The pain of his anger toward God.

However, she had no one to blame but herself. It was her impulsive behavior that had gotten her into this position. He'd told her he didn't want her, yet she'd practically forced him to marry her.

Well, he could have his leadership! She wouldn't make herself vulnerable to him again! She ground her teeth and flounced onto her side, glowering at the dark wall.

Sometime in the morning hours, the gentle rhythm of his breathing lulled her to sleep.

When she woke with the sun, he wasn't on the bed beside her. And in the light of morning, she couldn't seem to summon her anger from the night before.

Despair over a lonely future? Despondency over his lack of attraction to her? Rejection?

Yes. She felt all those things.

And the worst of it was, she was now faced with a decision. Did she truly believe the words she'd spoken to him the night before? That God worked all things for the good of those who loved Him and were called according to His purpose?

Because here she stood, smack dab in the middle of what certainly felt like a valley of the shadow of death.

Death of her dreams.

Death of her love—no, never her love. She would love him until they day that she died.

But how long would he cling to his anger? Even if the surgery was a success, there were other accidents that could take him from this earth in the blink of an eye. Was he thinking about those? She and her siblings and mother certainly knew a little about that kind of tragedy.

She tilted her face toward the ceiling. Closed her eyes. *Lord, I trust You. But please, help me to see the good in this, because it's true what Wash said. I'm having a hard time finding it right now.*

She rose wearily to dress.

One thing she knew. She would never make herself vulnerable to him again.

She only hoped that she would be able to keep both his family and hers from knowing how deeply his rejection had hurt her.

Chapter Twenty-three

Harlan had sent one of his men back to the alehouse the night before. It had been a risk, but not a great one because he'd made sure to move camp as soon as the man had left for town.

And the risk had been worth it, because they'd connected with him again this morning and he had returned with news.

It seemed that Butch's oldest son would be having a surgery today.

And it was perfect timing because Harlan was done playing around. He'd tried subtle. Also tried not-so-subtle. None of it had worked. So now it was time to go to the mats.

Yesterday there had been a redheaded woman with the men. She had to be the woman that Butch's oldest son had married on the day of the fires. And there was of course the other wife too. She looked a lot like Maisie. So until now he'd left her alone. But she was not Maisie.

He would remember that. He could remember that.

Maisie wasn't here.

Not Maisie.

If the Nolan men hadn't cared about their damaged fences, if they hadn't cared about dead animals, and if the entire town had shown up to rescue them when he'd burned their buildings . . .

well maybe it was time to do something that they would care about—something the town couldn't rescue them from.

Maybe killing their women would get the point across.

It had certainly changed him, hadn't it? Made him move on. But—he shook his head—he would not think of that today.

Today he would focus on the plan.

Wash was sitting at the breakfast table with Pa's Bible open before him when Zoe emerged from their room. No one else was up yet, and he knew the moment he looked at her that she was still riled.

Her footsteps faltered, but then she smiled and continued toward him. "Good morning." Her voice was cheery. Too cheery.

"Morning. You're up early."

"I figured I'd better make myself useful around here."

Jinx rose from his spot on the rug they'd placed for him near the fireplace. He padded over, tail wagging, and Zoe bent to give him a scratch. "Come on, boy, let's get you your breakfast." To Wash, she added, "I'll just get the coffee going. How did you sleep?"

She breezed past him and sailed into the kitchen, which was only divided from the table by a sideboard.

He nudged the Bible away and folded his arms against the cleared space. "Slept fine, thanks. You?" He watched her move to the sink and put the pump handle to use.

Had she heard anything he said last night? Believed him when he said she was temptation itself?

By the way she was working that pump handle like she might be flailing a rattlesnake, he didn't think so.

She moved to the stove and plunked the metal coffee pot onto the center. "Slept fine too. Thanks for asking."

That was a lie. Because when he'd woken with the first rays of the sun, she'd been shifting and murmuring restlessly and had even whimpered a time or two. He'd fled the room before he could give in to the temptation to comfort her. Then he'd come here to delve into the passage in Ephesians about how husbands ought to treat their wives—like Christ loved the church. That meant sacrificing his own wants and desires for her greater good. So far, he was doing okay at that, but thank the Lord his surgery was today because he wasn't sure how much longer he could hold out. If things improved, well then, maybe . . . He coughed and refused to let his thoughts go there.

Zoe scooped coffee grounds into the pot so fast that her hand was a blur of motion. That done, she tamped the lid into place. "There. Now, it's your turn, Jinx."

The dog's whole hind end wiggled when he wagged his tail.

She bent to cup the critter's face. "Who's a good boy? Jinx is a good boy. Come on." She stood and hefted the bucket of kitchen scraps and boiled corn mush that Jinx was fed from. The dog followed her happily onto the porch and Wash could hear the sound of her voice murmuring to the dog as she scooped food into his dish. The screen door squeaked open then and she returned the scrap bucket to its place. "I'll just head out to the coop and fetch the eggs. Be right back." She snatched up a basket and disappeared through the kitchen door again.

Wash hung his head and gripped the back of his neck. *Lord, I'm afraid that in trying to do what I felt was right, I've hurt her. Is she right? Have I not been trusting You like I should? I feel like I've been trying to trust You. But You of all people know that I'm pretty good at failing. No doubt, this has been the hardest thing I've ever faced. But then I think You know that too. Just help her to know that I truly do love her and value her and want to be a good husband.*

Maude stepped into the room from the hallway, tying an apron at her back. "Oh, good morning." She smiled. "You're up early."

He raised a hand of greeting. "Zoe's out collecting the eggs and already got the coffee going."

"Wonderful. I'll just start the bacon frying then."

Wash closed Pa's Bible and returned it to the little table in the corner of the dining room. "I don't have much of an appetite this morning, so nothing for me, please. I'll just go out and see if Zoe needs any help with the eggs."

Maude smiled conspiratorially. "Sure."

He let her think what she wanted and went in search of his wife. He paused outside the coop and watched her leaning into the roosting boxes. Her basket already contained several eggs. "Zo, what's going on?" He leaned against the chicken wire, his fingers looping through the holes.

"What do you mean? I'm collecting the eggs like I told you I was." She smiled, forced cheer ringing in her voice. "Then after breakfast, if you don't mind, I'd like to head into town and pay a visit to Jacinda at her dress shop. I have no clothes and if I'm to return to teaching next week, we can't have that." She giggled.

It grated on his nerves.

"Anyhow, I need to get her working on some skirts and blouses for me. It will be a bit of an expense. But I should have enough put by to—"

"Zoe, stop."

Her attention flew to him. Her brows shot up and this morning's first true revelation of her emotions etched little grooves into the skin around her lips.

The kitchen door opened. "Zoe?" Maude called. "If you hand me just a few of the eggs I can get them started."

Her snapping eyes still on his face, Zoe stepped out of the coop and purposely latched the door. By the time she turned to face Maude, her false smile was back in place. "I was just finished." She extended the basket. "Several good layers I see."

"Yes, Jackson bought those hens from . . ."

The women disappeared into the kitchen, leaving Wash standing by the coop with discouragement sweeping through him.

By the time he returned to the house, his siblings and father had all joined the fray and Zoe seemed determined to be the life of the party. At the breakfast table—where he sat despite his lack of appetite—she teased his younger brothers about all the homework she was going to have to assign to catch them up after their week off from school.

The boys groaned good-naturedly, and everyone laughed.

After that, she barely settled into her seat by his side for more than ten seconds at a time.

She would take a bite and then hop up to fetch Pa more coffee. Then another bite followed by a declaration that the boys needed more milk, which she fetched from the ice box in the kitchen. Jackson asked Maude about jam for his toast and Zoe leapt up before anyone could move, saying she would get it.

Wash wanted to kick his brother under the table, and might have, if it wouldn't have sent a shockwave of pain through his own leg.

Jackson scarfed down his toast then mentioned that he had to put in some hours at the mill today due to a large order from Cle Elum. He said he would meet them all at the clinic later.

Zoe jumped at that declaration. "Would you mind dropping me off at Jacinda's, Jax? I need to get her sewing some clothes since all of mine went up in the blaze. Then I can just walk over and meet you all at the clinic come time for the surgery."

His oblivious brother nodded. "Sure. I'm ready whenever you are."

Zoe stood. "I should help Maude with the clean—"

Maude waved a hand. "It's fine. You go on."

"Well, all right then." Zoe's hand settled on his shoulder ever so briefly. "I'll see you in town." And with that, she was gone, followed by Jackson out the door.

"Lincoln. Grant. Get to your chores, boys," Pa said.

As his younger brothers moved to obey, Maude cleared a stack of plates into the kitchen and started washing them.

Wash felt a little sick. He studied his folded hands on the tabletop. In trying to do what was right by her, he'd obviously . . . well he wasn't sure what he'd done, but she certainly hadn't been herself this morning.

Pa turned his coffee mug in a circle on the table. "She's just worried about you, son. She'll settle after your surgery, you'll see."

Wash gripped the back of his neck. Forced a smile. "I'm sure you're right."

The problem was, he wasn't sure. Not at all.

And the future stretched out before him—one long canvas without a dab of paint on it to give any guidance of how this might play out.

Zoe's morning passed in a haze.

Jacinda of course had been more than happy to set aside her project to take measurements and help Zoe pick out new materials. But that hadn't taken long and then the remainder of the morning had stretched interminably. She'd gone to the schoolhouse and was pleased to see that other than a coat of finish, the porch had already been repaired.

Gratefulness filled her. She wasn't sure if she could have handled another tragedy. And losing the schoolhouse—and all her books—certainly would have been that.

After that, she'd gone to Dixie's for a cup of coffee and a muffin. She hadn't been able to eat much of a breakfast, what with trying to keep up her good humor and avoid Wash's narrow-eyed scrutiny, and her stomach rumbled with appreciation at the sight of the raspberry confection.

She dawdled over that for as long as she could—even to the point of rudeness before she finally left her payment with Cora and stepped onto the boardwalk once again. There was still plenty of time before she needed to be at the surgery, so she decided to go for a walk.

Wyldhaven Creek was beautiful this time of year with the cool clear water burbling over mossy rocks and the banks burgeoning with green grasses that waved in the breeze. She crossed the bridge and meandered toward the east, simply enjoying the quiet solitude of nature.

Harlan kept well back in the trees as the redhead moved farther and farther from town. He hadn't expected it to be this easy. Certainly hadn't expected her to wander right to him all on her own.

Only another mile or so and she would be far enough from town that he could be well clear of the area by the time anyone in town could pinpoint his shot and get help to her. She would be long gone before anyone could reach her. Then they would see just how committed the Nolans were to remaining on their spread.

And this way he didn't have to hurt Maisie.

He frowned. No. Not Maisie.

Maisie wasn't here.

He carefully maneuvered around a large ponderosa, ducking under the branches as he tracked parallel with her. He was mindful of each step, treading lightly. He'd once tracked a Nez Percé squaw in just such a manner, and it filled him with a thrill of excitement to be on the hunt once again.

Chapter Twenty-Four

Reagan went first thing in the morning to the post office and had Ben send a wire for information about Harlan White. The postman had promised to bring it over as soon as he heard anything back.

The evening before, Reagan had brought Merle Olann a meager meal, but the man had refused to talk without a deal. Reagan hoped that he would be hungry enough this morning that the temptation of a hearty breakfast might change his mind. That and the news about all that Jerry had told them might be enough incentive to make him realize that he needed some leverage.

As a banker in Wyldhaven, he was finished, but if the man was smart, he'd want to save his life. And with the new information he'd read this morning about who would be on the circuit this month, if Merle wanted to do that, he was going to have to share something useful.

Reagan walked into the jailhouse with Zane and Joe on his heels and plunked the newspaper through the bars onto the floor of Olann's cell. "Page five. Read it."

Olann rose slowly from his cot and took up the paper.

Reagan waited only until he'd opened it to the right page before continuing. "Yesterday I told you that the judge in our county doesn't take kindly to repeat offenders. That was Judge

Green. Unfortunately for you, Judge Green seems to have been taken sick with consumption. He's been reassigned to a warmer climate for his health."

Merle's eyes lit up until Reagan lifted a finger.

"That's bad news for you, Merle. Because look who's replacing him. Judge Palmer. When comparing these two judges, saying that Judge Green didn't take kindly to repeat offenders, would be like saying that he didn't like lemon drops."

Merle frowned at him in confusion.

Reagan looked at Zane. "Did I say that right?"

Zane shook his head. "Not sure you got it quite right, Reagan." He angled himself so that Merle wouldn't see his wink.

A look at Joe revealed him also shaking his head, humor dancing in his eyes.

Merle still looked confused.

"Let me put it another way. If Judge Green didn't take kindly to repeat offenders, Judge Palmer would like to strap every repeat offender to a barrel of liquid nitroglycerin and make them hike a shale path down the steep side of a cliff."

Merle's eyes widened.

"Is that clear enough?"

The man nodded.

Reagan looked at his deputies. "I think he gets it now."

Zane patted him on the shoulder. "Good job." He gave Merle a sympathetic swing of his head. "Tough break for you, Merle."

Reagan poured himself a cup of coffee and then sank into his chair, propping his boots on the corner of his desk. "Tell you what, Merle." He deliberately sipped his coffee loudly. "I'm hungry. Zane and Joe are hungry. We're going down to the diner to enjoy a nice leisurely breakfast. And when we come back, I'm going to have a plate of Dixie's biscuits smothered in sausage gravy with a couple of eggs and some bacon on the side."

Merle pretended interest in the paper, but Reagan heard his stomach growl.

"When I walk through that door, if you are ready to tell me what you know about this Harlan White you mentioned yesterday, then that plate of breakfast will be all yours. But if not . . . Well, there's a stray dog that's been hanging around. I'm sure he'd be happy to scarf it up."

Reagan stood and took another sip before plunking his tin cup onto the stove beside the coffee pot to keep warm. "While you're pondering how hungry you are, I'm begging you to also seriously ponder the state of your future. I like Judge Palmer. Judge Palmer likes me. One word from me to him on how helpful you were in the apprehension of a man who may have burnt down one of our citizen's spreads . . . Well, that would go a long way to softening the judge's stance on your future, I'm sure."

Joe nudged Reagan's arm with his hat. "You should also let him know how helpful Jerry Hines was in his chat with us yesterday."

"He *was* very helpful, wasn't he?"

Zane and Joe agreed heartily.

"Hear that, Merle? How helpful Jerry was? He had some interesting things to say about you, by the way."

"Very interesting," Zane added.

With that, Reagan followed Zane and Joe from the jailhouse, leaving the man to read the paper and ponder his future.

"Think it will work?" Joe asked as they headed toward the diner.

Reagan shrugged. "We'll see how smart he is."

Elijah Harrow was in his clock shop, helping Aurora Clay and her charge, Tommy, when, through the window, he saw Zoe leave the boardinghouse porch and head across the Wyldhaven Creek bridge. He frowned. He didn't like to see her wandering alone like that. Especially not with all the strange happenings of late.

Aurora was still bent over the case of pocket watches, trying to decide which one to purchase for Preston for his upcoming birthday.

"Th-that one looks n-nice." Tommy pointed.

"It does." She hummed. "Do you think he'd like the wolf or the bear better?"

"B-bears are nicer than w-wolves. B-but w-wolves are p-pertier."

Aurora smiled. "True enough, Tommy. They're the same price so it's just a matter of choosing the design."

Elijah could no longer see Zoe from the windows of the shop. For some reason, more tension than the situation warranted filled his chest. "Mrs. Clay, if you will pardon me, I've just seen Zoe walking alone. Will you two be okay, if I leave the shop for a few minutes?"

"I l-like Zoe!" Tommy proclaimed.

Aurora smiled. "We know you do." To Elijah she said, "Of course. Take your time."

"Thank you." He snatched up his hat and hurried from the store leaving the bell jangling behind him.

By the time he reached the bridge, Zoe had wandered so far that he still couldn't see her. He hurried in the direction that she'd taken. *Lord, I'm not sure why I'm feeling so concerned. Please just keep her safe.*

It was the silence that first sent a prickle of unease down the back of Zoe's neck. She paused on the creekbank and tilted her head to listen.

No birds chirped. No squirrels chattered. Not a chipmunk had stirred across her path.

She looked up and down the creek and rotated in a circle to take in the brush and trees all around, but no one seemed to be near.

Still, perhaps she'd wandered far enough from town on her own, especially with that foul man, Harlan White, in the area. She ought to have thought about him before roaming so far.

Her tangled thoughts had been so focused on Wash and his continued rejection that she'd meandered for longer than she intended to. It was time she got to the clinic anyhow. His surgery would be starting soon. She truly did want to be there for him, even if his rebuff had cut her to the core.

Not back toward town! Something had spooked her.

Harlan slung his rifle off his shoulder. They weren't as far out of town as he would have liked, but he would be quick and vacate the area as soon as he took the shot.

He hurried through the trees to get ahead of her and find the perfect location. It wasn't long before he found a tree branch that protruded from a trunk at just the right height and angle to function as a rest. A break in the branches between him and the creek provided the perfect small opening he needed. He settled the barrel of his gun onto the V of the branch, took a calming breath and sighted in.

As soon as she stepped into his crosshairs, it would be done.

He drew in another slow breath. In slowly through his nose. Out slowly through pursed lips.

He could hear her footsteps now, rustling softly in the grass.

He closed one eye. Ready.

"Zoe!"

He jolted upright.

Someone calling to her from closer to town! But they were too late!

He focused once more on his task.

She stepped forward. He could see the white material of one of her sleeves now.

Calm. Be calm. In . . . Out . . .

One more step . . .

And there she was. She lifted her arm in a wave. "Hi, Papa!"

Harlan squeezed the trigger.

Just as Zoe lifted her arm to wave to Papa, her foot landed on a fist-sized rock on the path. It rolled beneath her boot. "Oh!" She flailed her arms to keep herself from falling backward.

Something bit into the back of her arm with a sharp sting. And then she was on the ground, with all the air knocked out of her, listening to the sound of a gunshot reverberating through the air.

Gunshot? Surely not. She must have been stung by a bee. Maybe a wasp, because it certainly hurt more than a bee sting would.

"Zoe!"

She heard Papa's cry as if from a long way off. Her ears rang and the ground was damp beneath her arm. She tried to sit up.

"Stay down, Zoe. Stay down." Papa Harrow dove on her, pinning her to the ground. With one hand pressing one of her shoulders to the ground and his pistol gripped in the other, he lay beside her in the tall grass that wavered along both sides of the path.

"What happened?" Zoe reached for the pain at the back of her arm and blinked when her fingers came away bloody.

"I've got a gun!" Papa yelled, searching the area all around them. "Just show your face, you coward. Just show your face!"

"Papa? Somebody shot me!"

"Shhh, Zoe. I know. Just stay still."

Harlan slammed his teeth together.

With the tall grass on either side of the path, he could no longer see his quarry. He would need to get closer to finish the job.

But he was too close to town. They would have already heard his shot. And whoever that man was—her pa, apparently—he claimed he had a gun.

Harlan hadn't survived this long by risking his hide in stupid confrontations that he might not win, and he wasn't about to start now.

Blazes! He hated not completing a kill.

He withdrew into the trees, and quietly slung his rifle strap over his shoulder once more.

When he'd gone several paces, he viciously kicked a pinecone. It jounced off the evergreen needles and sent a covey of quail cackling in all directions.

His day would come at another time, but that didn't mean he had to like the delay!

Zoe lay quietly next to Papa. She was starting to perspire beneath the blazing sun.

He lay beside her, searching the brush and trees from which the shot had emerged.

"Papa? I'm feeling a little woozy. Like I did the time I broke my arm. Do you think we can go into town now?"

"Not yet. Let me take a look." He bent to see the back of her arm, and she saw him wince. He tugged a silk hanky square from his jacket pocket and set to rolling it into a strip. "It's a miracle you're alive, Zoe! What were you thinking walking out here all alone?"

She felt a little sheepish. "I wandered farther than I planned to. Just a lot on my mind today, I suppose." But then her anger surged. "But this is Wyldhaven, Papa! I walk from the house to the school by myself all the time."

He tilted her a thin-lipped look. "You always have the twins and Aidan with you."

She had to concede that his point was true enough. "Well, a lot of good *they* would do me if someone started shooting at us! Who would want to shoot me?" She gasped as she remembered the man, Harlan, once more. "Yesterday, Butch had a run-in on the street with a nasty man named Harlan White. Do you think it could be him? Why would he shoot me? I didn't even speak to him."

Papa shook his head. "I have no idea. But I'm hoping the law heard that shot and will be here in a moment. I suppose that's as good of an explanation as any. I'll mention it. Here. Raise your arm a little if you can."

Pain seared through the muscle as she followed his instruction. That was followed by another more intense zing when he cinched the silk bandage into place.

Behind them, she heard hoofbeats. She raised her head, thankful to see Reagan, Joe, and Zane riding their way. The men reined up and leapt down.

Zane aimed his shotgun toward the tree line and searched it with a wary eye, while Joe came to her side with a canteen. "Here you go, Zoe. Are you okay?"

She sat up cautiously, a tremor vibrating through her. "I think so." She tried to keep her head below the level of the grass as she sipped some of the cool water. "Should we be worried that they might shoot again?"

Joe exchanged a frown with Reagan.

The sheriff stepped forward. "Tell me exactly what happened."

Zoe waved a hand. "I came for a walk. I had just turned around to head back to town when I heard Papa call to me. I slipped on a rock. I think that's what saved me." She lifted her arm to show them how close the bullet had come.

"Much too close. I'm glad you're okay, Zoe," Sheriff Reagan said.

"Tell him about Harlan," Papa said.

The sheriff's gaze sharpened on her. "Harlan White?"

Zoe waggled her head. "You already know that he had a run-in with Butch. I just can't figure out who might want to take a shot at me. His name was the only one to come to mind."

"Could this have been an accident?"

Papa Harrow shook his head vehemently. "No! This was no accident."

The sheriff cocked a brow at Joe.

Joe gave a shrug of one shoulder. "Revenge, maybe?"

Reagan turned and swung into his saddle. "Well, I don't like people taking pot shots at my citizens. Let's find him and ask him what his motivations are."

Joe moved to join his boss, and Zane mounted up as well.

Papa Harrow waved a hand in the direction of the trees. "The shot came from somewhere over there."

"You get Zoe back to town, and we'll see if we can track this varmint down." The sheriff put his heels to his mount's sides and ducked beneath a branch as he disappeared into the trees with Zane and Joe right behind him.

Papa stood, holstered his gun, and reached down to help her stand.

She swayed for a moment before feeling her balance return.

He offered his arm, then settled his warm sun-spotted hand over hers. "The law will take care of this now. Let's get you to the clinic. All that matters is that you get taken care of."

"Papa, I don't want Wash to know about this before his surgery. I will go to the boardinghouse and Dr. Griffin can see to my arm there. But I want a clean blouse before I go to the clinic to see Wash. After his surgery will be soon enough for him to hear of this."

Papa's brow furrowed, but he nodded his consent. After a few steps, he asked, "Want to tell me what's on your mind? What brought you out on your walk, I mean?"

She flapped a hand to dismiss his concern. Of course she couldn't tell him the whole of the matter. "Just concerned for Wash's surgery, I suppose. Concerned about the fire at the Nolans. Concerned about the fire at the schoolhouse."

"And now concerned about being shot at."

"Sheriff Reagan and Zane and Joe will catch whoever it was." *Please, Lord, keep them safe.* She tossed a glance over her shoulder to where the men had disappeared into the trees.

"Yes. We have good lawmen, don't we? It seems that Olann set the fire on the schoolhouse porch to buy time for him and Jerry to skip town. But the sheriff still managed to catch them."

"I was there yesterday when it happened. Have you heard what they did that got them arrested?"

Elijah shook his head. "No. Nothing."

Zoe pondered for a moment before saying, "It must be something serious because I got the impression yesterday that the marshal was waiting to interrogate Jerry until Wash and I left the clinic."

Elijah rubbed her hand. "It's never good when the law is after you!"

"I suppose not." They crossed the bridge into town. "Thank you for coming after me, Papa." She felt another tremor work through her. "I don't know what I would have done if . . ."

Papa patted her hand. "The Lord was with us. I just felt an urge to go after you—so strongly. I even left poor Mrs. Clay in the store by herself. I'm just so thankful that I listened." He thumbed at the moisture glistening in his eyes. "Now . . ." He helped her up the boardinghouse steps. "Into the dining room and sit. I'll have Dr. Griffin come right down."

Zoe rose up on her tiptoes to give him a kiss on the cheek. She stopped him with a hand to his arm. "Wash and I were just talking about how the Lord works all things for the good of those who are called according to His purpose. Papa, you are one of those good things that the Lord did for our family. I love you."

He sniffed and dipped his head to give her a kiss in return. "I love you too, sweet girl." He flapped a hand. "Now, go sit. I'll be right back." With that, he left her, taking the street at a jog.

Zoe stepped into the entry and Cora gasped the moment she caught a glimpse of her. "Zoe!"

Zoe glanced down at herself, surprised to see how much blood was on her blouse. She held up her good hand. "I got shot. Papa went for Doc. I just need a place to sit."

"Here! Right here!" Cora motioned her to the bench that sat to one side of the check-in desk. "Will you be all right if I go and fetch you a tumbler of water?" Cora eyed her dubiously.

Zoe smiled. "Yes. Thank you."

Cora was off like a flash of lightning. "Dixie that shot we heard was not a hunter!"

It was only a moment later that Dixie and Cora bustled back into the entry with water and clean rags. And Dr. Griffin and Papa were not far behind them.

Doc cleaned her arm and shook his head several times as she conveyed what had happened. "This is a deep scratch, Zoe. It bled a lot. But it sure is a miracle that it's not worse. I don't even think it requires stitches. Though you'll have quite a scar there from now on." He bandaged her arm with a long white strip of cotton and tied the ends of the strip in a neat knot. "There. I'll want to take a look at it in a couple of days, but I have a feeling we'll be out to your place anyhow, to check on your husband's leg." He smiled.

Zoe darted Papa a look. "He didn't see, did he?"

Papa raised his hands. "I was discreet."

Zoe turned her attention to the doctor. "I don't want Wash to know about this until after his surgery. Can you please not tell him?"

Doc scratched behind his ear. "I don't suppose I need to say anything to him, considering you are fine. But he is waiting for you. Wanted to see you before he goes into surgery."

"Yes." She stood. "I'm rather late, aren't I."

Dixie held out a white blouse.

"Thank you." Zoe accepted it and moved into the little water closet near the base of the boardinghouse stairs. She emerged a moment later wearing the clean blouse and feeling more like herself again.

Papa, Doc and the two women remained where she had left them.

She smoothed her hands over her skirt. "I'll head to the clinic now." She took in the women with a glance. "Please be praying that Wash's surgery goes well."

"We will," Dixie assured as Cora nodded beside her.

Papa walked with her onto the boardwalk and then gave her a hug. "I will be praying too. Your mother and I have been, ever since the news reached us through Aidan last night." He hesitated. "Did Belle have a chance to speak to you?"

Zoe grinned. "No. But I have a strong inkling that she might have some happy news to share! Kane had Maude pack a picnic lunch yesterday. And there was apparently a circlet in his pocket. Maude was pretty excited to tell me about it last night."

Papa chuckled. "I'd best keep my lips shut. Just try to find her when you have a moment?"

Zoe had no idea when she might find the time, but all she said was, "I'll do that."

He motioned toward his shop. "I have customers waiting, so I need to get back inside. Doctor Griffin will walk with you down to the clinic to ensure you don't get lightheaded."

Zoe offered the doctor a smile of gratitude, and then followed him down the street, steeling her emotions for the afternoon ahead.

Chapter Twenty-five

Wash was relieved to see Zoe enter the clinic right on the heels of Dr. Griffin. After the way she'd left the house this morning, he really wanted to speak to her before going under the anesthesia.

He was already dressed in a long shirt that looked more like a gunnysack than anything else. The doctors had placed him on a table that had wheels and there was a stack of pillows at his back.

He felt conspicuous and nervous with his whole family gathered around him. Even Jerry, who was still handcuffed to one of the other beds, kept looking at him.

Zoe's gaze settled on him, and he reached a hand toward her, needing to feel her there by his side.

Surprise lit her eyes for a moment before she moved, but then stepped forward and settled her hand into his. He gave her fingers a gentle squeeze. "Hi."

Before she had time to respond, Dr. Griffin and Dr. Polson arrived at his side. Both of them wore clean cotton breeches and long-sleeved shirts rolled up to the elbows.

"Hello, Nolan family." Dr. Griffin smiled and then reached out to touch Wash's good leg. "Wash, how are you doing?"

He lifted one shoulder. "Good as can be expected, I'd guess."

Doc smiled. "You're in good hands. I've assisted Polson with a number of surgeries in our new surgical theatre now and I can assure you that his skills are a wonder to behold."

Wash swallowed. Glanced over at Polson. “I’ve done my praying, so now I’m in God’s hands and yours.”

Dr. Polson smiled. “My hands aren’t quite as skilled as the Great Physician’s, but I’m pretty good for a mere mortal.”

Everyone chuckled nervously.

Dr. Griffin stepped forward once more. “We have a room with several chairs and some books and Dixie has assured me that she’ll have dinner delivered to you all in a few hours.”

“A few hours?” Zoe gasped. “How long is this going to take?”

“Well,” Dr. Polson tilted his head to one side. “That’s hard to answer before we get in there and see what we are facing. Rest assured that we’ll move as quickly as we can while at the same time doing our best to give Wash the healthiest possible future.”

Wash’s stomach curled. He didn’t hold out much hope. And the talk about having him sedated for hours reminded him that he needed to speak to his wife. “I’d like to talk to Zoe alone for a few minutes, if that’s possible?”

The doctors indicated that was fine and stepped to one side.

Wash hugged each member of his family and then watched as Dr. Griffin led them down a hallway, apparently to the room where they would wait.

Dr. Polson strode over and pulled a curtain around Jerry’s bed to block his view of them, and then he vacated the room himself.

It wasn’t completely private. But it would have to do, he supposed. He turned his attention to his wife.

Beside him, Zoe was working her trembling lips in and out and all around. Her hand quaked in his grip and she blinked rapidly to hold back tears. Her voice was low when she spoke. “I’m sorry I was so snippy this morning, Wash. I don’t claim to have all the answers where tragedy and trials are concerned.”

“Neither do I.” He let his thumb graze over her knuckles. “I love you, Zo. Do you believe me?”

She frowned. Sniffed. "I want to believe you."

"Want to?" He tugged her closer until he could urge her to sit on the side of his bed. It rolled a little, causing her to squeak with surprise and readjust. They both laughed. He leaned forward then and touched the side of her face. "Don't want it, Zo. Know it. It's true."

She poked his chest. "Don't you dare die on that operating table."

He sat back, relaxing at her bossy normalcy. "I'll do my best not to."

He crooked his finger for her to lean closer, and when she did, he kissed her slow and sure and completely. The way her lips moved beneath his had his heart racing like a locomotive.

Behind her, Dr. Polson cleared his throat. "Everything is ready and we really should get started while there is plenty of light."

Zoe gave him one more peck and then stood and stepped out of Dr. Polson's way. "See you soon," she said.

This was it. It wasn't too late to change his mind.

Dr. Polson stepped in and pushed his bed until it turned Wash's back to the room. He tried to crane his neck to see Zoe above the stack of pillows, but the doctor pushed him through two swinging doors, and she was lost from his sight.

His mouth felt dry, and his pulse rushed in his ears. Still not too late, but . . .

No. He wasn't turning back. He was going forward. He would do this for Zoe. For the hope that they might one day be able to have a somewhat normal future.

They trundled down a hallway and past several rooms to another set of double doors at the end and then into a plain white room. Other than all the surgical instruments that lay on a steel tray, the only thing that was different about the room was the vast number of windows. Even the ceiling had some windows in it.

"The windows give us the most amount of light possible and make it easier to see what we're doing." Dr. Griffin must have seen him studying them. He approached and urged Wash to sit up before tugging the pillows from behind his back. "Today is a perfect day for your surgery because there's a light cloud cover that allows plenty of light but will prevent harsh shadows. Lay back."

Wash forced his hands to lay relaxed by his sides, willing down the panic as he remembered the severe pain he'd been in after his last two surgeries. His breathing was fast and shallow and the braces between the windowpanes wavered a little.

Dr. Griffin rested a gentle hand on his shoulder. "It's all right. In just a moment we'll give you a little cup to breath into and then the next thing you know, you'll be waking up."

"Yeah." He remembered that part.

Across the room, Dr. Polson scrubbed his hands in a basin of water. Dr. Griffin joined him and did the same.

Only a moment later, they returned to his side. Dr. Griffin stuffed a wad of white material in a cup-like contraption and then dripped several drops of a liquid from a glass vial through a little hole. "Ready?" he asked Dr. Polson.

He nodded.

Wash swallowed. Too late to back out now, even if he wanted to.

Dr. Griffin smiled down at Wash. "Just breathe easy, Wash. You're in good hands." He placed the cup over Wash's mouth and nose and the last thing Wash saw was Dr. Polson picking up one of the shiny metal knives.

Several yards into the forest, Reagan swung down from his mount and motioned for Zane and Joe to do the same. Up to this point, they had been following the hurried retreat of whoever had taken that shot at Zoe.

The man hadn't even been trying to hide his tracks, but here there was a fork in the path. A large boulder that had fallen to the base of the foothills forced either a trek to the east or west to skirt around it.

And the trail had gone cold.

Smart man.

The two paths didn't merge again for several miles—not until the other side of Hunter's Knob. And there were any number of trails off each branch of the path where a man could make his escape. It was imperative that they choose correctly if they had a chance of capturing their quarry today.

Reagan squatted and searched the path carefully for any sign of someone passing this way. Nothing.

"See anything?" he whispered to Zane and Joe, who were both searching farther down each branch. They had to be careful and speak minimally here as sound carried easily in these mountains, bouncing from rock to rock.

Zane shook his head, but Joe lifted a hand and pointed to something on one side of the trail.

Reagan motioned for Zane and they both approached.

"He's brushing his trail." Joe kept his voice as quiet as possible.

And sure enough, there in the dust of the path, lay a partially brushed-out footprint that had been missed in the man's hurry to hide it.

Reagan clapped Joe on his shoulder and gave a nod. With a jut of his chin, he indicated that they ought to keep moving down this side of the branch.

They'd only taken a few steps, however, when an uneasy premonition swept over him. He held up a fist for his men to stop. They both looked at him, brows raised.

What better way to throw them off his trail than to manufacture a sloppy brush-out while actually doing a good job of covering the way you truly wanted to go?

Was this man smart enough to try something like that? If only they had a little more information on him, they might know the answer to that. As of a few minutes ago, there had been no response to Reagan's telegram.

Going out alone was a risk, but in this instance, it was one that had to be taken.

He motioned for Joe and Zane to go on ahead on the current path and that he would take the other and meet them on the other side.

Zane shook his head vehemently. "We stay together!"

The blaze of passion in his eyes had more to do with the fact that the marshal didn't want to have to return home to his wife and report that her son had been killed today, Reagan would bet. Well, he couldn't blame the man. Ma could be downright formidable when she wanted to be. He didn't want Zane going off without backup any more than Zane wanted him to. And neither would he risk Joe's life either.

He pointed back to where the trail had been sloppily brushed out. "That could be a setup to throw us off his trail."

Joe and Zane exchanged a glance of understanding.

Joe tilted his head. "True. You think he's that smart?"

Reagan lifted his shoulder. "I don't know."

Zane glanced around. "If you brush your trail, there's normally a branch that you toss aside, right? I mean, he's not going to drag it with him the whole way."

"Right," Reagan said. "Okay, we go this way for a mile. If we haven't come across more prints or his rake, we double back and check the other way."

They moved ahead at a trot, each of them searching the ground and the sides of the trail for evidence of someone walking the path recently. At the end of the mile, they'd found nothing.

Hang it! Reagan could almost feel the man slipping through his grasp. "Double-time, fellas."

They turned and raced back the direction that they'd just come, with their horses trotting behind them.

Reagan prayed they wouldn't be too late.

Harlan figured that his old trick must have worked to fool the lawmen. It had been at least ten minutes since he'd heard them on his tail. He hurried forward with satisfaction. "Simple solutions for simpletons."

He tossed aside the branch that he'd been using to wipe his trail and took the smaller trail toward the west at a run. He had to get to the men in camp and get them moving out of the area. Once there, they would take a few days to rest up and let things simmer down, and then they'd be back.

He burst through the brush that hedged in the canyon entrance where they'd made their camp and paused to prop his hands on his knees. Whooeee! He needed to do more riding and less running and that was certain.

He only took a moment to catch his breath. "Pack up, men. We ride in five minutes."

As usual, most of them were slow to respond, though, Ted jumped up and went to work saddling his mount and Harlan's.

Harlan drew his pistol and aimed it at the head of the nearest man still lounging against his saddle by the fire. "I said we pack up. Now."

The man put his hands up and clambered awkwardly to his feet. "All right. All right, boss. Give a fella a few seconds to adjust to new information, would you?"

Thankfully, all the others were moving now too.

Harlan holstered his pistol. "When I give an order, you don't have to think. You just have to do!"

"Yes, boss." The man hefted his saddle into his arms and started toward his horse, which was picketed with the others near the canyon wall.

Harlan stormed toward Ted and quickly set to shoving his effects into his knapsack. Razor blade and piece of shiny metal. Coffee cup. Yesterday's shirt that he'd washed and left to dry on a nearby sage bush.

"What happened?" Ted asked. He was cinching the last saddle into place.

"Law's coming." That was all Harlan was willing to say about the matter. Ted didn't need to know everything.

When he'd left earlier, he'd instructed everyone to stay put. He'd hoped to have the whole Nolan situation in hand by the time he returned. Would have too, if it hadn't been for that gal's snoopy pa!

Reagan had begun to feel downright irritated by the time he reached the footprints on the other branch of the trail. They'd fallen too far behind. The man had a much longer head start now and it would take some doing to find him.

He wasn't brushing his trail anymore. They'd found his broom a way back. But despite that, the man was being careful about where he put his feet and following a trail always took longer than making one. They needed to be moving faster or they were going to lose him.

He'd been on foot, which meant he had to have a horse hiding back in these hills some—

"He was on foot!"

Zane and Joe pulled up and looked at him.

"That means he likely had a camp nearby, don't you think?"

Joe tilted his head. "Seems likely." His eyes lit up. "There's a nice box canyon up in the hills not too far from here. Had to stay there one time when I got caught out in a storm. Has a good overhang. Plenty of fuel. It would sure make a good—"

"Take us to it." Reagan motioned for Joe to lead the way.

"Reagan, are you sure?" Zane always did like to do things methodically.

Reagan looked at Joe and indicated the direction they'd been running. "Is this the most logical way to get to that canyon?"

Joe nodded.

"Then I'm sure. We're already behind in the race. If he's there, we might catch up, but if not, well, I guess we can come right back here and start again. Let's go."

Harlan's men were idiots! Every last one of them. Well, maybe except for Ted. Several of them were still getting their saddlebags tied to their horses. And another couple were still cinching saddle straps. One was filling his canteen from the creek.

He ought to just ride off and leave them. But if the law caught up to them, Harlan had no doubt that every last one of them would testify that he'd been the one to burn the Nolan spread. Plenty of them had helped, but they'd still pin it on him.

At least none of them knew he'd tried to kill the girl. Killing a woman wasn't something even his men would likely put up with. That was why he'd gone out alone. But now, if the law showed up and they heard about the shot . . . Well, the timing would be a might suspicious.

"Let's go! Let's go! Let's go!" he yelled.

That made a few of them give the appearance of some hustle.

He grunted and slapped his reins into one palm. "Ted, do you think I'm being foolish to want this property so bad? I mean, Gregory was a fool. And he did lose the property in a card game. And the Nolans bought the land fair and square from the gambler that won it."

Ted didn't reply.

He was a good listener.

"I just wanted to do it for Maisie, you know? She will like it here."

Ted glanced over at him. His brows nudged up. "For Maisie, boss?"

"Yeah. Don't you think she'd like that land? Pretty rolling pastures. A nice little creek meandering through—headwaters of a creek no less. Good control over the rest of the spreads with that. I can just see Maisie sitting and rocking on that spacious front porch. Maybe I'll screen it in for her."

Ted seemed intent on studying the pommel of his saddle. "It is a right pretty little spread and that's certain. I'm sure she'd like it. In fact, why don't we ride out and fetch her right now?"

Harlan shifted uneasily. But he couldn't quite pin down what had made him uneasy. Ted's words had been casual. And he certainly would like to bring Maisie out right away. But . . . "Can't." He'd better not say more than that.

"Can't? Why not, boss?" Ted searched his face.

Harlan busied himself with adjusting the saddlebags on the far side of his mount. "Just can't is all! Now stop pestering me with questions!"

Fortunately, Ted didn't comment further.

Well, it made no never mind.

The last man had just swung into his saddle and they were ready to ride.

"Let's move!" he called.

Chapter Twenty-six

Reagan and his men had just reached the entrance of the boxed canyon when they heard a man's voice yell, "Let's Move!"

He motioned for Zane and Joe to take cover, one on either side of the path. Then he planted his own shoulder into a tree and leveled his rifle on the trail. If they timed this right, they'd have the outlaws surrounded before they knew what hit them.

A group of seven riders emerged from the boxed canyon.

Only one of them had bushy white hair, long sideburns, and a red face.

Reagan centered his sights on that man. "Everybody put your hands up. We've got you surrounded."

The group of riders pulled their mounts to a stop and several hands shot into the air.

The one who had to be White, looked around in a panic.

"Don't move, White. I've got a bead right on you and I'm a good shot. I won't miss."

"Neither will I."

Reagan blinked. One of Harlan's men—the one riding right behind him—had pulled a pistol and had it aimed at his boss's back! Reagan hadn't even seen the man move.

Harlan looked more shocked than any of the rest of them. "Ted, what are you doing?" He swore. "You no-good, dirty rotten traitor."

"Sheriff," the man with the gun called. "I'd like to reach in my pocket and get my badge, if you don't mind."

"You keep still," Reagan snapped. It could be a trap to throw them off. "The rest of you, down on your bellies in the dust. Toss your weapons."

The riders complied right away, but Harlan remained on his horse. Intently, he searched the forest. His horse bobbed it's head from the tension on the reins.

He was going to run!

"Harlan, I won't tell you again," Reagan yelled. "Down on the ground."

Harlan didn't listen.

"Ha!" He put his heels to his horse. It leapt over the nearest man in a long clean arc.

"Don't shoot him!" The man named Ted yelled.

But it was too late.

Reagan's bullet took Harlan in the chest before his horse had even completed the jump. Harlan tumbled out of the saddle, fell with a loud *whomp*, into a patch of sagebrush, and clutched at his chest. "You . . . shot . . . me." Blood spurted from his lips.

Joe was already on the man and disarming him.

Reagan swung his rifle toward Ted, who still hadn't dismounted.

"I'm a Pinkerton agent! I'm not a threat!" Ted yelled, raising his pistol toward the sky. "Please come check my badge because I need to ask that man some questions before he dies!"

Reagan motioned with his barrel. "Throw down your weapons."

The man immediately complied. "He's suspected of killing his wife. I was hired to find him and figure out what happened to her and where she is."

Remaining where he was, Reagan gave the man a nod. "Show Zane there your badge."

Zane stepped from his cover and looked at the badge. "Looks bona fide, Reagan."

Reagan felt himself relax. "All right." He tipped his head for the man to move toward White. "Ask your questions."

His stomach turned. He hated that part of his job. Taking a life was never easy. Never got easier, either.

He and Zane went to work tying the hands of each of the men on the ground as they listened to Ted's questions.

He fell on his knees beside Harlan. "Harlan, it's me, Ted. Can you hear me?"

"Ted. You've been . . . a good . . . friend." Harlan sputtered.

"Afraid you got me wrong, Harlan. I was no friend. Now I gotta tell you something. I've seen wounds like this. And you're not going to make it. Within moments, you're going to be standing before your maker. So I'm giving you this one chance to tell me what happened to Maisie?"

"Maisie . . . dead."

Ted hung his head. "What happened to her?"

Harlan clutched at his chest as a gurgling sound filled his throat. His focus blurred into the distance.

Reagan looked down.

But Ted wasn't ready to give up. He shook Harlan's shoulder. "What happened to her, Harlan?"

Harlan's gaze slowly returned to Ted's. "She was . . . gonna leave me. Couldn't let her."

"I know that. What did you do with her?"

"She's . . . she's . . . buried." Harlan's eyes fell closed this time.

"Where?" Ted clasped his hands behind his neck. "Where, Harlan?"

Harlan made no response.

Ted violently pounded his chest. "Where did you put her?"

Harlan's eyes jolted open with a gasp. "In . . . barn."

"In the barn." Ted fell into a sitting position with his arms wrapped around his knees. He rocked a little. "In the barn." Tears tracked down his cheeks.

Reagan gripped the back of his neck. It seemed the man had more feelings about the death of this woman named Maisie than a mere Pinkerton would. But they could deal with that in a moment. He motioned for Joe to keep an eye on the Pinkerton and then strode to the other men. "Listen up. Someone just took a shot at a woman from my town."

Every last one of them looked up in surprise. Even the Pinkerton.

"I need to know if it was any of you?"

All of them shook their heads.

One of the men lying on the ground spoke. "We've all been together here in this boxed canyon since last night. Not one of us left except for Harlan and he just rode back into camp a few minutes ago, said the law was on his tail, and we needed to ride out, right smart."

The Pinkerton and the others all nodded to concur.

"What about the fire a few days ago?" Reagan asked. "How many of you helped him with that?"

No one seemed to want to answer that question.

"Even you?" Reagan pinned the agent with a glower.

"I didn't know what he was doing until it was too late. I'd ridden to Cle Elum for supplies and to send an update to my boss. When I returned, the spread was already ablaze, and people were there putting out the fire. That being the case, I chose not to blow my cover."

Reagan swung his hand in a let's-round-it-up gesture. "Let's get everybody into town and we'll get all their stories straightened out."

Zane yanked one of the men to his feet and held onto him until he had his balance. "We need a bigger jail!"

Reagan sighed.

Mostly Wyldhaven was calm and peaceful with no need for even one jail cell, much less the two they had. But this was definitely going to tax their quarters, and that was certain.

Thankfully, the judge was due through town next week.

Zoe paced the waiting room from one end to the other, unable to remain in any of the seats for more than a few seconds. Her arm ached, but thankfully, she'd been able to keep her injury from Wash.

Across the room, Lincoln and Grant worked on a puzzle. It was a map of the United States glued to a board and then cut out along the state lines. She made a note that she ought to get several for her classroom. It was a great teaching tool.

Hours passed. Dixie came in with a rolling cart laden with wonderful smelling dishes. But Zoe couldn't bring herself to eat a bite. Washington's brothers, on the other hand, had no problem tearing into Dixie's pot roast and potatoes. Even Butch ate a hearty plate.

Maude approached a few minutes later and pressed a teacup into Zoe's hands. "Try to at least drink something."

"Thank you." Zoe wrapped her cold hands around the warmth of the cup. Despite the wondrous sunshine outside, she was feeling chilled and on edge.

Time seemed to stretch on interminably, and the sun had turned the sky into a soft shade of mauve before the doctors returned.

Zoe leapt to her feet from the chair where she had been sitting near the window. A tight fist of apprehension knotted her stomach.

Then Dr. Polson smiled. "The surgery went just about as perfectly as any surgery could go. There were indeed bone fragments in his knee joint. And I was also able to clean up and do some repair to the muscle that was damaged by the bullet." He shook his head. "I'm not sure what kind of surgeons the cavalry is hiring these days, but it looked to me like they should be butchers, not doctors."

Butch stopped by Zoe's side. "So you think he will be in better shape now, Doc?"

"I'm quite confident of it."

Zoe's gaze zipped to Dr. Griffin. The soft gleam in his eyes reassured her even more. "Dr. Polson did all he could to repair the damage. It's too bad he couldn't have been the original surgeon. Wash would have been in much better shape from the start. But now we can move forward from here."

Zoe sank back into her chair with relief, but popped right back up again. "Where is he? Can I see him?"

The doctors smiled. "He's in one of the surgical recovery rooms. He's still asleep, but should wake up any moment now. You are welcome to sit by his side."

Following Dr. Griffin's long strides, Zoe whisked down the hall and rushed into the room.

Wash lay on a bed with a thin mattress, his jaw slack and his head canted to one side, but he was inhaling and exhaling blessed deep breaths. His chest rose and fell, and he had a pulse—she checked.

Suddenly her tears began to fall and her legs trembled to the point that Dr. Griffin helped her into a chair.

She covered her face with her hands. "Thank You, Jesus. Oh, thank You for bringing him through!"

Charlotte lay in her bed the next morning with one hand resting gently on the flat of her stomach. Was Dr. Griffin right?

Was a child really growing inside her? It filled her with such a thrill and yet overwhelmed her with such a burden for the future as well. Would she be a good mother? She hoped that Isaiah would answer yes to that question because she'd tried to be the best mother she could to him.

That brought on another worry. Would Isaiah feel less loved? They hadn't intended to adopt, but the Lord had brought him to town, and it had simply seemed the right thing to do. The thing they'd *wanted* to do. And my how she loved that boy! But would that change with a child of their own in the house?

Her eyes fell closed. "Oh, Lord, I don't want Isaiah to feel spurned or rejected in any way because of this!"

Reagan stirred beside her. He hadn't arrived home last evening until well past midnight. He'd fallen into bed and been snoring before she could even find the words to share their good news.

Now in the predawn light that filtered through the curtains, she turned her head to watch her husband sleep. He lay on his stomach, his head facing her, and his chest rising and falling in a deep even pattern.

She eased to her side and tucked her hands beneath her cheek so she might get a better look at him. He was still as handsome as ever, though there were some crow's feet crinkling the corners of his eyes now.

From his interactions with Isaiah, she knew he was going to be a wonderful father. Already was a wonderful father.

He opened his eyes and pressed up onto one elbow. He squinted toward the window and then looked back at her. "You're awake early." He rubbed his fingers and thumb across his eyelids.

She smiled gently at him. "I am at that. I've been enjoying watching you sleep."

He quirked a brow at her. "I'm sure you've got better things to do than that. Busy day today?"

"Not really." Her heart thumped with an upbeat rhythm.

He groaned and hung his head. "Wish I could say the same." He started to climb from beneath the covers.

"Dr. Griffin wants me to stay in bed and rest for a few days." She tucked her lower lip between her teeth to hold back a smile.

He froze. Turned so he could look at her. She couldn't quite read his expression in the dim light. Maybe he hadn't heard her.

"I said, Dr. Griffin wants me to rest—"

"I heard what you said, Charlie. Why does he want you to do that? Are you sick?" He leaned toward her and placed one hand to her forehead.

She couldn't withhold a chuckle. "I am not sick."

He frowned, then settled back on the bed with his elbows propping him up. He studied her for a long moment, puzzling through their conversation, no doubt. "Charlie, are you saying what I think you are saying?"

She was having too much fun dragging this out. "That depends. What is it you think I'm saying?"

He leapt out of bed and quickly lit the bedside table lamp and then he was right back by her side and pulling her into a sitting position. "Are we having a baby?" He curved his hands around her face. "Please tell me we're having a baby." A sparkle of hope lit the blue of his eyes.

Her laughter rose from the very heart of her as she looked up at him. "You, Sheriff Callahan, are going to be a daddy."

Reagan's whoop surely would have Isaiah knocking on their door at any moment to make sure they were all right. He wrapped her in a bear hug and swung her from side to side. After only a moment he set her back and gripped her shoulders. A streak of moisture shimmered on his cheek in the light from the lamp. "When?"

"Not until January sometime."

Reagan threw back his head with another whoop, and then he hauled her out of bed and danced her across the room and back.

With her hands on his shoulders, she laughed and shushed him. "You'll wake Isaiah for certain!"

"Well he needs to know that he's going to be a big brother!"

Charlotte lowered her eyes. She forced her concern past her lips. "Do you think we can love two children equally, Reagan?"

He slowed. "Of course we can. Why?"

She brushed at a wrinkle in his night shirt. "It's just that I love that boy so much and I don't want to ever love him any less. With a child of our own—" She waved a hand. "Not our own. I think of Isaiah as our own, too. A child of our seed maybe is a better way to put it. Well, do you worry that we'll begin to love that child more? Because I never want that to happen. It would crush me to know I'd hurt Isaiah in any way."

Reagan eased her back onto the edge of the bed and cupped her face once more. "The wonderful thing about love, Charlie, is that it's an emotion that never runs out. No matter how many souls we have in our lives to lavish it on, there is never a short supply."

She worried her lip with a frown. She supposed he was right about that, though she'd never quite thought of it that way before.

Reagan bent and settled a kiss against her forehead. "The very fact that you are concerned about it, means that everything is going to be fine, Charlie. Isaiah will be thrilled and our love for him will remain steady even as it expands for this other little person too."

She felt the tension in her shoulders ease. "Yes. I think you're right, but it relieves my mind to hear you say so."

Reagan suddenly straightened. "Doc has you on bed rest?" He tossed a horrified glance to where he'd just swung her around their room. "And I've just been dancing you all over the place!"

Charlotte reached out to gather both of his hands into her own. "It's fine. I've just been having some lightheadedness and Doc said that can be common in the early days. I'm simply to monitor myself and if I feel too tired, I'm to lie down and rest."

"Have you been nauseated?"

She shook her head. "Not even a little. Only the small moments of dizziness. And they always pass quickly."

He stepped back from her then and danced around the room like a pugilist, punching his fists through the air. "I'm. Going. To. Be. A. Father!"

She laughed as she watched him until he once more spun into the space in front of her.

He looked down with chest heaving and eyes gleaming. "Get dressed, Charlie. We have to wake Isaiah, right now!"

Charlotte tilted him a look and pointed his attention to the clock. "It's not even five yet. Why don't you come back to bed and try to sleep for another hour before we share the good news?"

Reagan's shoulders slumped, but he did snuff the lamp and then crawl back onto the bed beside her. He leaned against the headboard and pulled her into his arms, and Charlotte relished the steady beat of his heart rapping out a tattoo beneath her ear.

Reagan rubbed her back and kissed her head, and Charlotte's eyes drooped closed as the surety of his love wooed her back to slumber.

Chapter Twenty-seven

Wash woke in the comfort of his own bed. A soft sun beam streamed through the bedroom window, warming his feet beneath the down tick. He stirred. Stretched.

Beside him, movement drew his attention. He looked over to see Zoe standing beside the bed smiling down at him.

"Good morning." She folded her hands before her. "How are you feeling today?"

He lifted his leg and assessed it carefully.

This was the tenth morning after his surgery. And until today he had continued to quash the hope that the surgery really had made a difference in his pain levels. But even on the first day after the surgery, he had been amazed at how much better he'd felt. He had chalked it up to the fact that he wasn't putting any weight on it yet. However, the next day Dr. Polson had come out to the house and encouraged him to take a few steps. There had been pain of course, but it had been dull and tolerable, not the sharp flames that he had lived with each time he took a step for the past year.

Hope for the future had flared.

He had again quickly banished it.

But then yesterday he had felt even better, and he'd been able to navigate the entire length of the hallway and living room and back again to his bed. He had almost cried tears of joy at the ease with which he'd accomplished it. Thankfully, he'd managed to restrain himself.

Now he looked up at Zoe with a smile. "I still feel weak as a newborn foal, but I'm amazed at how little pain I am feeling."

"Well, Doctor Polson said it would take some time for you to regain the strength you've lost in that part of your leg over the past year. So that is to be expected. I'm just so relieved to see you recovering so well. Now, if you want to sit up . . ." She hefted a pillow from the bed beside him. "I'll bring you a tray of breakfast."

For the first time he let optimism over the future take control. It would take work to recover his strength, yes, but he'd never been one to shy away from hard work. What had discouraged him for so long was the impossible agony. Even if he continued to have this level of pain in his leg for the rest of his life, it felt manageable. And for the first time, he dared to let himself believe that he'd be able to provide for Zoe and a family in some way. He might not be sure what that way was yet, but the mere possibility of it raised his spirits.

As he watched her lean close to tuck the pillow behind him, breakfast was the last thing on his mind. He waited until she'd stretched past him for another pillow, then while she was already off balance, he hooked one hand around her waist and tugged her down onto the bed beside him.

"Oh," she squeaked as she fell across his chest.

He grinned at her. "And what if I'm not ready for breakfast yet?" Her cheeks flamed and she lowered her attention to where her hand had propped against his chest. "Everyone's awake. The doctor will be here any minute."

"Let him wait."

She pulled in a measured breath. Lifted her gaze to his and Wash felt his pulse ramp up. This woman, this beautiful soul, was his for the rest of time. He would cherish her and forever be grateful that the Lord had seen fit to give a fool such a treasure. "I love you, Zoe."

She rolled her lips together. Tears of happiness gathered in her eyes as they searched his. "I love you too."

He leaned toward her. Brushed her soft lips with his own. Her eyelashes fell against her cheeks as she offered her mouth in sweet surrender. He slid his hand further behind her back, drawing her nearer, and when she settled her hands on either side of his face, he swept his hands to her arms to urge her to hold him tighter.

She gave a little gasp.

He jolted back to assess how he might have hurt her. "Sorry. Are you okay?"

"Yes, yes. I'm fine." She smoothed her hands against his nightshirt.

His eyes narrowed. "What is it?"

"It's noth—"

A knock sounded on the door. "Wash?" Pa called. "Doc's here."

Wash growled in good-natured irritation. Blast Polson's punctuality.

Zoe scrambled from the bed, tucking in her blouse, and smoothing her skirts.

He lowered his voice and winked at her. "We could just ignore the door and pretend we aren't here."

With a pointed look that said he ought to behave, she stepped over to open the door. "Good morning, Dr. Polson. Please, come in." She moved out of the man's way.

He strode in and set his bag on the table inside the door. "And how are you feeling this morning?"

"Feeling fine." Wash angled his eyes toward his wife. "Zoe was just bringing me breakfast." He liked the way her cheeks flushed prettily.

"Good. Good. Glad to hear it. I'm very pleased with your recovery so far. Off with the bandages, if you please."

Wash withdrew his leg from beneath the tick and set to unwrapping his bandages. "The sutures have been itching some. Is that normal?"

Doc nodded. "Perfectly. In fact it's a good sign of healing." He bent over the incision. "Wonderful. I don't see any signs of infection, and everything seems to be healing up as expected. Very good." He pressed gently against the stitches. "Any pain?"

Wash shook his head. "Not really."

"Good. And here?" He pressed again.

Wash shook his head.

"Marvelous. Let me get you a clean wrap." Polson stepped to his bag and withdrew a bandage. As he turned back toward the bed, he gave Zoe a look. "And how about you? How is your arm today?"

Zoe cast Wash a bit of a wary, wide-eyed glance.

"And your leg? I haven't had a chance to ask about that till now."

If possible, Zoe's eyes grew even wider. "I'm fine, Doctor. Nothing to worry about."

"What's wrong with you?" Concern tightened Wash's chest.

Zoe tossed the doctor a bit of an irritated glance before turning a smile on Wash. "Nothing is wrong with me. Let's just concentrate on you. You're the patient here."

The doctor bent over him and began to wrap the clean bandage, blocking his view of his wife. Wash leaned to the side to maintain eye contact. "What aren't you telling me?"

"Nothing. If you'll excuse me, I'll let Dr. Polson finish up here and go help Maude in the kitchen. Then I have to be off to the school. I'll see you this evening." She breezed from the room. But there was a telltale wash of red creeping up her neck.

Right. He'd forgotten momentarily that this was her first day back to work. She'd given her students an extra week off so that she could remain home to care for him, but today she would return to teaching. Wash pinned the doctor with a look. "What is she not telling me?"

Dr. Polson winced ruefully. "I didn't realize that she wouldn't have mentioned any of it to you. I apologize. I didn't mean to step into the middle of something."

"Into the middle of what, Doc?"

Dr. Polson sighed. "If you'll forgive me, Mr. Nolan, I think that should be between you and your wife." He finished tying off the bandage. "Now, if you don't mind. I'd like to have you take a longer walk today. So up, up."

Heaving a sigh, Wash stood and with the doctor's help, dressed and donned his boots. For thirty minutes, the doctor had him walking all around the house, up and down the porch steps, and across the yard, even.

Through it all, Wash was amazed at how wonderful it felt to be able to walk with so little discomfort. He concentrated on all of the doctor's instructions, doing the exercises as commanded. During the whole ordeal, he couldn't wait for the doctor to leave so that he could find Zoe because he needed to talk to his wife.

However, by the time Dr. Polson left, Zoe had already gone to the schoolhouse.

Well, he would just have to figure out a way to get into town because he wasn't waiting until this evening.

She owed him some explanations!

It took Zoe all morning to get the kids settled into even a resemblance of industriousness.

First, she had the little ones sweep, while the older ones dusted cobwebs, washed windows and chalkboards, and blacked the stove. She maintained that a clean environment was the best aid to learning, and was satisfied with the job her students performed on this gloriously sunny Monday morning.

Now each of the students had been rewarded with a whole hour for reading. Zoe ought to be doing some lesson prep for the rest of the week, but her mind wandered.

She felt light and free and wholly hopeful for the future.

But she was also discouraged and weary. Exhaustion seemed rooted deep in her bones.

The judge had arrived and the trials had taken place over the past few days and poor Mrs. Hines had been a ruin of weepiness every time Zoe had caught a glimpse of her recently. Poor Jerry had been sentenced to ten years for his part in the cheating scheme. Zoe could still hardly believe that the man had been stealing from all of them for months now. How had he been able to look them in the eyes?

Mrs. Olann had left town before the trials had even started, taking little red-haired Carmen and her other children with her, and Zoe had no doubt that part of her fatigue was over the fact that she was going to miss that sweet little girl sitting in the front row each week and asking questions with her dear lisp.

Zoe couldn't imagine leaving a town while her husband was jailed and waiting for a trial, but it had come to light that apparently this wasn't the first time Mr. Olann had been in jail. And she was thankful that Carmen hadn't been around to see her papa sentenced to fifteen years—part of which had been because of his attempted murder of Jerry to cover his tracks.

With her elbows propped on her desk, Zoe shuddered. Imagine! All these years their banker had been a crook and none of them had known it! On top of that, he'd convinced a formerly upstanding citizen to cheat and steal. That also disheartened her.

Though she hadn't attended any of the trial because she'd been home taking care of Wash, she'd heard that Kin had been a wonder in his role as prosecutor in each case.

Even Harvey's men had each received five years for their part in burning the Nolans' spread. All except the Pinkerton agent, Mr. Beck, who had been sent on his way in peace. It seemed Harlan White's wife had been a close friend of Mr. Beck's during his early years, and now he bore the burden of informing her family and recovering her body for a proper burial.

Her gaze settled on poor David Hines, seated in the back row of the school. He was supposed to be reading, but was instead staring out the window, and Zoe couldn't bring herself to chastise him for it.

So far, Priscilla had remained in town, but Zoe couldn't help but feel a burden over wondering what would happen to David if—likely *when*—his stepmother decided to leave. He wasn't Priscilla's son. Would she care for David? Or just skip town, leaving him behind? She obviously wasn't qualified to run the mercantile on her own.

Zoe prayed the woman would do right by the boy. She also prayed that David wouldn't lose touch with his father completely.

Despite all the man had done, she hoped he would come out of jail a better man for his punishment.

"Hello? Mrs. Nolan?" Lincon's voice pulled her from her reverie.

Zoe bit back a smile at the sheepish look on his face as he waved for her attention. "Yes, Linc?"

"May we please be dismissed for the lunch hour, Miss Kas—I mean, Mrs. Nolan." His face flushed, but there was a bit of pride shining in his eyes to have her sharing his own last name now.

Zoe glanced at the clock. Her brows shot up. "Oh my! Yes. My apologies, children. You may be dismissed for lunch. And since I'm fifteen minutes late in letting you go, you may have an extra fifteen minutes on the other end of the hour. Be back at one fifteen."

Some of her students would hurry to their houses in town to eat, while others who lived farther away would remain in the schoolyard to eat and play.

The schoolhouse soon emptied, and Zoe opened her desk drawer to fetch her own lunch. Her shoulders fell. She'd forgotten her lunchpail on the counter in the Nolans' kitchen this morning in her haste to escape before Wash pestered her with too many questions.

She was thankful that he'd had a couple days to recover from his surgery and that his healing was going so well, but she'd wanted him to have a few more days before burdening him with the knowledge that she'd almost been killed. And since the bruise on her leg was almost healed now, she'd hoped never to have to mention that particular injury to him.

Well, no matter. She'd passed days before without having a lunch and she would survive this one too.

She decided to take a little break in the sunshine. She stepped out the schoolhouse door and paused on the bank of the creek. The path stretched before her, but she couldn't seem to make herself move.

The creek rushed by like an army on a warpath. It filled her with trepidation simply to stand here, but, determined to overcome the fear, she forced herself to remain where she was. It was just Wyldhaven Creek. Simply water burbling over stones. Nothing more.

But the sound of it ramped up her pulse and made a thin sheen of sweat break out on her forehead. She drew in the calming scent of the nature all around her. Willed her pulse to settle.

The Lord had protected her, and she didn't want Wyldhaven Creek to forever hold terrifying memories. It did help to know that the man who'd taken that shot at her would never be able to do so again, even though it was a weight upon her to know that he'd been killed. The sheriff had said it wasn't her fault and that her getting shot at had helped them track the man down in the first place. So she tried to be grateful for the way the Lord had worked things out, but it still weighed on her.

"Zo?" Wash spoke from behind her.

She spun to face him, her eyes tearing up at just the wonderful sight of him there. He was dressed in a brown suit coat and tan slacks—looking kempt and handsome as he always used to. She could see the shape of the bandage around his knee and calf beneath his trousers. And he still had a cane in his hand, but his face looked rested and at ease—something that had been missing from his countenance, she realized, since he'd returned home.

He lifted her lunchpail. "You forgot this. Jackson was headed to the mill and gave me a ride."

She smiled. "My knight in shining armor. I was just lamenting that I'd have to go hungry till this evening." She motioned to the grassy bank. "Knowing Maude, she packed enough for two. Join me?"

"Don't mind if I do." He settled on the grass beside her, but before handing her the pail, he looked over at her. "You, Mrs. Nolan, have been keeping things from me, it seems?" He propped one hand on the grass behind her and leaned close until his shoulder touched hers.

She hung her head and plucked a blade of grass. The creek still marched militantly. "Nothing so important as your recovery."

He propped his chin on her shoulder and when he spoke, his breath was warm on her cheek. "Zoe, nothing is more important to me than you. But no one will tell me what happened. So please . . . put my mind at ease. Are you okay?"

"Yes." She tilted her head against his. "I'm fine. Honestly."

He eased back and touched her chin so that she would look at him. "Good. Please tell me what happened. Start with your leg?"

She worried her lower lip with her teeth. So much for keeping that from him. "When we fell after the wedding, I . . . whacked my leg on a pew, I think."

He winced. "And nothing was broken?"

"No. Doctor Polson checked it that very afternoon, right before we learned about the fire."

Wash sighed. Dropped his chin against his chest. "I wish you felt you could confide in me."

This time it was her turn to touch his cheek to get his attention. "I *do* feel that I can confide in you. But I also wanted everyone to concentrate on you and your healing. My injuries are superficial." She batted her hand through the air.

His eyes narrowed. "'My injuries' . . . Doctor Polson also mentioned your arm. What happened to it?"

"Well . . ." She cleared her throat. "I went for a walk before your surgery, just to clear my head a little and . . . I'm all right, and the situation has been taken care of so there's nothing to worry about."

"Zo . . ."

She pushed a tremulous breath through her lips. "That man, Harlan White, took a shot at me."

Wash stiffened. "He what?!"

Zoe angled toward him. "Wash, it was the craziest thing, but the Lord really protected me. I stepped on a stone, and it rolled beneath my boot. I threw my hands up like this to catch my balance as I was falling backward, and the shot just clipped the underside of my arm here."

His eyes fell closed.

"Doctor Griffin looked at it and said it might leave a scar, but that it will heal up just fine."

His head tilted toward hers, and he pressed a gentle kiss to her shoulder. "We really have had a tumultuous start to our marriage haven't we?"

Zoe laughed. "You can say that again."

For a long moment they sat in silence and then Wash draped his arm around her shoulders and drew her close. He spoke softly, his voice warm and sure. "The Lord is my shepherd; I shall not want. He maketh me to lie down in green pastures: he leadeth me beside the still waters. He restoreth my soul: he leadeth me in the paths of righteousness for his name's sake. Yea, though I walk through the valley of the shadow of death, I will fear no evil: for thou art with me; thy rod and thy staff they comfort me. Thou preparest a table before me in the presence of mine enemies: thou anointest my head with oil; my cup runneth over. Surely goodness and mercy shall follow me all the days of my life: and I will dwell in the house of the Lord for ever."

Such peace washed over Zoe in that moment that her eyes filled with tears. The sound of Wyldhaven Creek seemed to transition from a rushing torrent to a soft soothing song of contentment. Her thrumming pulse eased into a steady rhythm and the tightness in her chest immediately relaxed. "Thank you for that reminder. I'm ready for some green pastures and still waters."

"Me too." Wash pressed a kiss against her temple. "God has our future firmly in His hands, Zo. I don't know exactly what it will look like—we might have more trials to face—but I know we can trust the One who does know."

"I do too." Zoe could have quite contentedly spent the rest of the afternoon right there with her husband by her side, but she had students to teach and a rumbling stomach. "Now what about that lunch?"

Wash grinned at her. "Oh you thought I was serious? This is just an old tin bucket I found on my way here."

She laughed. "It is not. That scratch has been on my pail for I don't know how many years." She reached for it, but Wash playfully snatched it from her grasp, and as he teased and flirted, Zoe suddenly realized that she hadn't felt this level of contentment since Wash had quit writing to her all those months ago.

He finally relented, but only because he was hungry himself, he proclaimed, and as she took a bite of her sandwich, she closed her eyes and angled her face toward the sky. *Thank You, Dear Father, for all that You've done for me—for us—despite my tendency to rush ahead and try to take things into my own hands. Keep leading and guiding us, and please provide a job for Wash that won't be too taxing on his leg.*

She felt Wash's gaze warming her face. When she glanced over at him, he gave her a wink. "This is nice, sitting here, sharing lunch with my best friend again. I've missed you, Zo. I didn't realize how much until you showed up on my porch with your valise in your hand."

She smiled. "So no regrets?"

He shook his head. "Never." He leaned close and after a surreptitious glance to make sure no children were in sight, he gave her another wink and a lingering kiss.

She could get used to lunches like this. She really could.

After a moment, she eased back. "I think I might have to forget my lunchpail more often now."

He laughed, pressed one hand to his chest, and gave a mock bow. "I'll always be happy to come to your rescue, my lady."

A movement along the path by the creek drew their attention.

Zoe's brows shot up. It was Taulby walking their way, but he wasn't alone. Beside him was the short blond woman that she knew to be Mr. Heath's great-niece! Zoe's smile stretched her cheeks for a moment, but then she noticed that they were both very serious.

The girl kept her face lowered.

He paused before them, a somber sorrow filling his eyes. "Good afternoon."

Wash stood and helped Zoe to her feet. Then offered his hand to Taulby. "Afternoon."

Taulby motioned to the woman. "This is Anja Johansen."

Zoe nodded. "What's wrong?"

Taulby glanced at the woman for a moment, but she couldn't seem to rally herself. "I'm afraid it is bad news that we carry."

Not again. Zoe scooted closer to Wash, and felt her tension ease slightly when he slipped his hand around hers. "Oh?"

"It is Mr. Heath, you see."

Wash and Zoe remained quiet.

"I'm afraid that he has passed away during the night."

"Oh no." Zoe covered her mouth. She fixed her attention on the woman. "I'm so very sorry for your loss. For all our loss."

"Yes, so very sorry," Wash added.

Anja plucked a tall blade of grass and shredded it in her fingers. "Thank you."

Taulby shifted and it was the way he set his big broad hand so tenderly on Anja's shoulder that filled Zoe's heart with relief and a hope for his future. It appeared that she hadn't broken Taulby's heart too badly, after all.

Taulby dropped his hand and clasped it behind his back. "We have been asked by Sheriff Reagan to inform everyone that there will be a funeral followed by a town council meeting in the morning at the church. He regrets to pair them so closely, but since all will be in town, it only makes sense to this business take care of all at once, and Anja has agreed. He asks that you come if you can. Also, some work to save us, would you be able to this news tell to your families?"

Wash dipped his chin in agreement. "Of course. Miss," he swept a gesture to include Zoe in his next words, "please let us know if there's any way we can be of help."

She dipped her knees in a curtsy and thanked them again. As she and Taulby moved on down the path, Zoe rested her hand on Wash's arm. "I'd best return to the classroom. Looks like the children will be getting another day off so that we can attend. What is this going to mean for us as a town, do you think?"

Wash patted her hand. "We'll be fine. There will be a period of adjustment, and I'll wager we'll need to elect a mayor now to do all the things that Mr. Heath has done through the years, but we'll be fine." He leaned down and gave her a quick peck on the cheek. "Zoe?"

"Yes?"

"Thank you for choosing me, even when I was so unchoosable."

Seeing Taulby again must have stirred up this conversation.

She smiled. "I will choose you for always, Wash."

"Lucky me. See you at home tonight?"

She nodded. And as she watched him walk away, she was filled with the certainty that he was right. Despite the town's loss, they would be all right. The people of Wyldhaven had proven that they were not daunted by trials.

Chapter Twenty-eight

The church was packed the next day when Wash and Zoe arrived with the Nolan family. They made their way inside and Zoe marveled at how well Wash was getting around despite being only eleven days post-surgery. She was afraid he might be overdoing it, but Dr. Polson had said that as long as he continued to use his cane and stopped walking when he felt pain, that he should be fine.

It felt a bit odd when there wasn't enough room on the Nolan pew for her. Even more odd when Wash motioned for her to lead the way onto the bench where the Olanns had normally sat on the right side of the church just in front of the Carvers' bench.

Zoe did a double take when she saw her sister sitting next to Kane. Zoe had been preoccupied with nursing Wash and with lesson planning and now realized that too many days had slipped by since she'd heard the news about their engagement.

Belle didn't seem perturbed, however. She grinned bigger than Jinx at milking time and held up her left hand so Zoe could see the gold band on her finger. Zoe thought it was sweet that Kane had offered Belle that symbolic gesture even though it wasn't very common for people of their set to do so.

She reached for her sister's hand and examined the intricate vine that was inscribed into the metal. "It's beautiful! I'm sorry I haven't stopped by."

Wash reached past Zoe to offer Kane his hand. "Bully for you."

"Thank you!" Kane beamed.

Zoe offered Kane a grin. "Welcome to the family."

He settled a hand against Belle's back. "Wouldn't want to be part of any other."

Belle leaned back and snuggled into the crook of Kane's arm. "Did you hear about the trials?"

"Yes. At least bits and pieces. Enough." Zoe waved a hand. "I'm honestly glad that the judge was already scheduled to be here last week."

"Oh, yes. Me too! Papa says that Mrs. Hines is putting the mercantile up for sale."

Zoe felt her insides crumble a little for poor David. She really hoped that Priscilla would take good care of him.

Kane jostled Belle with his hand. "Don't gossip, Belle." He gave her a squeeze to take the sting out of the words.

Her sister looked over at her intended. "How is it gossip if it's true?"

Beside Zoe, Wash made a sound that let her know he was fighting a laugh.

Kane gave Belle a pointed look and Zoe felt her cheeks bunch. It seemed that Belle had finally met her match in Kane Carver.

His voice was even and gentle when he replied, "Even if it's not gossip per se, it's best to leave people's business to them and not spread conjecture. I think that's how we would want to be treated."

Belle flounced a little and adjusted her skirts. "Well, I guess that's true enough. There is a scripture about that, isn't there?"

Kane's mouth quirked. "There is, yes."

"If I could have everyone's attention!" Sheriff Callahan's voice rose from the front of the room.

Zoe gave her sister and Kane a little wave of farewell, then turned to face the front. Movement on the other side of Wash caught her attention and she glanced over to see Kin sliding onto their bench behind a man in a very fine double-breasted dress jacket. The man undid a couple of the buttons as Kin leaned past him to speak to Wash.

"Wash, this here is Mr. Royce of Royce Lumber Industries," he whispered.

Wash sat straighter and immediately thrust out his hand. "Sir, it's very good to meet you."

Zoe felt her breath hitch. This must be the rich patron! Sheriff Reagan was still speaking from the front of the room, but she was completely intent on the conversation happening beside her.

Mr. Royce leaned closer to Wash. "Might we find time to speak after this meeting concludes?"

"Of course," Wash agreed.

With that, both men turned their attention to the front of the room, and Zoe followed suit even if her curiosity was burning.

"And now," Sheriff Reagan was saying, "I'll turn you over to Parson Clay."

Parson Clay rose somberly. He eulogized Mr. Heath and talked about how they likely wouldn't even be here if it weren't for his founding of Wyldhaven. He read some scriptures and made a crack about Mr. Heath dancing around the throne in heaven. "Likely all the angels had to duck his cane when he tossed it!"

Zoe laughed along with the other congregants. Her gaze landed on Anja, who sat all alone on the front pew, smiling and wiping the tears that streaked her cheeks. Her heart went out to the woman. What would she do now that her uncle was gone? Had he left her anything?

After a few more comments and a time of urging those gathered to be ready when their time came to meet their maker as Mr. Heath had been, Parson Clay instructed that everyone should step outside for the burial. "After that, we'll give everyone a fifteen-minute break and then ask that you meet back here to discuss some recent events and needs of our town."

Everyone waited for Anja to depart the church first and it did Zoe's heart so much good to see Taulby slip out of the back row and swing into step right behind her. It made her happy. She only hoped they could work things out.

Wash gripped her hand, and they followed the flow of traffic out to the graveyard on the far side of the church property. Sheriff Reagan, Deputy Joe, Marshall Holloway, and Dr. Griffin carried Mr. Heath's coffin to the hole that someone had already dug. With Kin, Jackson, Ewan, and Mr. King helping, they carefully settled the box onto the ropes and then lowered it into the hole.

As the parson spoke, Wash tugged Zoe closer to his side and dropped a kiss against her temple and she had no doubt that he was envisioning that he might have needed to stand through a similar ceremony if Harlan White's shot had taken her down as intended. A shiver worked through her. She closed her eyes and sent up a prayer of thanks for the Lord's protection.

After Parson Clay closed in prayer and Anja had dropped in a handful of dirt, several men set to work with shovels to fill the hole and people separated into groups to visit.

Mr. Royce motioned that he would like to step to one side, and they all moved to the shade near the wagons, with Kin following.

Zoe followed and as they approached the place where Mrs. Hines stood beside David, Zoe saw Taulby and Anja stop in front of her.

"Mrs. Hines," Taulby said in his steady deep voice, "It is very sorry we are for your troubles. I think in this I can help."

"Oh?" Priscilla wrapped one arm around David's shoulders, drawing him nearer.

And that gesture softened Zoe's heart toward the woman ten-fold. She didn't have to worry about David. He was going to be taken care of, she suddenly knew it without doubt.

They were abreast of the group now, and Taulby continued. "The mercantile I would like to buy. And Anja, here in town will stay and the sales she will manage."

Zoe smiled as she passed. The last glimpse she got was of Mrs. Hines's eyes filling with tears of gratitude. As they moved on, she heard the woman say, "Oh, my, that is such a relief, Mr. Ecklund. Such a relief. David and I are going to move to Tacoma so we can be near to the prison and visit Jerry as often as we can, and . . ."

Her voice faded away as clusters of congregants separated Zoe from the conversation, but she'd heard enough to have her heart eased. Anja would have work, Taulby would still have her nearby, and the Hines family would have trials, but hopefully they would come out the other side the stronger for it. Of all the crazy things, Zoe realized that she would miss Mrs. Hines's strident personality. And that was something she never thought she would say.

When they had reached the relative privacy of the space next to the Nolans' buckboard, the newcomer turned to Wash and stretched out his hand again. "I'm sorry that we haven't had the chance to meet in person until now. I'm very sorry for the severe injury my son caused."

"Thank you, sir. I appreciate that. But, as you can see, I'm doing so much better now after a recent surgery."

"The cavalry never offered you a surgeon?"

Wash and Kin exchanged glances and Zoe concentrated on her fingers. How much easier things would have been for Wash if the surgeons had been adequately trained.

"Two, sir. Unfortunately, it wasn't until this third surgery from our surgeon here in Wyldhaven that I've found a great measure of relief from the pain."

"I'm very sorry to hear that." The man's feet shuffled, drawing Zoe's attention to the high gloss of his shined black shoes. "As you might surmise from my arrival, Mr. Davis here tracked me down. He says that you haven't been receiving any of my recent payments?"

Wash hung his head and gripped the back of his neck. "No, sir. But I don't want you to feel like you have to—"

"Nonsense." Mr. Royce cut him off. "Of course it is right that I help you since it was partially my fault that—Well . . ." He brushed away that line of conversation. "I'm happy to help. In fact I insist upon it. And you'll be happy to know that we've spoken with the sheriff on this matter and he investigated the issue. It seems that this banker, Mr. Olann, was indeed receiving my transfers, but was putting them into one of his own accounts instead of into yours."

Zoe's jaw dropped. Of all the cheek! Stealing was bad enough, but to steal from a man who had gone off to fight for his country and come home wounded, why, that just about made Zoe's blood boil!

"Rest assured that I kept a careful accounting, and we'll get you every penny that I've sent."

Wash scuffed his cane through the dirt. "Thank you, sir. That will be very helpful to my family at this time."

The man nodded. "I heard about the fires. Sounds like you've had a rough go of it."

Wash smiled. "It's been a bit of a month, yes sir."

Kin clapped Wash on his shoulder. "I'm working with the sheriff and Mr. Royce here to make sure we get everything sorted. I'll let you know as soon as the money is in your account."

Zoe's brow crimped. "Will we even have a bank in town after today?"

Kin cast an auspicious glance at Mr. Royce but made no reply.

Mr. Royce got a bit of a twinkle around his eyes. He looked at Wash. "Kin says you are right good with numbers?"

Wash frowned even as he waggled his head from side to side.

Kin offered, "He's just being modest. He was top of our class. Even beat out Zoe here and she's a teacher now."

Zoe rolled her eyes. "Hey! We tied a time or two as I recall."

Mr. Royce chuckled as she'd hoped he would, but his gaze was still on Wash.

Zoe felt all jittery inside. Was the man going to do what she thought he was?

"Not sure if you've heard," Mr. Royce said, "but the bank was put up for sale immediately upon Mr. Olann's conviction." He waited a beat. "I purchased it."

Wash's head snapped up and Zoe pressed her fingertips to her lips when she caught sight of the light of hope shining in Wash's eyes.

Kin gave her a wink from across the circle.

Wash seemed to be holding his breath.

Mr. Royce pulled a face. "The only problem is that I don't really want to move to Wyldhaven to run this new purchase of mine, so I'm looking for someone to do that for me."

Wash remained perfectly still, continuing to wait.

"I looked into your service record, Mr. Nolan, and since I arrived in town a few days ago, I've been asking around about you. Both your record and the word of people who've known you all your life make me certain that I won't regret my offer. I would like for you to run the bank here in town, if you want to."

Wash seemed frozen. But the light of hope from his eyes had expanded to ease his posture. "Don't get me wrong, Mr. Royce, sir. I would love to do that. It would, in fact, answer several of my prayers. However, I have no experience in running a bank."

The man waved a hand. "After you've recovered sufficiently, I would like you to spend two weeks at my Seattle branch. We'll train you and try to answer all of your questions and after that, you can wire anytime if you need answers. One of the perks of modern technology!"

Wash was suddenly grinning from ear to ear. He stretched out a hand. "Well, now, that sounds right fine."

"Wonderful!" Mr. Royce pumped his hand heartily. "How does two hundred dollars a month sound?"

Zoe barely managed to restrain a gasp. Why, that was more than twice what she'd expected the salary to be!

Mr. Royce waved a hand. "Just to start. After we get you trained, we'll raise your salary commensurate to your skills and the position."

Sheriff Reagan started ringing the church bell to call everyone in to the town meeting.

Wash was shaking his head in awe. "That sounds fine, sir. More than fine."

"Good. Good. I'm very happy this all worked out. I know you won't let me down. Well," he glanced toward the church. "I'd better let you all get to your town meeting, and I have a train to catch. Take time to recover and let's have you start at the bank in, say . . . three weeks? That will be the first of the month. It will also allow me to get everything set up—the new sign hung, the vault's lock changed, that sort of thing."

"That sounds fine, sir."

"Good." The man gave a firm nod. "Now, there's one patron of the bank that I'd like to meet in person since he had such a large account. I wonder if you can point me in the direction of a Mr. Isaiah Coleman?"

When they all three chuckled, Mr. Royce frowned.

Kin pointed to where Isaiah was playing catch with several other of the town's boys. "That, sir, is Mr. Isaiah Coleman."

Mr. Royce's brows shot up and then he began to laugh. "Well, I'll be." He lifted a hand in farewell and strode across the yard.

Zoe watched as he approached Isaiah and spoke to him.

Isaiah immediately doffed his cap, tucked his baseball glove beneath his arm, and thrust out his hand.

She felt someone studying her and turned to find Wash scrutinizing her. "So? What do you think?"

"I think I'm about to explode with the excitement of it all. But I mostly want you to be happy. Do you think you would enjoy such work?"

He turned his gaze to where Mr. Royce still talked with Isaiah. "It wasn't what I planned for my life. But I've always loved working with numbers, as you know. Pa used to have me do the books for the spread." He frowned. "But that was before I left for the cavalry. I haven't been helping him much, recently."

Zoe looped her arm through his and looked up at him. "But that was then. And this is now. We can only go forward."

He dipped his gaze to hers. "I'm happy to go forward with you by my side and I do think I'll enjoy the work. It's a huge relief, honestly. If my leg pains me too much, I'll be able to sit down for some of the time."

Seeing that Kin had stepped away to join Cora entering the church, Zoe settled her chin on her husband's shoulder. "And the salary certainly is nice, so . . . perhaps we could revisit the conversation about having children?"

Wash turned and settled his hands at her waist, tugging her closer. "I've been meaning to talk to you about that." He pumped his brows, and his focus slipped to her lips.

With her arms draped behind his neck, Zoe tilted him a coy look. "Oh, have you now."

"I have indeed, Mrs.—"

A loud commotion drew their startled attention toward the church steps.

"Nolan," Wash finished. "Speaking of children . . ." He grinned.

Zoe beamed too.

For Parson Clay had hold of Aurora's arm as he helped her down the church steps, and she was walking gingerly with both hands curved around her stomach. Dr. Griffin had his bag in hand and was hot on their heels.

Parson Clay looked as pale as a sheet. "Just a little way to the house, Rory. Just a little way." He scuttled ahead and then rushed back to her side so fast that he had to clap a hand to his hat to keep it on his head. "Do you need me to carry you?"

Aurora pegged him with a glower and transferred one of her hands to her lower back. She froze with a wince and breathed sharply for a moment and then seemed able to gather herself. She started along the path toward the parsonage again. "I'm having a baby, Preston. I'm not dying! I'm fully capable of walking. Please" —she motioned him toward the house— "just get the water on like Dr. Griffin asked."

From behind the couple, Dr. Griffin looked over at them with a huge grin and a wink.

Wash's hand rubbed a warm circle against her back. "Promise you'll talk nicer to me when our time comes."

Zoe laughed. "I make no promises. You know how temperamental redheads can be!"

He chuckled and lowered his head toward her. "Now where were we?"

Zoe's vision was suddenly blurred with tears. After so many months of struggle, the Lord truly had led them to green pastures and still waters, and she felt like her cup of hope for the future was suddenly running over with possibilities.

Please Review!

If you enjoyed this story, would you take a few minutes to leave your thoughts in a review on your favorite retailer's website? It would mean so much to me, and helps spread the word about the series.

You can quickly link through from my website here: http://www.lynnettebonner.com/books/historical-fiction/the-wyldhaven-series/

Want a FREE Story?

If you enjoyed this book...

...sign up for Lynnette's Gazette below! Subscribers get exclusive deals, sneak peeks, and lots of other fun content.

(The gazette is only sent out about once a month or when there's a new release to announce, so you won't be getting a lot of spam messages, and your email is never shared with anyone else.)

Sign up link: https://www.lynnettebonner.com/newsletter/

ABOUT THE AUTHOR

Born and raised in Malawi, Africa. Lynnette Bonner spent the first years of her life reveling in warm equatorial sunshine and the late evening duets of cicadas and hyenas. The year she turned eight she was off to Rift Valley Academy, a boarding school in Kenya where she spent many joy-filled years, and graduated in 1990.

That fall, she traded to a new duet—one of traffic and rain—when she moved to Kirkland, Washington to attend Northwest University. It was there that she met her husband and a few years later they moved to the small town of Pierce, Idaho.

During the time they lived in Idaho, while studying the history of their little town, Lynnette was inspired to begin the Shepherd's Heart Series with Rocky Mountain Oasis.

Marty and Lynnette have four children, and currently live in Washington where Marty pastors a church.

Made in the USA
Monee, IL
30 July 2024